What the critics are saying:

All Hallows Heartbreaker:

"This was one gem of a book. Funny, fast-paced, and sexy as all-get-out...Dylan is one seriously hot hero, sweet enough to make my teeth ache, yet dominant enough to make my knees weak...Tongue-in-cheek throughout most of the book, Emmy had me laughing out loud a number of times...I definitely recommend this novel to all fans of erotic vampire stories." – *Barb Chan, Just Erotic Romance Reviews*

"A wild romp of raunchy sex, laugh-out-loud humor..." – *Kathy Samuels, Romance Review Today*

Love Bites

"One thing is certain, Delilah Devlin eaves a masterfully written story of vampires, seduction, murder, and mystery with My Immortal Knight: Love Bites " ~ *Romantic Times*

"...congratulations to Ms. Devlin for creating a masterpiece. The novel has intense suspense that was thrilling and delightful. The fast pace of this story kept me mesmerized and kept me guessing as to what was going to happen next in the story...Quentin and Darcy have such explosive sexual tension that you could actually see the heat rise from the pages of this story...I recommend this fiery vampire romance for everyone who loves a truly amazing story." – *Holly Susuan, Just Erotic Romance Reviews*

Twice Bitten
My Immortal Knight I & II

By Delilah Devlin

TWICE BITTEN: MY IMMORTAL KNIGHT 1 & 2
An Ellora's Cave Publication, August 2004

Ellora's Cave Publishing, Inc.
1337 Commerce Drive
Stow, Ohio 44224

ISBN #1-84360-895-2

My Immortal Knight: All Hallows Heartbreaker © 2003 Delilah
Devlin
ISBN MS Reader (LIT) ISBN # 1-84360-660-7
Other available formats (no ISBNs are assigned):
Adobe (PDF), Rocketbook (RB), Mobipocket (PRC) & HTML

My Immortal Knight: Love Bites © 2004 Delilah Devlin
ISBN MS Reader (LIT) ISBN # 1-84360-763-8
Other available formats (no ISBNs are assigned):
Adobe (PDF), Rocketbook (RB), Mobipocket (PRC) & HTML

Edited by *Briana St. James*
Cover art by *Darrell King*

Warning:

The following material contains graphic sexual content meant for mature readers. *Twice Bitten: My Immortal Knight* has been rated *E-rotic* by a minimum of three independent reviewers.

Ellora's Cave Publishing offers three levels of Romantica™ reading entertainment: S (S-ensuous), E (E-rotic), and X (X-treme).

S-ensuous love scenes are explicit and leave nothing to the imagination.

E-rotic love scenes are explicit, leave nothing to the imagination, and are high in volume per the overall word count. In addition, some E-rated titles might contain fantasy material that some readers find objectionable, such as bondage, submission, same sex encounters, forced seductions, etc. E-rated titles are the most graphic titles we carry; it is common, for instance, for an author to use words such as "fucking", "cock", "pussy", etc., within their work of literature.

X-treme titles differ from E-rated titles only in plot premise and storyline execution. Unlike E-rated titles, stories designated with the letter X tend to contain controversial subject matter not for the faint of heart.

Also by Delilah Devlin:

TWICE BITTEN

MY IMMORTAL KNIGHT I
ALL HALLOW'S HEARTBREAKER
&
MY IMMORTAL KNIGHT II
LOVE BITES

Delilah Devlin

ALL HALLOWS HEARTBREAKER
MY IMMORTAL KNIGHT I

CHAPTER ONE

"Dylan, watch your back!"

At his friend's warning, Dylan O'Hara spun on his heels and ducked beneath a sweeping claw. He feinted to the left, and then surged upward, slamming the creature into a damp brick wall. "You will heed me!"

Arms immobilized, the beast shuddered and bared its teeth, a flash of white in the scant moonlight penetrating the narrow alley.

In its most primitive form, the creature couldn't understand him. Dylan sighed. This might take some time.

Behind him, wood splintered and metal rang against rock. "Quentin, you'd better finish your end quickly," he shouted, careful not to look away from the vampire. "We've more problems waiting at The Cavern."

"I'd be happy to oblige, but this one won't release its prize." Quentin grunted in accompaniment to the thud of heavy fists pounding flesh.

Dylan's vampire renewed its struggle.

Battling his own mind-stealing anger, Dylan barely pulled his throat away from a mouthful of jagged teeth. He slammed the creature into the wall again. "I will outlast you, bitch."

Intelligence glittered in the creature's dark gaze, and then her features relaxed, morphing instantly from snarling vampire to the cotton-candy sweetness of a teenaged girl. "Mr. O'Hara, I'm so sorry. You can let me go now."

The "Mr. O'Hara" made him feel at least a couple of centuries old. Dylan glared at the dark-eyed girl whose mane of curly, brown hair framed a pale face with sweetly bowed lips. "Who made you, little girl?"

She transformed again, from sweet sixteen to seductress with a single lap of her tongue around blood red lips. "You may," she whispered.

Dylan rolled his eyes. "Your sire. Who was your sire? And how do you know my name?"

Her lips formed a moue. "Why, Nicky *made* me. And every vampire knows *you*."

Muffled blows continued to sound behind him, and he shouted to Quentin, "For fuck's sake. He's only a mosquito. Can't you finish him on your own?"

"Inexperience doesn't mean the bastard hasn't got a wicked right hook," Quentin replied.

A loud crash and dull thump followed—flesh met metal. Then silence.

"Quentin, have you finished?"

"Not quite," Quentin said, and then groaned.

The girl peeked over Dylan's shoulder.

He pressed a finger to her lips. "Not one word."

Her glance darted back to his, and she nodded too quickly.

He kept his finger pressed to her lips. "And you don't move an inch, or I'll dust you."

Her eyes widened. Maybe she was a virgin to the vamp lifestyle, but she knew enough to fear a Master Vampire's threat. She nodded slowly.

Dylan turned to aid his friend, not the least surprised to hear the scurry of footsteps heading toward the street. With a shrug, he realized he didn't care the girl was getting away. He could always catch her later.

Quentin had the foresight to remove his shirt before entering the fray, and he rose from the ground to stand bare-chested, facing a male vamp in full-blooded frenzy.

The vamp's face was contorted with bloodlust and his fangs formed two greedy rows, the long incisors curving over his lips. Carrying a human at his side like a bag of potatoes, he swung his free arm and connected with Quentin's jaw.

Quentin landed next to a trash bin. When Dylan approached, he smiled crookedly. "I've got him softened up."

Dylan slid a stake from the top of his boot. "I told you, Quent, we haven't time to play."

The beast lumbered from side to side, the girl under his arm flopping like a rag doll. Blood, spattered on his Linkin' Park T-shirt and blue jeans, indicated she wasn't the vamp's first victim of the night.

To fight a vampire at the peak of his bloodlust, Dylan needed an extra push. So he let his own lust take him by degrees, careful to balance waning human intelligence with increasing vampire strength. He thrilled to the heightened strength and awareness—bloodlust being a dangerously close cousin to his dark sensuality.

Skin on his cheeks and forehead stretched to accommodate rising plates of facial armor. Fangs slid from his gums, pushing shorter incisors behind them. Dylan curled his lips and snarled a warning at his opponent.

When the other male vamp threw back his head and roared, the rag doll at his side stirred, and she wriggled to free herself from the vampire's grasp. The vamp dropped its gaze to the girl, and Dylan leapt to push the stake deep into its chest.

As Dylan's face reformed and his teeth retracted, the vamp staggered, finally relinquishing its hold on the girl. With a great sigh, the creature fell to its knees. Features blurred, then reshaped.

A blond, sparse beard covered the chin and jaw of another teen. The youth's fearful gaze met Dylan's the instant the young man's body disintegrated into dust.

"Goddamn, Nicky."

Quentin stepped past him, heading for the girl. She lay on her back, eyes closed tightly. Even from a distance, Dylan heard her heart hammering. Quentin bent over her, his mouth at her throat.

Dylan shuddered, thankful his friend had taken charge of the girl, certain he wouldn't have been able to stop himself from draining her dry. He'd been too long without fresh blood…and a neck was a tender bit of flesh.

After a long moment, Quentin raised his head, blood smearing his lips. "Open your eyes, little girl."

Her lids lifted slowly, expression dazed.

"You partied too much with the boy, and he got a little carried away." His voice soothed. "You want to go home now."

"I want to go home," she said in monotone.

Quentin pushed a strand of her hair away from her forehead. "Did he drive you here, sweetheart?"

She blinked slowly. "I drove my car to The Cavern."

"How very convenient," he murmured. "Time to go home."

"I want to go home," she repeated.

Quentin helped her to her feet, and she walked to the end of the alley, staring straight ahead. His heavy hand landed on Dylan's shoulder. "We're done here, Dylan," he said quietly. "Let's make sure she gets to her car."

With one last glance at the empty, crumpled T-shirt and blue jeans, Dylan rose to his feet. "How many kids do you think Nicky had to go through to make this one?"

Quentin snatched his shirt from where he'd hung it on a nail and shrugged into it. "Why would he even want one this young?"

"Younger humans are more resilient. Teenagers stand a better chance of surviving the transformation. And they're all out tonight, it being Halloween. Easy pickings."

"Bloody hell. We should be glad he isn't turning babies in Spiderman outfits."

Dylan raked his hand through his hair. "Let's get out of here."

They left the alley and walked toward the violet neon sign marking the entrance to The Cavern.

Just as the girl passed them in a little red Civic, soft misty rain began to fall.

Dylan raised his face and inhaled, welcoming the moisture.

"Fuck me!" Quentin said. "It's raining again. Hurry along, now."

"My friend, you're too fussy. How can you not love the rain? It smells like home."

"I hated home every damned day of my life. Why the hell do you think I was in the Caymans when I was turned? London is forever dreary."

Dylan shook his head. They were poles apart in most things, but bound by their immortality. More than lifelong friends. "Seattle's as close to Ireland as I've found in the world. The weather's soft, and the rain makes everything..." He took a last deep breath. "...clean."

* * * * *

Later, Dylan surveyed the growing crush of bodies undulating to the techno beat on the dance floor below. It was Halloween, but the vamp-savvy crowd had foregone the costumes for the excitement of mingling with the real thing. "Just another Saturday night at The Cavern," he mumbled. He was growing bored with the scene beyond the one-way mirror of his soundproof room. Bored and horny.

"I wonder what young Nicky has planned for tonight," Quentin said from the black leather sofa.

Dylan shot a glance at his friend whose appearance was completely unruffled after their skirmish in the alley. "I thought he was beneath your notice."

"Just wondered." Quentin took another sip of brandy from the snifter Dylan had poured. "It being Halloween and all. Americans get so excited about that sort of thing."

Dylan checked the cuffs of his shirt. They were frayed and smudged with grime. "Just remember," he said, pinning his friend with a glare. "Nicky's mine."

Quentin lifted a single aristocratic brow. "Are you going to stake him or invite him to dinner?"

Dylan ignored the jibe and unbuttoned his shirt. At times, Quentin's British drollness grated on his nerves. "I'll talk to him—first. He's trying to take over, you know. He's building his own army."

"I'm shivering in my boots. An army of mosquitoes."

"Be afraid. He can't control immature vamps. You saw what happened."

"Wasps, then."

Dylan drew the curtain closed, shutting off the view, and then shrugged off his shirt. "They're already leaving carnage in their path. Before long, the police will be poking their noses in our business. At least Nicky doesn't have that little girl in the alley to add to his ranks."

"Should we have left her alive? What if she remembers and brings the police down on our heads?"

"She was unconscious most of the time," Dylan said. "Thanks to your persuasion, she'll think she dreamed the rest of it."

"Well, there are plenty of willing hosts here tonight. Nicky's army doesn't need to kill."

Dread lingered like stale blood. "You know damn well Nicky doesn't consider whores a suitable meal."

"It's true. He doesn't like to stop at a little nibble." Quentin's eyes narrowed. "But what about you? Are you going to end your fast?"

"We're not talking about me. I'm not a menace to human society."

"Dylan, you have to feed. As it is, you're likely to rip the head off your next host, if you don't take the edge off with a little sex first."

"I'm in control."

Quentin snorted. "Not for long, if you don't feed. There are plenty of hosts below, willing to take your cock and your bite. Why not go for it?"

Dylan lifted an eyebrow. "Are you offering to pimp for me?"

"Not bloody likely. We don't have the same tastes."

"And I'm tired of a steady diet of drugged up whores."

Quentin's grin stretched wide. "We could do a foursome."

"I'd rather go without."

Quentin's expression grew serious. "Then make yourself a mate."

A fading memory of a redheaded angel caused a dull ache in his chest. "You know I wouldn't risk a woman's life for that."

"For fuck's sake, you're a stubborn bastard. Take a human lover."

"Maybe I should. It's not like I'd have to fall in love with her. Humans are too short-lived." Dylan strode past Quentin to the coat rack next to the door and selected a black leather vest, buttoning it closed. "Let's patrol the floor. Make sure everyone plays nice tonight." He opened the door and looked back at Quentin.

"Oh, all right." His friend heaved a sigh. "You sure know how to suck the life out of a party."

Before Dylan reached the bottom step of the stairs, he sensed a change in the crowd. Every vamp in his view stiffened. Their expressions grew expectant.

Dylan lifted his nose to the air and sniffed. Beneath the usual cloud of cigarettes, perfume, and sweat, something fresh and sweet — and infinitely carnal — wafted in the air. His body tightened in anticipation. Tonight was the night.

Without looking over his shoulder, Dylan yelled, "Find her!"

* * * * *

Emmaline Harris adjusted the snug fit of her bustier and patted her breasts to make sure everything that mattered was covered. She'd ditched her shawl in the coatroom near the door and was beginning to regret the exposure.

"Damn Monica and her costume," she muttered. When Monica had lent her the Vampira outfit, she obviously hadn't taken into consideration the two-cup difference in their sizes.

Emmy took another deep gasp of air and headed toward the center of the dance floor. That's where Monica was most likely to be.

Emmy didn't recognize a soul. This West Seattle tavern, next to the waterway and Elliot Bay, wasn't the sort of place Emmy was accustomed to.

"Excuse me. Pardon me," she said, as she sidled between gyrating bodies, but soon realized no one heard her above the deafening music. And worse, she was the only person dressed for Halloween. "Monica is so dead. Why did I bother with an hour of makeup and this stupid costume when everyone else is wearing Dollar Store fangs?"

"Talking to yourself again?" Monica drawled into her ear.

Emmy whirled. "Don't do that!"

"I see you made it," Monica said, grinning. She flicked a lock of brown hair over her shoulder. "I knew the outfit would be delicious on you."

Emmy took in her friend's appearance and frowned. "Your fangs look pretty darn good, up close. But your blue jeans and tank are the scariest," Emmy grumbled. "What's with this place? Don't they know it's Spooky Night? Or did I get my days crossed?" Then she realized Monica hadn't even bothered changing what she'd worn at lunch before coming to the club. Monica must have been in a hurry. Must be a new man.

"Come," Monica said, grabbing her hand and pulling her toward a dark corner. "Now that you're finally here, I have friends I want you to meet."

Emmy tried to dig in her heels. "When you say friends, you mean guys, don't you? Monica, I don't think I'm ready for this whole getting-back-up-on-the-horse-that-kicked-you thing."

"Shut up, Emmy. My friends will love you."

"I'm sure they will, with my boobs pushed up to my chin and this tourniquet squeezing my waist to nothing. I'm sure I've lost a few brain cells already to asphyxiation."

Emmy tugged, trying to free her hand, but Monica continued to pull her toward the corner. "You should rethink this whole blind date thing. Your friends aren't going to know the real me. When they see me in daylight, they'll think I exploded!"

Monica looked over her shoulder. "Trust me. That will never happen."

Before Emmy could utter another protest, Monica halted in front of a group of young men. Emmy's heart sank. "You know I almost thought this might be the night, but Monica—" she pulled her friend close enough to hiss into her ear, "Are you out of your mind? They're teenagers! What are you going to do, introduce me as Auntie Em?"

"Not them, silly. Him!" Monica placed a hand in the middle of her back and shoved.

Startled, Emmy had only a moment to note a black leather jacket that clothed a tall, lean frame, and then she was hugging it to keep her balance. "Sorry, that was awfully clumsy of…" She looked up into a cold, harshly sculpted face, framed by dark hair that brushed the shoulders of the jacket. "…my friend."

"What have you brought me, Monica?" the man asked. The smile playing at the corner of his lips didn't relieve Emmy's sense of unease.

"An appetizer," Monica drawled, then giggled.

"You know, I'm not the least bit hungry," Emmy said, trying to lighten the atmosphere that had suddenly grown dense as mud.

"I almost always am." The man looked down at Emmy, and then leaned forward.

She screwed her eyes closed and sucked in her lips. *No way is he going to kiss me. Monica, what were you thinking?* Instead of a kiss, he licked the side of her face.

Her eyes flew open. "I think I'm coming down with a bug." Not averse to licking, but concerned they hadn't been introduced, Emmy couldn't stop her nervous prattle. "Licking me could be hazardous to your health. I might have Monkey Pox. I should go home and call the CDC."

Before she could back away, his arms wrapped around her like a vise.

"Then again," she said, pushing against his shoulders, "maybe I should just introduce myself since Monica hasn't seen fit." She strained to look behind her, but her friend was nowhere to be seen. "Typical," she muttered.

She turned back to find the man nuzzling her neck and emitting a growl that would have sounded incredibly sexy, except that it tickled the side of her neck. "Stop that!" Turning her head to close access to that particular avenue of attack, she squealed when he hoisted her high in his arms.

His mouth was now level with the exposed flesh of her breasts, and there was too much breast thanks to Monica's bustier. Her creamy flesh was a beacon for perverts to feast on.

Only this perv wasn't getting any. "Oh no. No breast-licking. I mean it. Or my boyfriend is going to—"

"Join us?" Despite the deep shadows, Emmy detected amusement in the man's expression as he gazed up into her eyes.

"Not likely," she said, lifting her chin and sniffing. "He doesn't like to share."

"Is that right?" A smile stretched across his face, his teeth flashing brightly. "Tell me about him. I'd like to know my competition."

"Well I'm sure he doesn't have nice pointy teeth like yours, but he's big as a bear and jealous." Emmy had a stray thought that she sounded like Little Red Riding Hood. She almost laughed, but her predicament was getting less funny by the moment. The predatory gleam in her captor's eyes was making her nervous. "You don't want to upset him by being here when he arrives."

"What does he look like? So I'll be sure to call him over."

Her last boyfriend had been an unimpressive shrimp. "Well, he's big. And dark. Darker than you. His hair has a little wave, and it's...longish. And green eyes." She'd always wished for a lover with green eyes.

"Is there more?"

"That's it." She bit her lip. "D-did I tell you he's big?"

The eyes of the devil who held her narrowed above his crocodile smile. "You know, I don't think you have a boyfriend, least not one who sounds like he'll give me any trouble." His voice dropped to a sexy rasp that sent a shiver of alarm down her spine. "You're going to have to convince me you aren't just delaying the edible here."

"The inevitable, don't you mean?" Emmy blinked and almost lost the thread of the conversation when he laved his tongue along the side of her neck. "Oh I wouldn't try to delay anything—if you were my boyfriend, that is. Although I must say, if I didn't have a boyfriend," she gulped, "which I may or may not have, I'd probably still not want to date you."

"I think you would," he whispered in her ear. "You're dying for a walk on the wild side."

A shiver of awareness crept along her spine. Alarmed because she was responding to his seduction, she tried one last time to deny him. "I'd never go out with you. You're the dangerous type. And a girl knows there's no future in a relationship with a dangerous man. I may not be the best judge of men, but even I know that."

"Good God, does the chit ever come up for air?"

Emmy jerked toward the voice that sounded behind her. It belonged to a man who was gorgeous in a proper, stiff-upper-lip sort of way. A white dress shirt tucked into gray slacks clothed a long, lean frame—rakish, and he was blond.

Now the man standing next to him could have been tailor-made for the role of her boyfriend, because he was everything she'd described and so much more. Tall for one. Nicely muscled, if his bare arms were any hint of the corded sinew beneath his clothing. Broader—filled out in all the manly places Emmy liked to have filled out. And more dangerous looking than the scrawny ape licking the tops of her breasts. He'd do.

She smiled brightly. "Darling!"

CHAPTER TWO

Momentarily stunned by her exuberant greeting, Dylan stared at the woman Nicky was about to ravage. With her body crushed against his nemesis, Dylan had an excellent view of the lush curve of her waist, which blended into wide hips — and an ass a man would die to pump against. To his photosensitive eyes, her hair reflected the radiance of a sun in its blonde strands. The skin of her shoulders, rosy with blushes, made his mouth water.

His cock twitched behind the fly of his blue jeans.

Quentin coughed, breaking the spell the woman's brilliant smile had cast.

"Nicky. You know the house rules," Dylan said, his voice roughened by his instant attraction to the woman. "No civilians."

"I like this one. So refreshing." Nicky nuzzled her neck and grinned lazily. "She's a meal and a half. We could share."

The woman slapped Nicky's shoulder. "Oh no. I don't go for that kinky stuff."

"Put her down. Now." Dylan glared daggers at the younger vamp, even as he wondered at his sudden urge to rip Nicky's arms off.

Nicky returned his glare, appearing nonchalant about raising Dylan's ire. "Keep your knickers on — as you Brits say."

"You damn well know — I'm Irish."

Nicky shrugged. "I was only having a bit of fun." He lowered the woman to the floor.

Unsteady, she grabbed Nicky's arm then smiled thinly at Dylan. "Well, that was entertaining. I think I'll go find my girlfriend, Monica."

As she walked past Dylan, he snaked an arm around her waist, pulling her to his side. "Are you talking about Monica with the brown hair and blue eyes?"

She tried to shrug out of his embrace, but only managed to set the fleshy tops of her luscious tits jiggling. "Are we doing this again? I'm tired of the game. And I won't be surprised if you both haven't left bruises. You guys must be doing some serious steroids."

Dylan's gaze lifted to her face. "You aren't going to find Monica."

Her wide hazel eyes met his gaze for the first time. Despite the sexy dress and the thick makeup on her eyes and mouth, there was a lively intelligence reflected in her gaze. And she was an innocent. She hadn't a clue about the smoldering fire she'd lit in his loins.

"Why?" A frown creased her brow. "Has she already left?"

Dylan resisted the urge to draw a deep breath and bathe his hypersensitive sense of smell in her scent. "Listen, Monica isn't your friend anymore."

The sound of Nicky's mocking laughter angered Dylan. To him, everything was a joke. Human life was cheap.

"Like I'm going to listen to *you*." She struggled against his embrace, then frowned when he didn't let her go. "She's been my friend forever."

"Right now, she's only thinking about her hunger." He knew—his hunger had hardened his dick to stone, and his fangs inched down from the roof of his mouth.

"You know, you're right. Why whenever we have lunch together, she doesn't go on and on about her boyfriends or her bad Brazilian wax job. No, she goes straight for the breadsticks!"

The urge to shake her until her teeth rattled warred with the need to take her to the floor. Dylan realized she was aggravating the shit out of him, but he wasn't bored. And there was only one way he could think of to make her shut up. Ignoring Nicky's avid stare, he leaned down and kissed her.

For him, the contact was electric. Her lips were soft and lush. Her breath sweet and minty. Her tongue hesitantly traced the fangs on either side of his mouth, and he thought he'd never been so hard.

He retracted his teeth. He wanted to savor her innocence.

"Nothing like broadcasting your interest to the world," Quentin mumbled.

Dylan opened his eyes to see Nicky walk away. He pulled back from the woman. "You didn't see me from the front, Quent. There's no way he missed this hard-on."

The woman's mouth gaped, and her glance fell to his groin.

"Good work shutting her up." Quentin's expression was once again irritatingly droll.

"Just make sure Nicky doesn't get up to any more mischief tonight," Dylan said. "He's already staked a claim on her."

"Righto. I suppose you're going to look after the girl?" Quentin drawled. "About bloody time."

"Sod off," Dylan snarled.

"Hello! I'm here," the woman said. "I don't know why men think they can talk over a woman's head just because she's blonde."

Quentin's gaze was alight with humor.

"You've better things to do, Quent. Get lost." To the woman, Dylan said, "You're coming with me."

"Now look here," she said, pushing against the arm that anchored her to his side, "I don't know you from Adam. I don't even know your name. Why the hell would I go anywhere with you?"

"Name's Dylan O'Hara," he said flatly, then lifted her off her feet and headed toward the stairs.

"Wait a minute. Where are you taking me?" Her legs scissored and the sharp spikes of her heels found his shin.

Exasperated, he put her down and glowered. "Dammit. I'm rescuing you."

Her hazel eyes rounded. "You think you're saving me from the bad guy?"

He stepped close, forcing her to look up at him. "I'm saving you from a *badder* guy."

"Oh!" Her eyelids dipped, lashes concealing the thoughts her eyes appeared to always betray. "You really think he would have hurt me?"

Touching a finger to her soft cheek, he said, "He wanted more than just your blood, sweetheart. You wouldn't have been able to stop him." He slid the finger to the side of her neck and felt her blood thrum as her heart beat faster.

"That's an odd way to put it. Can I stop you?" she asked, her breath shallow and rapid.

"Anytime you want. But you have to tell me you don't want me."

Her gaze lifted to his face. Fear and excitement warred in her expression. "I'm Emmaline Harris. Emmy, if you like."

His hand slid behind her head, combing through her hair, and then he tugged to tilt her face back. "Tell me to stop, Emmy."

"This is crazy. I just swore off men," she whispered. "I didn't want this."

His lips hovered an inch above hers, giving her time to change her mind. "Didn't want what, Emmy?"

The heat of a blush stained her cheeks. "To fuck."

"Bloody hell." Dylan clenched his jaw and willed himself not to pounce. His cock had been painfully hard before—now his balls felt ready to burst. And he'd thought she would be safer with him!

"Was I wrong?" she asked. The uncertainty in her voice produced a slight quaver. "I thought you wanted me too. It's like I conjured you. You're everything I ever wanted, and there you were. Just for me."

"What a coincidence. I thought you'd been made for me." Dylan's hand fisted in her hair. "I may hurt you."

A seductive smile tilted the corners of her mouth. "I'm counting on it. In fact, if what's pushing against my belly now is any indication, I think you're going to ruin me for any other man."

"Come upstairs with me." He released her hair and moved away. "It's your choice."

With a slow rub of her hip against his cock, she stepped past him and climbed the stairs.

He was right behind her—the sway of her hips, from side to side, the sole focus of his attention. Black velvet hugged her bottom as she climbed, revealing the faint indentation of her panties. Each step produced a tiny jiggle of her ass, sending a jolt of awareness right to his groin.

Before they reached the top of the stairs, Dylan adjusted himself to let his cock rise along the zipper of his jeans, popping the snap at the top for relief.

Thankfully, his leather vest covered the head of his penis. He brushed by her to unlock the door, welcoming the darkness inside the room. He became aware of her clutching the back of his vest, so he reached for the blinds and rolled them, letting in the light from the dance floor.

When the door closed behind them, silence fell over the room. Emmy walked to the window. "Can they see us?"

"No. It's one-way glass."

She pulled up the blinds, exposing the window. "I didn't realize there were so many people here. Can they hear us?"

"No more than you can hear them. The room's soundproof."

She looked over her shoulder and her skin pinkened. "Dylan, lock the door."

With his heart pounding in anticipation, he complied. When he turned back, he found her standing in front of the window, peeling down the top of her bustier. Her breasts sprang from their confinement, milky-white globes, crowned by large rosy areolas. As he walked toward her, he noted the large circles were dimpled and her nipples pouted.

Emmy leaned forward and pressed her breasts to the glass, then raised her arms and flattened the rest of her upper torso against it. "Oh, it's so deliciously cool. You're sure no one can see me?"

Dylan closed in, standing just behind her. With his nose pressed to her apple-scented hair, he widened his legs and pressed his cock to her backside. "No one can see us. Is this how you want it?"

"My skin aches. Could you untie the laces of my bustier?"

Hunger clawing at his belly and groin, Dylan's hands shook while he plucked the silk laces along her back to loosen the corset. Finally, it fell to the floor leaving her creamy back bare. He smoothed his hands around her shoulders and down her spine, achingly aware of her fragile body and the warm, fragrant blood just beneath her skin.

She moaned and pushed her velvet-covered bottom against his cock. "The button. There's a button and a zipper. Open them."

Dylan found them easily and pushed the skirt past her hips to the floor. He'd been right about her ass. Round and pink—he gave it a little slap and watched its delicious jiggle. His body screamed with the need to ram deep inside her.

Now, the only thing between his cock and her ass were red silk panties. He shoved them down her legs, then knelt to pull them off, lifting one foot at a time. When he rose, he licked the back of her thigh, the crease where her legs and buttocks met, then the dimples above her heart-shaped ass. He skimmed his hands over her from shoulders to her round buttocks and squeezed.

She shuddered. "Dylan, I'm feeling things."

He smiled, and dipped to kiss her shoulder and the tender corner of her neck. "You bloody well better be."

"Strange things," she said, her voice ending on a whimper when his hands circled her hips to play with her pussy. "It's not like I'm a virgin, but...I've never felt like this."

"Tell me what you feel," he said, and deliberately licked away Nicky's scent from her neck.

"Tingly, hot—like something's going to explode. I'm scared."

He scraped his teeth against her neck and groaned. The blood was just beneath the surface. Not yet. "Sounds like the buildup to an orgasm, love. Haven't you ever had one before?" To remove himself from temptation, he knelt behind her and nudged her legs apart with his hands.

Her buttocks rose and she gasped. "I thought so. At least, my heart raced and I felt wet...down there." A tremor ran down her legs.

With both hands, he parted her buttocks and leaned forward to lap at her down-covered pussy. Her seam oozed a fragrant gift of excitement. "You're certainly wet now." Dylan licked between her labia, tasting the salty-sweet cream.

She jerked, and then pushed her hips back and higher, giving him greater access to her soaking cunt. "Ooh! Keep doing whatever it is you're doing. Don't stop."

Two fingers parted her outer lips, and he fluttered his tongue against the thin, tender folds inside. He drew them between his teeth and sucked.

Instantly, Emmy shrieked and bucked. "I'm gonna die. Ohmygod, I'm gonna die."

Her body shook with her sobs, but Dylan didn't stop. He slid his tongue inside her juicy cunt and speared in and out while his thumb rubbed in circles over her hooded clit. When her breath came in rhythmic pants, and her thighs stiffened against his cheeks, he sensed she hurtled toward her climax.

Teeth slid from the roof of his mouth a moment before he turned his head and sank his incisors into her quivering pussy, piercing her clit and inner lips.

Emmy screamed a long ragged howl. Her cunt throbbed with pleasure.

Small capillaries burst and spilled a trickle of blood into Dylan's mouth. As he sucked, he continued to mouth her tender flesh—until long after the pulses tightening her vagina slowed. Retracting his teeth, he healed the tiny wounds he'd made with the lazy lap of his tongue. He turned his head and kissed her inner thigh.

"Did you just bite me?" she asked, her tone incredulous.

"Yes." He leaned away from her. "Did you like it?"

"I didn't know you could do such a thing. And it hurt! But…" Still pressed to the glass, she glanced over her shoulder. "…is that what an orgasm's really like?"

Not knowing which issue he should address first, Dylan rose painfully to his feet. One need had been partially slaked, but by now his cock had to be turning blue from constriction. He unbuttoned his vest and shrugged it off, not caring where it landed on the floor. Gritting his teeth, he willed his shaft to relax, and then he reached for his zipper.

"Good lord! You're not wearing underwear. Should you be doing that?"

His hand hesitated and he opened his eyes, hoping she wasn't asking him to end their interlude.

Emmy had stopped hugging the window and was staring at his groin.

From the front, she was proving lethal to his self-control. He'd always been partial to blondes—and she was the real thing. "Should I be doing what, Emmy? Do you want me to keep my pants on?" He grimaced against the pain. "I'll stop now, if you tell me."

"That's not what I meant. But your zipper." She pointed at his groin and blushed a deeper rose. "Won't you hurt yourself with the zipper?"

"Stop talking about it, and I might be able to get him down a bit." He closed his eyes against the sight of her and took a deep breath.

"Oh. Can I help?"

"No!" Taking another deep breath, he eased the zipper down slowly, wincing as the metal teeth scraped his cock.

He heard her gasp. "Holy shit! Now I'm not sure which will hurt worse, your bite or your dick."

Dylan jerked, and the zipper pinched his cock. "For fuck's sake!" He ripped the zipper down the rest of the way, then doubled over in pain. Air left his lungs in a single strangled gust.

"Oh, I'm sorry." Emmy's hand patted his head. "What can I do? Can I help?"

Still clutching his groin, he raised his head and stared at her.

Her eyes were wide with concern. "Your face is bright red. Are you all right? Can you breathe? I know the Heimlich."

"What the fuck?" He shook his head in confusion. "Just sit!"

When she sank onto the edge of the leather sofa, Dylan felt it safe enough to turn his back. He reached for the edge of his desk to steady himself. Gradually, the pain ebbed, and he straightened.

Nervous laughter bubbled. "Oh! I meant CPR, not the Heimlich. No wonder you looked at me like I'd grown two heads."

Dylan shook his head, and then surprised himself with a single bark of laughter. He turned back to the sofa. Emmy still hugged the edge, her skin ghostly pale against the dark leather.

She bit her lip and raised her arm to cover her breasts. "I suppose the mood's gone, huh? What with you injured and all. I'll just get dressed."

His gaze swept over her breasts, rounded belly, and the nest of pale hair between her legs. "If you give me a minute to recover—"

Emmy chewed on her lips, and then bounced from the sofa and walked toward him, stopping just in front of him.

With eyes on her breasts, he pushed his jeans down his hips and struggled to free a leg.

"I could…" Emmy's gaze fell to his cock, widened, and she licked her lips.

Dylan hopped on one foot and pulled a leg from the jeans.

"…could kiss it better."

He landed on the carpeted floor on his backside, and then laid back, his arms stretched wide. "You are a menace! I give up. Sex with you may be the death of *me*." He felt a tug on his calf and looked down the length of his body, eyebrows raised.

Emmy was pulling his pants the rest of the way down his second leg. She blurted, "Well you don't think after seeing that dick that I could just walk away?"

CHAPTER THREE

Emmy pulled off his pants, relieved that finally they were on equal ground. He was flat on his back. Naked as she was. Although, equal wasn't exactly the right word for him. His dick was extraordinarily above equal. Stellar and mythic were better words that came to mind.

Redder than the rest of his skin, his cock rose from a nest of straight black hair. Hair that appeared the same color and texture as the fur on his chest. Something she'd noticed as soon as he'd taken off his leather vest.

On closer inspection, she noted his penis was thicker than her wrist and long with deep veins running down the side. It was crowned by a smooth, round head and as beautiful as the rest of him.

While she was naked and ordinary. Only ordinary wasn't the right word, either. *Über*-ordinary, maybe. No, ridiculous— that's what she was. Her ass was enormous. Her breasts were flabby. And she hadn't shaved her bikini line. Perhaps she'd better get dressed.

Her gaze fell again to his mighty sword.

"Don't get shy now," he said. "Or are you forgetting the part about kissing it better?"

How had she ever had the nerve to say that? Of course, she was always saying the first thing that came to mind. Then again, he sounded a little worried. Like he was afraid she might not go through with it.

A dick of mythic proportions didn't come by twice in a lifetime. She bit the edge of her lip and knelt beside him. "You'll have to show me what you like. My ex-boyfriend said I do it all wrong."

"He was a bloody idiot." Dylan reached for her hand and pulled it toward his cock. "Start like this." With his hand over hers, he moved her up and down on him.

The skin that slid over the rigid shaft was velvety-soft and hot. "I've done this before." She increased the speed.

His eyes closed tight. "If you use some spit, you can move faster and squeeze while you do that."

Seeing his eyes closed, she felt slightly less self-conscious. Ready to try something new. Cupping her free palm to her mouth, she spit, then slid both hands around his cock. "Squeezing is good?"

"Oh yeah. A little twisting too." His hips lifted off the floor at her first sideways caress. But his eyes stayed closed.

She must be doing it right. Relieved, she twisted her hands in opposite directions as she pushed and pulled. "What about the other thing?"

"Other thing?" he gasped, and opened his eyes.

"A blow job. I'm not very good at that either."

"God help me." Dylan sighed and put an arm behind his head. With his head raised, his green eyes could see everything she did.

Her hands slowed and she waited for his next instructions, determined to get it right.

"Stop moving your hands," he said, his face taut.

Startled, she stopped instantly. Maybe, she'd hurt him.

"You were doing it right, Emmy." He raised his hand to comb his fingers through her hair. "Too right."

She let out a relived sigh. "Would you like me to do the other thing now?"

"Just put your mouth wherever you want," he said, his voice gruff and low.

The "wherever you want" confused and excited her. Her ex had always insisted on her swallowing his cock right away.

She leaned over him and tried to decide where to start first. Head, shaft, or the sac below?

She kissed his balls, smoothing her lips over them. Only, it wasn't enough. She stuck her tongue out and laved one, but it rolled away. Determined to hold it still for a licking, she sucked one into her mouth and caressed it with her tongue.

A deep moan and lift of his hips told her she was on the right track. She opened her mouth wide and sucked the other into her mouth.

"Emmy," he said, his voice strained. "Straddle my face."

"Huh?" So surprised by his request, she let him pull her around, until her pussy hovered above his mouth and his penis tickled her collarbone.

The now familiar stroke of his tongue had her back curling like a cat to press her pussy into his face. His mouth closed over her labia, and he sucked and stroked, making her forget her purpose until the shaft of his dick nudged her chin.

She tilted his penis and lowered her mouth over the silky-smooth head. When his teeth sank into her tender flesh, she squirmed and moaned—and bit into his dick.

With a single, deafening roar, he lifted her from his body and pushed her to the side. "What the hell do you think you're doing?"

"What you did to me." Tears filled her eyes. She'd done it all wrong, again. Her hands covered her breasts. *I'm so stupid.*

With his hand fisted around his cock, Dylan cursed. "Son of a—" His gaze met hers, and he grew still, his face tight with a grimace. "It's my fault. I should have explained. There's a difference between you and me."

"Right. The man-woman thing." She sniffed. "Yeah, you Tarzan. Me Jane."

"No." He let go of his dick and combed his fingers through her hair again.

By now his petting calmed her. She turned to his hand like a cat seeking an ear rub. "I just did it wrong."

"No, dear. I can bite—you can't. At least not hard."

She glanced down. Angry red teeth marks marred the shaft. "I'm sorry." Then she realized he was still engorged, fully erect. "Does it hurt much? Can I try it again?"

"No!"

Deflated, her shoulders sank and her heart slowed to a dismal thump.

His finger lifted her chin. "Emmy, let's just fuck."

Emmy searched his eyes for any sign of pity for her inept performance, but saw only raw desire. Once again encouraged, she said eagerly, "Show me what you want. Contrary to my previous error—I really am a quick learner."

Kneeling in front of her, he helped her into position, her legs spread wide over his lap. "You're in charge. Take as much of me as you want."

Accustomed to being commanded by a more experienced partner, Emmy awkwardly planted her legs on either side of him and rose high enough for him to place his cock against the opening of her vagina. With her hands on his shoulders, she lowered herself a few inches, letting gravity pull her down his shaft.

"That's it," he said, and his hands on her ass helped her rise.

She sank again, slowly, making sure she savored every sensation as his cock drove upward, past her labia, into her channel, stretching her. Then up she rose again.

Soon her breath came in little pants, sweat breaking over her skin. When she noticed moisture collecting on Dylan's upper lip, she stopped worrying about it. Instead, she slid her moist breasts against his chest, swirling her nipples in his hair.

Up and down. Down and grinding—her swollen clit seeking the friction of the hair covering his groin. She needed him deeper and harder. She wanted another orgasm. "Ooh!" Her voice rose as she bounced faster. "Oooh!"

Dylan's strong arms closed around her, stopping her movement.

She slapped his shoulders. "I'm losing it! Let me move."

His arms tightened. "You're not losing it. Sometimes pausing makes your orgasm more powerful."

"Really?" She stopped struggling and found her face was level with his. Staring into his eyes, she noted flecks of brown and gold, the colors of the forest at the start of autumn. His irises weren't entirely green.

Dylan blinked and pulled back his head. "What's wrong?"

"Nothing. I'm just catching my breath." Then something occurred to her. "Do you realize we've never kissed? Here you are with your dick all the way up me, and we haven't kissed."

His eyebrows drew together in a frown. "I beg your pardon. I kissed you. Remember? Downstairs, in front of Nicky."

Dylan's nipples were flat, brown circles with tiny nubs in the center. She wondered if they'd dimple like hers when kissed. "Who?"

"The *badder* guy." One of his hands closed over hers, halting her exploration. "The one licking your neck. Do you remember now?"

"I remember. It seems so long ago." Satisfied Dylan hadn't bypassed a rule of modern lovemaking, Emmy laid her head on his shoulder. "So are you going to show me that more powerful orgasm?"

His hand stroked her head. "Have you caught your breath?"

She peeked at his face, thrilled at the lusty look in his eyes. "Will I be needing it?"

"Oh yes." He smacked her ass. "Now get off me."

She groaned noisily and closed her legs around his back. "I don't want to."

"Emmy, do you like the feel of me inside you?" he asked, his voice a sexy growl next to her ear.

"Mmmm-hmmm. That's why I'm not moving."

"And if I tell you I can be deeper inside you?"

Emmy's belly tightened like a spring. This was something else she knew about. She unwound her legs and pushed off his lap, his cock sliding from inside her with a pop. In an instant, she turned and went down on her hands and knees. "Doggie style, right?"

He coughed. It sounded suspiciously like a laugh. Then hands closed over her buttocks, parting them. A single slide of his cock between her cheeks had her arms trembling. Then he slid his long shaft inside her soaking pussy, pushing inexorably inside. A long stroke out, and he drove back inside—*hard*.

Emmy started the climb, jerking and whimpering softly as he pounded into her, until her arms collapsed beneath her, and her head sank to the floor. But his hands anchored her hips as he continued to slam against her ass, faster and faster.

Suddenly, her breath caught, and her world tilted. "Ohmygod! Ohmygod!" she chanted, slanting her hips upward to take him deeper still. Another stroke, and then the tension in her belly snapped, and her cunt began to milk his cock, throbbing and clasping.

Still he moved inside her. At the same maddening pace.

As the pulsing inside her slowed, a nagging thought stopped her cold. Perhaps, she wasn't woman enough to get him off?

Again, she rose and pushed back to meet his strokes. When his hands squeezed her ass, she was reassured. The sound of flesh slapping flesh resounded each time his belly met her ass, warming her skin and her heart.

Excitement coiled in her belly, and she arched her back. "It's happening again!"

* * * * *

Dylan's hips pistoned faster, Emmy's soft bottom cushioning his belly at the end of each sharp stroke. Her moans tightened his balls until he had to come or they would explode.

An itchy tingle in his gums announced the downward glide of his teeth. He halted instantly and prayed for restraint. He'd already scared her once.

"No, don't stop now," Emmy wailed and pushed back, trying to take him deeper inside.

With a curse, he stopped the movement of her hips.

"Is this another pause to make it stronger?" she asked, her breath gasping.

Dylan raised his gaze to the ceiling, willing himself to resist the dark lust that swept over him. Instead, it centered between his thighs.

Emmy bucked, her head flung back. "Please, do something. Move!" Her hair settled, strands of her blond hair clinging to the sweat on her back.

He wanted nothing more than to wrap her hair in his fist. "Hold still, Emmy. I'll hurt you."

A shudder wracked her shoulders and her head sank to the floor again. "Do you want to bite me again?" she asked, and then peeked over her shoulder.

He clenched his jaw, his long teeth spearing the inside of his upper lip.

"It's okay," she said softly. "Weird, but okay. Besides, it didn't hurt that bad." A smile lifted the corners of her lips. "And I came."

He shook his head, trying to deny the quickening that pushed at the skin of his cheeks and forehead. "Don't look at me, Emmy."

"Just do it." With a shrug that he felt pull at his groin, she faced away. "Whatever gets you moving again. Fuck me, Dylan."

"Come here," he said, guiding her buttocks down as he knelt behind her. Still connected, he pulled her into his arms. Her back leaned into his chest, and her buttocks were cradled by his groin.

As his hands settled over her belly, he commanded, "Give me your neck," and he nuzzled through her hair to find the corner of her shoulder, drowning in the scent of apple blossoms and her desire. Goosebumps rose beneath his palms.

Emmy tilted her head to the side. "Tell me what you want."

Dylan lapped the side of her neck, his tongue preparing her fragile skin. "Trust me to make this good for you."

A little gust of laughter jerked her rounded belly. "You've already given me better than my boyfriend ever did in over four years."

Primitive, surging anger instantly reshaped his face, and the muscles of his body hardened to steel. He thrust upward.

"Ohmygod!" she cried. Her hands raised behind her head to twist in his hair.

Dylan slid his hands beneath her to cup her buttocks and he squeezed. His voice almost a snarl, he said, "Move on me, baby."

Her knees on either side of him, she lifted up then sank back down on his cock. Her sigh of relief ending on a moan.

Dylan glided his tongue over her skin one last time, then sank his teeth into her neck, just breaking into the skin.

She struggled against him. "I'm not sure—"

His hands rose to her breasts and he fondled them, tugging at the nipples until she eased back once again.

"There's more?" she asked, her breath hitching when he deepened the bite. "It's incredible."

His teeth slid into her until blood rushed into his mouth.

"Ohmygod!" she repeated, rotating her hips on his cock, grinding down. She writhed, her buttocks sliding on his thighs. Then, with his mouth still upon her neck, she bounced against his lap in short jerks.

When her shudders grew deep, starting in her thighs and rising to her belly, Dylan's humanity was nearly lost. A rumbling started deep in his throat that increased with the volume of her moans. He flexed his thighs, lifting them both as he pumped into her. Faster and faster, the blood screaming through his veins, and then his cock burst with a stream of come.

He groaned against her neck.

"Please," she said, gasping.

Dylan withdrew his teeth immediately and realized that he, too, was trembling. At once, he licked the punctures on her neck until they closed. Then he dropped a hand to the curls between her legs.

She widened the space between her legs and continued to rock against him.

As he twisted a nipple between the fingers of one hand, fingers of the other combed through the fine hair until they found the slick button of her clitoris.

He glided his fingers down to where his dick was embedded in her pussy. Capturing cream from their combined come, he returned to her clit and circled on it, the pad of his finger rubbing harder and harder. When she began to keen, he plucked her clit, squeezing in rhythm with the rough treatment of nipple.

"Dylan!" she cried, a moment before she collapsed against him, panting.

Long strokes over her belly and thighs calmed her breathing. Her head lolled on his shoulder, and she looked up. "If I make it home, I'm staying in bed for a week."

He rubbed his cheek against the soft skin on her shoulder, assuring himself his face had returned to its human mask. "I'll see you home."

"You don't have to," she said quickly. "I won't make this into anything more than what it is."

"And what is it?" he asked.

"Wonderful. But just a fuck." Her gaze darted away.

Her blunt words knocked the breath out of him. He wondered why. He'd gotten exactly what he'd set out to find tonight. Uncomplicated sex. Still, he couldn't stop the sudden surge of anger. "Whether you want to see me again or not, you're stuck with me whenever the sun goes down."

"Only in the dark?" One blonde brow arched. "What are you, a vampire?"

CHAPTER FOUR

Dylan gave her a heated stare.

Disappointed he hadn't returned a smart-ass comment, Emmy wondered if her blunt words had shocked him. She'd only said "it was just a fuck" to let him know she had no expectations. If he knew he'd rocked her world, he'd probably run screaming into the night.

Not that Dylan appeared to be a screamer, but most men got butterflies when a woman appeared too enthusiastic in their company.

No, Emmy wasn't going to cling. If their interlude was all she'd get from this unusual man, then she'd walk away proud she'd earned her first orgasm. She'd certainly worked hard for it!

Emmy giggled, then looked up into his face again. "Is there any particular reason we're stuck with each other at night?" Her heart pitter-patted, hoping he hadn't said it in the heat of passion. Perhaps he'd finally seen her without his passion-lenses and decided not to be seen in public with her huge butt.

Dylan sighed, then said, "Love, would you mind getting up now? We need to talk."

Here it comes, she thought. *I won't cry. I won't let him see how disappointed I am.* She rose from his lap and bent to pick up her clothes from the floor.

"Not yet," he said, his strong fingers wrapping around her arm.

All that glorious muscle had been hers — at least for a while.

He guided her to the sofa. "Take a seat. We'll talk."

After she had settled onto the cool seat, she wished she had her skirt to cover her thighs, which spread like butter over the leather.

He knelt beside the sofa, his eyes level with hers, the gold flecks glowing in the sea of deep green. His finger tapped her nose. "Emmy, pay attention."

Hoping to forestall some awful 'I'm letting you down easy speech,' Emmy blurted, "You really don't have to do this." Her hands wrung in her lap. "I'm a grown-up girl. This was great, but I can make my own way home now."

His brows drew together. "Emmy, you're not going anywhere without me."

Her heart lurched, wanting to soar, but she kept hold of the tethers. "Dylan, you don't have to say that. I'm not expecting anything to come of this. Can't we just say we had a grand ole time and I can leave?"

"Don't you want to see me again?" he asked softly.

"Of course I do," she admitted, feeling as awkward as a teenager waiting to be kissed. "I was just trying to make this easy for you, in case you wanted an out."

"I want to see you again, too."

She released the tethers and smiled as her heart lifted toward a clear blue sky.

"But there's something else." His voice was deep and serious.

The traces tied to her heart tangled in the trees. "You've already got a girlfriend?"

He blinked. "No, Emmy, I don't have a girlfriend."

"You're bi! Was that your boyfriend I saw you with earlier? I can see why you'd be attracted—he's very handsome."

His finger pressed against her lips. "I'm not bi. I'm not trying to brush you off. I just need for you to listen to what I say."

He glared and kept his finger mashed to her lips until she nodded. When he took the finger away, Emmy tightened her lips and slid her hands beneath her thighs.

He rose to his feet. "Your life is in danger." Dragging a hand through his hair, he paced in front of her. "Your friend Monica is working for Nicky now. And Nicky's very dangerous. In fact, he's a murderer."

His cock swayed between his legs in the most amazing way, and then she realized what he'd said. Alarmed, she said, "Then we have to help Monica."

He halted. "Monica can't be saved. It's too late for her, Emmy. And you must never see her again."

She waved her hand in dismissal of the foolish thought. "Why should I believe you? She sells housewares in the same store where I'm the bookkeeper. Saleswomen don't become murderer's groupies."

"While I'm sure there was a speck of logic somewhere in all that, I'm telling you the truth."

"I don't believe you. She's my friend."

"For the love of..." Dylan's hands clenched at his sides. "She's not the same girl. Nicky's changed her."

Emmy felt her lower lip push out, and sucked it back in quickly. How would he ever see it her way if she acted like a child? "Even if it were true, Monica would never hurt me."

Dylan threw his hands up. "Fine. Have it your way."

Emmy was a little disappointed Dylan had conceded so quickly. "Great." At least he'd quit ragging on Monica.

"Get dressed," he said, his tone brooking no dissent.

Ruffled by his curt tone, Emmy lifted her chin and knelt to retrieve her clothing. After patting the ground without results, she relented and looked at the floor. She gathered her clothing, then glanced at Dylan.

His arms were crossed over his chest and he was completely dressed. "Do you need help?"

She wondered how he'd dressed so quickly. "I've been putting my own clothes on for twenty-odd years now. I think I can manage." Only she was so irritated, she put her panties on inside out.

A single raised eyebrow mocked her.

"I did that on purpose." She slid her skirt over her hips and sucked her breath in to close the zipper at her waist, then she lifted her bustier and let it dangle from the end of her finger. When he didn't take the hint, she cleared her throat. "It would go faster if you laced it up for me."

Dylan cupped a hand to his ear. "I didn't quite hear you. Were you asking for my help?"

"You might be God's gift in the fucking department, but I can see why there's no girlfriend lurking in the shadows — you are a Grade A asshole!" She threw the black velvet bustier at his head and stomped toward the door, hand outstretched to the brass knob.

He slammed into her back, pinning her to the door. "You're completely mad," he said, his voice tickling her ear. "And what a temper. There's not a woman in this building who would brave my wrath."

"Of course, I'm mad." His body enveloped hers, making her feel incredibly small and helpless. "You'd drive a saint to commit murder. Besides, I'm not afraid of you."

Something warm and wet glided over the top of one shoulder.

"No fair," she complained, but she turned her head away to bare her neck. He had the most amazing tongue, slightly rough like a cat's.

"I know," he said, his tongue flickering over her skin to slide toward her ear. "You're having a perfectly good pout, and I'm ruining it."

"Yes, you a—" Her breath caught when is hands caressed the sides of her breasts where they were mashed against the door.

He shifted slightly away, and his hands moved around to cup them fully. "We could just stay here." His voice dropped to a low purr. "I could play with your breasts, since I didn't really have a chance to do them justice before."

Emmy moaned and rubbed her ass against his groin. "I'd love to, but I have to work in the morning. I should head home."

"Then I'll make sure you get home safely." He removed his hands and lifted his body away from hers.

Immediately, Emmy missed his weight. She turned to face him and leaned back to let the door to support her wobbly legs. "Because of Monica?"

"And her boyfriend—Nicky." He lifted his hands, his palms framing her face. "I'm not asking you to put your faith in me. I'm just asking you to allow the possibility they mean you harm."

Reluctant to even conceive her friend would betray her, Emmy nodded and accepted his help donning her bustier.

"Did you drive here?"

"No, I took a taxi."

"Good. We'll take my car. When we leave here, I want your vigilance. Tell me if you see anything suspicious."

Numbed by great sex and the depressing feeling her perception of her life was about to change forever, Emmy followed Dylan from the club. Except for her directions, the drive was quiet, and sooner than she wished, Dylan parked his BMW a block from her apartment building.

"Stay inside. I'll get your door." He let himself out, and walked around the car.

But he didn't immediately open her door. His head lifted, and his nostrils flared like a dog catching a scent in the wind.

The door latch popped with a soft click and he eased the door open, offering his hand to assist. "Stay behind me," he said, then led the way down the deserted street. They walked on the side of the street opposite the streetlamps, careful to keep in the shadows.

Emmy's nerves crackled with unease. Although she was sure Dylan was dead wrong about her friend, and not at all convinced Monica even had a steady boyfriend, she clutched the back of his vest. Monica told her every down and dirty detail of her life—how could she miss telling her best friend she was dating a serial killer?

When they were thirty yards from her front steps, Dylan stopped cold, drawing her deep into the shadow of a shop doorway.

Emmy looked both ways along the street, but didn't see a thing wrong. "Really," she whispered, "aren't you being just a little paranoid?"

"Quiet." His arm circled her waist, and he held her to his side. "Look to the left of the steps."

Emmy stared, but still didn't see anything except shadows. Until one shadow moved. A dark figure crept out of the darkness and into the light of the streetlamp. Then another stepped from behind a car.

Emmy gasped. One was Monica—but the other wasn't Nicky. Still, Emmy thought she recognized the man from The Cavern. He'd been among the young men in the group surrounding Nicky. "I don't understand," she said, trying to read Dylan's expression in the dark. "What would they be doing here—hiding in the dark? They're a little old to be egging my place. Halloween's over."

Dylan didn't reply, he turned and walked back the way they'd come, pulling her behind him. Emmy heard shouts, and without knowing why, she and Dylan broke into a run. The car loomed forever in the distance. With her sides aching, she gasped for breath, struggling to keep up with him.

Using the remote, he unlocked the doors and they both dove inside. The ignition revved to life, and he pulled out onto the street, executing a sharp U-turn. As the headlights swept the street before them, several men were illuminated. Something about their appearance didn't look quite right to Emmy.

Then she saw Monica, her glossy brown hair framing a face that looked like something out of a nightmare. Her cheeks and forehead protruded. Her brow was heavy and deeply furrowed. She bared her teeth and a jagged line of white appeared, framed by long incisors that glistened when she threw her head back. The howl that followed Dylan and Emmy down the street wasn't human.

Emmy welcomed the familiar roar of the engine and muted sounds within the car. The glare from an oncoming car startled her. She blurted, "That wasn't a goddamned mask! Was it?"

"No Emmy, it wasn't," Dylan said.

His calm reply wrapped a cold blanket around her shoulders. A shiver lifted the hairs on the back of her neck, and then the trembling began in earnest, shaking her shoulders.

Dylan's hand landed on her arm and she jumped.

"Easy now," he crooned. "I'm taking you to my place. They'll know where you are, but they won't be able to touch you there."

"How...how did you know they would be there?" she asked, the chill causing her to stammer. "Why do they...want me?"

His jaw tensed. His gaze slid toward her then away. "Because I want you."

Slowed by shock, her response came several moments later. "Then why...didn't you stay away from me?"

When Dylan glanced at her, his expression was stark. "I couldn't help myself."

"I don't understand. What's wrong with their faces?"

"They're vampires."

Despite her quaking unease, Emmy found that comment amusing. "Like 'I vant to trink you're blahd' vampires? No kidding, what was wrong with them?"

"I'm telling you the truth. They're changed. Not human." He swallowed, then said, "They feed on human blood."

Emmy remembered Dylan's fetish for biting, and all her senses clamored "danger". She licked her suddenly dry lips. "You're like them, aren't you?"

His eyes narrowed, but his gaze never left the road. "Leave it alone, Emmy."

She couldn't. She had to know. "You're one of *them*, aren't you?"

"Fuck!" His fist slammed against the steering wheel. "Yes, Emmy. I'm a vampire." He shot her an angry glance. "Satisfied?"

"Let me out of the car," Emmy demanded, her hands scraping the door panel in search of the handle.

"I can't let you out of my sight, Emmy. It's not safe."

"And I'm safe with you? Let me out of the car!" her voice rose, hysteria making it shrill. "Let me out of the goddamned car!"

Dylan's face hardened, and his hands tightened on the steering wheel. "Settle down, Emmy. It'll be all right."

"I want out," she screamed. She yanked on the door handle and pushed. The door swung outwards and she prepared to jump.

Dylan pulled the steering wheel to the right, and the door slammed closed. Before she could open it again, he'd engaged the safety lock. He had her trapped inside the car.

Emmy flew at him, raining blows at his head. "Let me out! Let me out!"

With the arm nearest her raised to protect his face, he shouted, "For fuck's sake! Cut it out!"

Emmy was beyond hearing. What she'd seen had frightened her so badly all she wanted to do was run. One of her blows reached beyond his arm, hitting his face.

In an instant, Dylan's features blurred and stretched, the upper part of his face pushing outward, his teeth lengthening as she watched, finally mute with horror. She shrank against the door.

Dylan roared, his hands still clutching the wheel, but no longer controlling the direction of the vehicle. The car swerved to the left, throwing Emmy hard against the passenger door, and then back to the right, bumping up onto the curb. They hurtled toward a streetlight pole, and Emmy braced herself, closing her eyes.

A loud, animal roar preceded the sickening crunch of metal, shards of glass tinkling against the metal pole. Slowly, Emmy realized they'd come to a halt and Dylan's upper body was draped across her. His face—his "normal" face—rested on her shoulder. He was breathing.

She shoved him away, determined to slide out of the car while he was unconscious. But the door handle didn't budge, so she punched the button for the automatic windows.

He stirred, straightening away from her. "Ballocks!" he said, and then groaned, clutching his head.

A whimper escaped her when the window slid down. She reached for her seatbelt latch—

His hand covered her fingers, stopping her from releasing it.

Her gaze darted to his face, dreading the possibility he'd changed again and was ready to rip out her throat.

Instead, a lopsided grin broke across his face. "Hell of a ride, sweetheart."

CHAPTER FIVE

"Are you all right?" Dylan asked, his hand reaching for her face.

She jerked away.

"Still skittish I see." He looked around them and cursed. "Looks like you have your wish. You'll have to walk."

He tried his door, but it too, was impossible to open. Instead, he lowered his window and levered himself out of the car.

As was his habit, he immediately lifted his nose to the breeze, checking for danger. Finding nothing strange in the rain-scented breeze beyond the acrid aroma of burnt rubber, he knelt beside Emmy's door. "Sweetheart, are you hurt?"

Bathed in the fluorescent light of the streetlamp, Emmy's expression grew more alarmed as he visually inspected her for injury.

She must have thought he was envisioning a menu. She drew away from him, fumbling with her latch. "Don't you touch me!"

"Perhaps you shouldn't be moving so quickly."

Stubborn to the bone, Emmy knelt in her seat and climbed over the console to his, then crawled out the driver's window. She landed in a heap on the far side of the car, letting loose an impressive string of curses.

Dylan sighed and got to his feet, eyeing Emmy as she stood, afraid to spook her into further acts of recklessness.

As it was, her hands lifted as though she were poised for flight.

He eased his hands into the pockets of his jeans. "You have a few choices here."

The headlights from an approaching car drew her attention from his face. Her shoulders lifted with her indrawn breath.

"You might want to rethink flagging them down for help. You don't know who's in the car."

"I'll take my chances," she said, stepping from the curb into the street.

Dylan raised his gaze to the streetlamp and planted his hands on his hips—rather than around her stubborn neck. "Emmy, will you stop to think? If I'd wanted to hurt you, I could have done so when we were still at The Cavern."

Her frown reflected her indecision.

As the car drew closer, Dylan took the choice away from her. With one bound he landed on top of the car. Before she could finish gasping his name, he landed beside her and dragged her into the shadows, his hand covering her mouth.

The car passed slowly as the driver peered out at the wreckage of Dylan's BMW.

Dylan held his breath, but didn't recognize the face of the driver. Then he heaved a sigh when he saw a child in the back seat, still dressed in his Spiderman costume. He was dozing with his face pressed to the window glass.

Not Nicky's crew. Not yet, anyway.

The car drove by and turned at the next corner.

Emmy's elbow dug into Dylan's waist and he released her, stepping back with his hands raised.

She scampered several steps away, putting distance between them before swinging back to level a blistering glare. "What is it with you vampires? Can't you take no for an answer?"

He fought a smile. She couldn't still be afraid if she was back to scolding him.

Frustration pushed her lips into a pout he wanted to kiss away.

He cocked one eyebrow, intentionally pushing another button. "Did I ask you a question?"

Angry red circles blossomed on her cheeks. "That's not the point, and you know it." She looked back at where he had held her in the shadow. "You move pretty fast. I didn't see you coming." Her eyes narrowed. "Is that another vampire talent?"

"Of course." he said, his voice pitched low.

"Don't you give me that sexy voice," she replied. "You're just trying to work your vampire hoo-doo on me, again."

This time he couldn't stop the smile from stretching across his mouth. "Vampire hoo-doo?"

"You know damn well what I'm talking about. You worked some kind of spell on me. I wasn't looking for a man tonight. Nope. I was minding my own business when you and Nicky-boy started arguing over me like two dogs over a bone. And bam! Not ten minutes later you've got me naked and panting—"

"Like a dog?" Dylan's smile grew wider and he took a step toward her.

She took a step back. "What do you think you're doing?"

"I'm going to kiss you."

"Are you nuts?" Her eyes grew round, but she didn't give another inch. "Didn't you hear a word I just said?"

His hands circled her waist, and he pulled her close, his hips pressing between her thighs.

"No biting," she said, her breath catching when her chest flattened against his. "Biting me is strictly verboten."

He lowered his head. "Is kissing?"

"Kissing is...just kissing, right?" Her hands crept up his chest then around his neck, her fingers sliding into his hair.

Dylan touched her bottom lip with his tongue, then licked along the seam of her lips. He felt her sigh as she opened her mouth, letting him inside.

Her surrender emboldened him, and he reached for her buttocks, his fingers squeezing the plump velvet-covered pillows of flesh as his clothed cock prodded her lower belly.

Her hands pulled on his hair, and she stuck her tongue into his mouth, sliding it over his teeth. When her legs widened to accommodate him, Dylan pushed against her, centering his cock on her pussy and rubbing, in and out. He had to get inside her.

What was it about her? He stroked her tongue, and her belly curved into him. His hand sought the small of her back and pressed her so close they aligned. She was a perfect fit.

But still a human. Dylan pulled back.

She followed his hips, moaning as she ground her crotch against him.

He ended the kiss, resting his forehead on hers. Needing space to put her back in the box that kept his heart safe. "We should wait until we reach my place."

"Too damn late," she muttered. "You did it, again."

"Did what?" he asked, willing his body back into submission.

"Your vampire hoo-doo. My pussy's so hot, I'll die if you don't fuck me now."

Blood pooled in his groin, making him hard as oak. "You do have a way with words, Emmy." Not a man to leave a girl hurting, Dylan drew a fistful of her skirt up her long legs.

Emmy's hands dropped to his waist. She unbuttoned the opening of his jeans and slid down the zipper. Eager hands shoved his pants down his hips, just far enough to free his cock.

One part of him was amused at her ardor, the other part was desperate to be inside her, and so he lifted her up by the buttocks.

Her legs rose and wrapped around his waist.

The head of his dick bumped against the soft hair covering her mons, then slid along her moist cleft.

Emmy groaned and flexed her hips, and finally, he was gliding inside her, swallowed from tip to root, enveloped in warm, wet heat.

His cock swelled, the skin stretching tighter, his balls aching for release.

"Move, you gotta move." Her voice, thick and plaintive, spurred him. Walking with her in his arms, he stepped toward his car and pressed her back against the passenger door.

With her anchored, he bent his knees and pulled out of her, relishing in the moan of protest that rose from her throat, before he slammed back inside her.

Her legs constricted around his waist, but Dylan pulled out again, and then rubbed the head of his penis along her drenched slit.

"Please," she begged, then pushed her hands between them. Before he understood what she was doing, the top of her bustier was pushed beneath her breasts and she'd opened his vest.

When the tips of her soft, naked breasts, rubbed against his chest, he felt his face tighten with the shifting of bones. He tried to lower his forehead to her shoulder, but she was pressing wet kisses to the side of his mouth.

"I need more," she said. "Hurry. Just give it to me hard." She slid her lips along his jaw and nipped the underside if his chin.

Unable to wait a second longer, he gripped her hips hard and pulled her down as he rammed upward into her. Then he lifted and lowered, nothing gentle left in the sweet pounding he delivered to her pussy.

The car creaked, her breath gusted, and he hammered faster. Emmy's arms tightened around his neck, her eyes closed tight. "Harder. Oooh! Please, harder."

Along with his face, his body hardened and his cock lengthened. Mustn't drink, he reminded himself, the last vestige of his human mind relenting to primal instinct.

Instead, his teeth sank into his bottom lip and his thrusts deepened, shortened, and finally hammered. Reaching so far inside he battered against the mouth of her womb.

Aware she writhed and moaned and pleaded, but unable to think beyond the tight, warm hole that gloved him, he continued to move. Faster. Harder. Deeper.

Until the warm place tightened like a fist, and she let loose a long, keening howl.

He thrust again, and then again, before flinging back his head to roar. His sex erupted deep inside the woman's belly. Marking her with his seed.

When sperm pumped inside, he lowered his head to her shoulder, shuddering as he dragged air into his starved lungs.

With the last pulse of his orgasm, Dylan's face realigned and the curtain of his bloodlust lifted.

Emmy's legs trembled as they unclasped his waist and lowered to the ground. Dylan lifted his head, wary of what he might see in her gaze.

Emmy's eyes opened and her gaze met his. Distress wrinkled her forehead, and her lips quivered.

She was afraid again.

Dylan cursed and lifted her off his cock, then wiped the blood trickling from his mouth with the back of his hand.

After she pulled down her skirt, he smoothed her hair back from her forehead. "Did I bite?"

"No. You also haven't come yet."

"What makes you think that?"

"Your man-thing is still hard as a rock."

He grinned. "Well, I didn't bite. And I won't. I promised."

Her face tilted to the side. "Can't you come without, um, a transfusion?"

"Of course I can. But it's a lot of work, and we can't stay here any longer."

"That was all for me?"

"Do you trust I won't hurt you?"

"Hell no! You're a man. You're into…pausing!"

Dylan was satisfied with that. She saw him as a man. "Will you at least stick with me until we can get to a safe place, tonight?"

Her eyes narrowed, and then she remembered her breasts were bared because her hands flew up to cover them and she turned away to adjust her top. "Trust me, he says. When every chance he gets, he has me flashing the world."

Dylan shook his head. Never mind he'd already had her luscious tits inside his mouth, or that she'd been the one to bare them in the first place.

She turned back to him, her chin jutting. "I'll go with you — for now. Until I can find a taxi, that is. I have work in the morning."

Dylan had no doubt she wouldn't be reporting to work in the morning. But her agreement was going to take some special persuasion. First things first. They needed to find shelter and fast.

He held out his hand. "Come on, sweetheart. We have to start walking."

Emmy stared at his hand like it was a snarling dog. If she touched it, he'd work his magic again and she'd be powerless to resist.

Now that she knew what he was, she understood why she'd surrendered so easily in the first place. His superpowers made him irresistible to women. Even to bookkeepers! She just had to resist his snake oil charm and the electric current that flowed from his body to hers every time they touched.

She'd resist or she'd be dead. Emmy hadn't missed his transformation from man to monster. And she'd seen the blood dripping from his mouth.

She hadn't cared at the time, because his body had grown a tensile strength that had made her weak with excitement as she held him between her thighs. And his mythic dick had attained a Titan's proportions. She'd lost her fears in an orgasm to end all orgasms.

Once she'd returned to herself, she'd been horrified at her abandon. Bookkeepers did not do it in broad...streetlight...with vampires. And they definitely didn't bare their tits every time a vampire used his bedroom voice.

"Are you coming?" he asked.

"It's still dripping down my legs," she muttered.

"Pardon me?"

"Never mind. Just lead on. And no tricks. I'm on to you now."

Dylan turned to walk down the sidewalk, keeping to the dark shadows next to the walls.

Emmy followed, too tired to question where they were going. Head down, she put one sandaled foot in front of the other.

A vampire. Wouldn't you know? Emmy Harris couldn't find herself a nice used car salesman. She had to go and find a sweet-talking vampire.

Dylan halted in front of her, and she bumped into his back. They'd left the shop fronts behind and were passing tall, abandoned tenements whose windows were dark mouths, many boarded up on the ground floor.

When Dylan turned onto the staircase leading into one such building, Emmy tugged on the back of his vest. "Dylan, this doesn't feel like a good idea," she said in a whisper.

He grabbed her hand and pulled her up the stairs. Just when she was sure he'd brought her here to ravage her so no one would hear her screams—and unsure whether that thought excited her or not—she heard the muted sound of music and laughter.

Past the wooden doors at the entry, her shoes clicked dully on the dirty tiled floor. Unable to see very far into the murky interior, she clung to Dylan's vest as he walked sure-footed toward the end of the foyer.

The music, a relentless techno beat, grew louder, echoing in the darkness. At the end of the hall, a sliver of light pierced the gloom.

Emmy wondered whether a homeless person had found shelter in the abandoned building, but then Dylan opened a door, and light spilled out, and Emmy encountered horror beyond her imagination.

CHAPTER SIX

Dylan tugged her inside, and the door closed, locking her in with monsters.

Lit only by flickering candlelight, the creatures in the room undulated. Not one of the many occupants looked their way. Engaged in sex and feeding, vampires and human lovers writhed against each other in an orgy of dance and sex. The pungent aromas of cheap perfume, cigarettes and cum were so thick she nearly gagged.

Emmy stumbled over the foot of a naked vampire as he pumped into a groaning woman where they lay, stretched across a shiny vinyl-covered couch. His back and buttocks rippling, brawny muscle flexing with each thrust. Emmy realized Dylan must look much the same when he wore his demon skin.

Others fornicated on the floor. One group consisted of a female and two males—one male pounding into the ass of the woman who was in turn going down on the other male.

On a chair, a woman straddled the lap of a vampire, whose mouth fed at her neck, blood dripping onto her breasts.

Dylan's arm slipped around her shoulders, and he brought her close.

Her gaze broke from the couple in the chair and rose to his face. She noted the taut set of his chin and the grim tightness of his mouth.

"Don't leave my side," he said. "This is a dangerous place for you, Emmy. If I had a choice, I'd never bring you here."

Too frightened to speak, she nodded, then followed as he led her through the people dancing in the center of the floor. Deeper into the smoke-filled apartment.

They passed through the living room and into another hallway where a couple fucked against the wall. When Emmy sidled past the female vampire, she hissed at her and then laughed when Emmy jumped. Aware the creature's gaze followed her down the hall, every hair on Emmy's body rose.

Dylan pushed into a room lit by moonlight, where a man and two women stretched across a large, bare mattress.

From the lax expressions on the women's faces, it was evident they'd just finished having sex. The male vampire was feeding from the wrist of a blonde woman, while a female vampire sucked blood from the top of her breasts. Based on the moans coming from the blonde, Emmy surmised blood-giving was a pleasurable thing.

Emmy's hand crept inside Dylan's, and he squeezed it.

"Viper," Dylan said.

The vampire on the bed raised his head and bared his teeth in a gruesome smile. Instantly, his ferocious mask collapsed. A handsome Hispanic man replied, "Dylan. Imagine how embarrassed I am. I've fed and not offered you a drink."

Dylan's hand tightened around hers. Emmy's fear raised a notch.

"I'm not here for a feeding," Dylan replied, his voice quiet and casual. "I need your car."

Viper's gaze sharpened and fell upon Emmy. "Don't tell me you picked up a snack in this neighborhood. Your little host isn't known to me."

Emmy pressed her body into Dylan's side, wishing she could hide. Viper's face might be handsome now, but it was alight with a malevolent curiosity.

"My car broke down. I'll have yours returned tomorrow with interest."

Viper smiled and slapped the thigh of the woman nearest him. "Leave us."

The women stretched, their nipples pointed and red. When the female vampire sidled past Emmy, she rubbed her breasts against Emmy's arm and leaned close to sniff.

Emmy forgot to breathe. Dylan reached around her and shoved the vampire away. Only when the door closed behind them, did Emmy dare relax.

Viper padded naked to the opposite corner of the room. He bent, exposing a round, hard ass, as he rifled through a backpack lying on the floor.

When he turned, Emmy couldn't drag her gaze from his cock. Were all vampires well hung?

Metal glinted in an arc when he tossed the keys to Dylan, and Emmy wondered how long she'd stared.

The wry grin that tilted the corners of Viper's mouth told her he'd noticed her interest. Then the dark rivulets at the side of his mouth reminded Emmy of what she'd just witnessed, and her stomach turned. She'd given herself to a bloodsucker, too. What did that make her?

Dylan pulled her from the room. He didn't release her hand until the doors of the apartment building closed behind them.

Immediately, she missed his comfort and rubbed her palm against her skirt. She was reading things into his actions—again. He hadn't intended to comfort her. He was just marking his territory.

They rounded the corner of the building to find a low-slung Jaguar parked in the alley.

The headlights blinked, and the doors unlocked with a soft click. Emmy crawled inside and laid her cheek against the leather seat. Her eyes closed and the hum of the engine swept her into sleep.

* * * * *

Dylan gently rolled Emmy to her side and unlaced the ribbon holding her top together.

She murmured a protest, but didn't wake. Just like she hadn't wakened when he'd hoisted her into his arms to carry her inside his house.

He swept away the last of her clothing and pulled up the bedding to cover her. Her blonde hair fanned around her pale face, a burning halo against the navy silk pillow cover. The creamy tops of her shoulders begged a kiss, but the purple half-moons beneath her eyes attested to her fatigue.

Still, he wished he could wake her to bury himself inside her one more time before he slept. Emmy's innocence was becoming a drug.

A soft chirrup from the intercom announced Quentin's arrival at the back gate. He closed the bedroom door and headed to the living room.

Quentin let himself into the room and flashed a triumphant smile. "You look bloody exhausted. Well done!"

"It's been a trying evening—and not for the reasons you think."

Quentin's eyebrows rose. "You didn't bed the girl?"

"I've yet to take her *in* a bed...but aye," Dylan said, "I've slaked that thirst."

"Oh ho! Better and better. Tell me, did she stop her chatter while doing the dirty deed?"

Dylan grinned. "She was relentless." He padded to the bar and poured whisky into two tumblers.

Quentin's face was alight with curiosity. "A spirited girl, then?"

"A passionate one." Dylan wished his friend would take his twenty questions to the devil. Something delightful awaited him in bed.

"She did appear made to pillow a man's thighs." Quentin collapsed elegantly into one of the brown leather chairs that flanked the fireplace. "There's a bit of chill in the air."

Dylan took the hint and ignited the gas flame in the fireplace. The large room was cold as a mausoleum. And vampires didn't retain heat.

Quentin raised a hand before the fire. "I didn't see the Beamer in the garage when I parked. Car trouble?"

Dylan took the chair opposite. "Of a sort," he murmured.

Quentin's gaze swung back. "Nicky's crew?"

"They were lurking near her apartment," Dylan said, letting the anger he'd banked roll over him. "Lying in wait for her to come home."

"No casualties?"

Dylan's jaw tensed. "I didn't let them get near enough."

"Nicky's gone too far," Quentin said, his voice tight with fury. "The Masters' Council has to act now."

"Most of them are too passive. Too damned comfortable to do what's right. They'll never act."

"Or worse," Quentin said. "They'll try to negotiate a holiday from death. As if one could talk Nicky into stopping."

"The council will wait, hoping one of us takes matters into our own hands."

"So they don't have to dirty their consciences with a dusting?"

"Exactly," said Dylan. He no longer had any qualms about taking the younger Master's life. Nicky had to die to spare Emmy's life.

"At least we've discovered for certain that she's in danger. We can take appropriate precautions in the coming nights."

"Unfortunately," Dylan said, "she knows what we are now."

"Well, shit. I'm sorry about that." Quentin's gaze sharpened. "I take it, the fact we're night owls didn't go over well?"

"Like a rock." Dylan glanced away. "She tried to escape me and the car kissed a light pole near Viper's."

"That's a tough neighborhood for a stroll after dark. So where'd you get the Jaguar?"

"It's Viper's."

"You took her to the Den?" Quentin's lips curled in disgust. "Were you mad? A girl like her?"

"I know. It wasn't as though I had a better choice."

"You need to join the cellular age. You could have called a cab."

Dylan threw back the drink and savored the burning trail it left on its way to his stomach.

"So how did she take it?"

Dylan closed his eyes. He'd felt her horror. "Wide-eyed as a school girl." *Does she think I'm like the hungry vamps at Viper's?*

"She didn't run screaming?"

"She was probably too frightened." Dylan wondered if demons plagued her dreams. "Tell me about Nicky."

"A priest couldn't have been more circumspect," Quentin said with disgust. "He snacked on a blood host, fucked a college student, and then went home."

"I'm surprised he cares enough to hide what he's doing."

"How certain are you that he's behind the vamps who were at your girlfriend's house?"

"His newest paramour, Monica, was among those waiting for Emmy at her apartment. Monica's her former best friend."

"Bugger. So she's already a killer. She'll feast on her friends first."

"What are friends for? They're so easy to lure away from their doors."

"You know you haven't done the girl any favors."

Dylan didn't need to be told. Instead, he changed the subject. "Her name's Emmy."

"Emmy? A sweet name."

"Yes. She's a bookkeeper."

Quentin grinned. "You're kinkier than I thought. So are you going to share this one?" he asked, with a sly tone.

"Fuck no." Jealousy niggled. "You try to seduce her, and I'll kill you."

Quentin sipped the last of the whiskey from his cup. "Sweet Emmy inspires so much violence."

"She will never see it," Dylan swore.

"Has she not seen your tender violence?" Quentin asked, his tone sly.

"I'm not sure."

"You hide your face? I'd not be doing that one in the dark. She'll glow like candlelight."

"That's too insignificant a flame."

Quentin's eyebrows rose. "A scorcher, is she? Best have a care that you don't go up in a blaze."

"My fingers are already singed."

"Braggart."

Dylan yawned. Dawn was approaching.

"I'll let the dogs into the yard," Quentin said. "Don't mind if I stay the day, do you?"

"Just keep to the other side of the house."

"Not planning to rest? Fuck. Don't say as I blame you."

Dylan rose from his chair. "I'll see you at dusk, friend."

"Lucky sod. I'm having another drink."

Dylan returned to the bedroom and slipped inside. He stripped in the moonlight and slid beneath the comforter, already warm with her body heat.

Emmy murmured in her sleep, but didn't wake when he pulled her on top of him like a blanket.

He intended only to hold her, but her hips rolled and her legs widened. Her warm thighs gloved his cock. She murmured, a soft feminine sound that filled the empty place in his heart as it swelled his cock.

The tip of his penis nudged her portal.

Liquid heat seeped out to bathe his head.

He gritted his teeth and forced his arms to relax around her. *Let her sleep, you horny bastard.*

Emmy's face rolled into the corner of his shoulder, and he lifted a hand to smooth her hair. He meant to soothe, but her mouth opened over his throat and sucked delicately against his skin.

Blood rushed from his extremities to his cock in an instant. And he waited, not sure if she'd simply kissed him in her sleep.

Then her hand slipped between their bodies and wrapped around him.

"Thank God, you're awake." Relieved she was the one taking advantage of his weakened resolve, Dylan glided a hand over her back, down to her buttocks and cupped a cheek. He slipped a finger into the crease between her buttocks and fingered the rose guarding her rear entrance.

Her gasp betrayed yet another point of innocence. He rubbed harder.

Her hands rose to his chest and she pushed away to look into his face. "Should you do...that?" she asked.

"Do you like it?" He dipped the tip of one finger past the tightly furled mouth.

Her eyes closed and her mouth formed an "O". It pleased him when her legs quivered around his hips.

"Shall I stop?" he asked, fully aware she was too far gone to permit him to stop.

Her reply didn't disappoint. She flung back her head, arching her hips, and pushed her ass against his hand to deepen the penetration.

He placed his other hand on her ripening breast and squeezed.

"Oooh," she groaned. Her hips lifted ever so slightly, pressing against the head of his cock, until it slipped inside her vagina. She ground down until she was fully seated—her soft bush grinding lightly against the base of his cock. In the darkness, her face strained, and her mouth opened wide around a gasp.

He reached for another pillow and placed it behind his head. The better to watch Emmy slowly fall apart. He'd help her lose her way.

Leaning forward, he sucked her breast deep into the cavern of his mouth and rubbed his tongue on the hard tip.

Emmy's hips flexed once, and she whimpered. She adjusted, straddling his hips, her knees fitted tightly to his torso. Then she levered herself up and down on his cock.

Dylan switched to the other breast, and her hand closed around the one he'd left. Still, she pumped up and down.

His finger swirled inside her ass, poking deeper and pulling out, and then pushed back inside.

Her hands sought his shoulders and she leaned forward, moving faster, shallow bounces jiggling her breasts and belly.

Dylan felt the first ripple along her inner walls, caressing him, pulling him deeper. Her hips slowed and rotated, as she pressed her clit against the base of his cock.

With spit on the tip of his finger he slid his hand between them and rubbed the slippery nubbin.

Her movements grew jerky before stopping altogether. "Please," she said. "Take over. I can't move."

Before she could blink, he rolled her to her back and hooked his arms beneath her knees, pressing them up and outward, spreading her wide. He planted his hands on either side of her and pumped his hips, cramming his cock as deep as he could get, then pulling out with a circling motion of his hips, before driving straight back inside.

Emmy's head thrashed on the pillow. Her moans strangled behind gritted teeth.

Dylan leaned down to kiss her and her eyes flew open. She returned the kiss, enthusiasm making her kiss wet and sloppy.

He laughed and lowered his head again to lap at her lips. When he withdrew, her hands gripped his hair to pull him back. This time her mouth sealed over his, and her tongue stabbed inside his mouth.

Now muted by their joined mouths, moans sounded from deep inside her throat and came with each panted breath.

He ended the kiss and leaned back. "Scream for me, Emmy."

CHAPTER SEVEN

At his urging, Emmy couldn't hold back another second. "Come with me," she said.

He shook his head and continued the deep thrusts that pounded against the gate of her womb. Buried to the hilt, he ground his pubic hair against her clitoris until she was so sensitive to the scrape, she thought she might come out of her skin.

But she wanted him with her. This one last time, she needed the whole enchilada. "Baby, bite me."

He stopped. His arms grew rigid and his nostrils flared. "Don't move," he said, his voice holding a tone of desperation.

"I want you, Dylan. All of you."

"Ballocks! Emmy, do you even know what you're asking?"

"For you to trust me to be strong?" She lifted her hands to his cheeks. "Do you think I haven't seen your other face?"

Dylan's eyes closed. "Then watch." His eyes opened—not the dark orbs she knew were green—but glowing golden circles that reflected the waning moonlight, like an animal's. *The better to see me.*

His cheekbones lifted, popping and cracking as his face reassembled into the monster mask, his skin stretched tight around it.

His lips curved above teeth that slid over his human set, long and razor sharp, the longest at the four corners of his smile. *The better to eat me.*

The most miraculous part of the transformation were the muscles that grew rigid and strained beneath his skin, stretching him outward, turning the arms that held her knees to stone. And his cock was one of those muscles, pushing deeper without a flex of his hips. *The better to fuck me.*

A low growl rattled in his throat, and Emmy doubted for a moment that she was really ready for this. His tongue, longer, rougher, swiped her throat. It numbed her skin. She relaxed. He'd considered her comfort—there was still part of the man inside the monster.

His teeth sank slowly into her neck, burning at first, then he drew, sucking her blood, and pure sensual heat spread from her neck, tightening her breasts and belly.

His hard body pushed inside her, pulled out, and pushed again. His thrusts were so powerful her buttocks left the bed with each stroke. Still he kept a steady rhythm that soon had her wishing for him to move faster, harder, rougher. And she told him so.

He growled in response—the Big Bad Wolf buried between her legs, and she reveled in the power to make him lose control and be the beast for her.

That she could inspire the beast in any man was a revelation.

Her hands sought his long hair, and she pulled, knowing the ache intensified the thrill. His cock stretched her, cramming inside her, hurting—wonderfully.

Then the low rumble in his throat grew louder, vibrating against her throat, and come shot into her, hot and messy.

"Dylan!" she screamed, her release rolling over her in scorching waves.

He released her legs, and she wound them around his waist, holding him tight while her pussy milked him. When the last contraction shook her, her hands fell to the pillow beside her head. She couldn't move a muscle. His passion had devoured her.

* * * * *

Emmy woke to find herself draped over Dylan like a quilt, his breath lifting the hair next to her ear.

She raised her head. Gone was her beast. Dylan's handsome face, slack with pleasant dreams, reflected the light of dawn creeping around the edge of the thick curtains.

She fitted her lips to his and kissed him, but he didn't move. If not for his shallow breath, she would have worried. Vampires, it seemed, really did sleep like the dead.

Too bad. Smashed against his chest, her tits ached for a little play. A definite downside to vampire boyfriends.

With a sigh, Emmy got out of bed and turned to draw the covers over him. Slowly, of course. She was allowed one last peek. He'd never know how hard she fought the urge to crawl back beneath the covers. But she was realistic enough to know that this had been a one-night stand. The longer she lingered, the harder it would be for her to leave with any grace. Dylan wasn't for the likes of her. He was gorgeous—she was ordinary. *And he's a vampire.*

She knew he'd object to her leaving because he was a gallant man and saw himself as her protector, but she had to face her problems on her own. If she stayed, she risked her heart.

Gathering her clothes, she dressed in the bathroom, and then called a taxi from the phone next to the light switch. She washed her teeth with a glob of toothpaste on her finger and did her best to smooth her bed-hair. She leaned into the bathroom mirror to check her neck. Miraculously, he hadn't left a mark.

She wished she could have lingered to bathe in the large whirlpool tub. Navy tile, chrome fixtures, and green plants in front of an ice block exterior wall inspired long leisurely bubble baths.

She could easily picture the two of them making love among the bubbles.

"Get a grip." Chiding herself for longing for something she could never have, Emmy left the bathroom and headed down the stairs to the front door.

Her hand was on the doorknob, ready to pull it open, when the patter of multiple feet skittered across the threshold outside. She peeked out one of the narrow windows flanking the front door.

Dogs pressed their noses to the glass. Big macho dogs with drooling jowls. One smashed his face to the glass and barked so loud it rattled the pane. She jumped and flattened her back to the door.

A honk sounded in the distance, and Emmy realized the taxi had arrived. "Shit!" At this rate she'd never make it to work.

"I see you met the pets," a familiar laconic voice startled her. The blonde man—Dylan's friend—sat in the shadows of the cavernous living room. And he was stirring. Must not be a vampire.

"Um," she said, kicking herself for how witty that had *not* sounded. "Do you know what to do with them? Will they bite me if I go outside?"

"Little girl, they will ravage you." Only the way he'd said "ravage" didn't increase her fear of the dogs.

"Are you one, too?" she asked, ready to risk dismemberment outside. After all, she had only assumed Dylan and he were friends.

"One?" he asked, with a lift of one finely arched brow.

"A bloodsucker." She rolled her eyes. "Of course you are. You're all arrogant as hell." Curiosity, spurred her to ask, "How is it that you're awake? Dylan's sleeping so soundly, I didn't wake him when I left."

White teeth and lips curved into a devilish grin. "Did you exhaust our Dylan?"

Emmy blushed, and then frowned at him to show her irritation at his lack of tact.

He shrugged. "I haven't slept yet. When I do, I'll fall into a deep, dreamless state, same as Dylan."

He spoiled the bored dilettante act with a long yawn.

"Are you going to let me out of here?" she asked, sure her taxi would leave her.

The dogs moved from the porch to the gate by the distant sound of their barks.

Quentin walked toward her on bare feet. Taller than Dylan by an inch or two, he was too pretty for Emmy's newly acquired taste. She wondered if her theory about their "proportions" would hold true, but didn't dare drop her gaze down the sharp-eyed man's body.

"You know," he said, stopping in front of her, "you'd be better off far away from here."

"Well, thanks for the advice, but I have a job," she said, raising her chin to show she wasn't the least bit intimidated. "And I like Seattle. You know, green, mossy, rain-every-fucking-day Seattle."

His grin was gleeful. "A like-spirited girl. Does Dylan know you hate this place?"

"I don't exactly hate it — it makes my hair frizz. And no, we never discussed it." And they never would. She was leaving. If Damian here would cooperate a little.

He grimaced and hunched his shoulders to stretch first one side, then the other. "Damn, I shouldn't have stayed so long in that chair."

So vampires could have backaches. That cheered her.

"He wants you to stay here, you know. It's safer."

Emmy shrugged. "It doesn't look like you guys can get around very well in the daytime. I think I'm pretty safe."

He nodded. "All right, then. I'll bring the dogs into the garage until you leave."

"Thank you."

His gaze bored into hers. "Just remember to be inside, behind a locked door tonight. Better yet, come back here before dusk."

"Sure," she said, knowing she'd never be back to let herself in for that kind of heartache.

"I mean it." He touched her cheek. "Be somewhere safe when darkness falls."

"I will," she promised, her mouth dry.

He walked past her on bare feet and disappeared down a hallway. Soon, she heard the dogs whine excitedly and run toward the side of the house.

She let herself out of the front door, sorry she hadn't had a chance to tell Dylan goodbye.

* * * * *

After returning home to change, Emmy was late for work. And the day only got worse.

Work dragged. The lack of sleep the night before left her muzzy-headed. Numbers blurred. She snapped at a co-worker. Her fingers hit the wrong keys. Errors inside errors appeared in much of what she entered all day.

Frustrated after reentering a long column of numbers, she decided to close down her computer and leave.

Worse than putting in a rotten day's work, she'd been grumpy all day. Mad at herself for not having the courage to grab for the gusto. She'd gone back and forth, trying to decide whether she should risk her heart and go after her bad boy vampire, or save herself the heartache and run now.

Leaving her office in the back of the store, she walked through Ladies Garments, where a cloud of warring perfume made her head ache. In Housewares, a saleswoman who normally staffed the children's section looked bored as she helped a customer choose a blender.

Emmy waited patiently. She'd been worried all day about Monica. She hadn't shown up for her shift, and she hadn't answered her calls. Ever an optimist, Emmy hoped Dylan was wrong about her friend.

The saleswoman finished with her customer and walked toward her. "Still haven't heard a thing. Are you going over to her place to make sure everything's okay?"

"I'm headed there now."

Emmy drove the short distance to Monica's apartment, noting with a healthy dose of worry that the sun was already slipping behind the horizon. Dylan had to be wrong about Monica. Even if Monica were a bloodsucker, she wouldn't harm her best friend.

Emmy had to know for sure what had happened to her friend. For all she knew, Monica might be injured and in need of help. Emmy's eyes could have been playing tricks on her the previous evening. Maybe Monica had played a joke, dressed in a vampire mask. It was something free-spirited Monica would do.

Besides, everything about last night seemed like a dream. Too frightening to believe. Perhaps, she'd been caught up in some sort of mass hysteria.

Hell, if it weren't for the pleasant ache between her legs, she might have convinced herself that Dylan had been a dream.

She let herself into the apartment with a spare key. Nothing looked out of place. Or at least nothing more than usual. Monica was a slob. "Monica?" she called out.

No response. She walked deeper into the apartment and headed down the hallway to the bedroom.

A part of Emmy was relieved to see Monica stretched across the bed, her hair in disarray, still wearing the same tank and jeans she'd worn the previous evening.

Remembering Dylan's warning, Emmy picked up a red spiked heel from the floor and walked toward the bed. "Monica?"

Monica's head lifted from the mattress. "Em? That you?" Her voice sounded raspy. But normal. A red line marked her face—an imprint from the wrinkled sheet. Monica's gaze dropped to the shoe in Emmy's hand. "Are you here to borrow my heels?"

That bit of normalcy eased Emmy's apprehension. She stepped closer. "Are you all right? I was worried when you didn't come to work today."

Monica rubbed a hand across her face and murmured, "I should have called in. After you left, the Halloween party was hellacious. I didn't get in until the wee hours."

Emmy plopped down on the bed beside her, relieved to talk to her friend. "You're not kidding. You wouldn't believe the things that happened to me last night."

"You mean tall, dark and horny?" Monica's gaze brimmed with mischief. "I saw him carry you away. You didn't put up much of a fight, so I left you to it."

Emmy blushed and gave her friend a sideways glance. "What about you and Nicky?"

Monica moaned. "There's something about vampire cock."

"You know?"

"I had the bites to show it."

Emmy chewed on the inside of her lip, before blurting, "Dylan said Nicky's dangerous."

Monica's expression grew sly. "Yeah. He is. And he's an amazing fuck."

Determined to set her friend straight, but floundering for a way not to make him more appealing to Monica's adrenaline addiction, Emmy asked, "How did you meet him?"

"I stopped for gas on my way home from work, yesterday. When I went into the store, he had a little shop girl up against the wall."

"Screwing?"

"No. Killing," she said matter-of-factly.

Heart in her throat, Emmy jerked to her feet, but Monica's hand wrapped around her wrist, tight as a manacle. "Monica?" she asked, very afraid she'd made a terrible mistake.

Monica's grip tightened as she slid off the bed. "Sorry, Em. Nicky wants to see you, again."

Emmy winced against the pain and tried to pull her hand free. "Let me go."

"No can do. He'll be here shortly." Her voice roughened and her face transformed. She flung her head back, shaking out her long brown hair. "Oh, much better. Nicky's smart. He knew you'd come looking for me."

Emmy raised the shoe with her free hand. "Monica, you don't want to do this. We're friends."

"But what are friends for, Emmaline?" She grinned revealing a row of shiny jagged teeth. "What are you going to do? Stab me in the heart with my Manolo Blahnik pumps? Don't make me angry."

Emmy swung the spiked heel at Monica's face.

With a howl, Monica released her wrist and raised her arms to cover her head.

Emmy pummeled her with the shoe, driving her back, until Monica's legs met the edge of the mattress and she fell. Emmy threw the shoe at her and bolted for the hallway, making it to the living room before Monica barreled into her back. The wind whooshed from her lungs and she struggled, breathless, to flip the heavy weight off her.

Monica climbed up her body until she lay draped over Emmy. Her nose snuffled against Emmy's neck. "Do you think he'll mind if I take a little bite?"

With her face pressed to the carpet, Emmy thought fast. Monica was growing heavier and stronger. Emmy feared what that meant. "What does Nicky do to people who disobey his commands?"

"Dust them." Her tongue laved the corner of Emmy's shoulder, nosing away the collar of her blouse.

"Think Monica. Did he want me whole? What did he say?"

Monica groaned. "Can't remember."

Knowing Dylan's mental faculties were impaired in his vampire state, Emmy injected a calm she wasn't feeling into her voice. "Will Nicky be angry with you, Monica?"

"Maybe."

"Monica, let me up. Let's talk about Nicky."

Monica licked her neck again. "Hungry."

"I could make you breakfast."

"Need blood. You have it."

Good going, Em. You just reminded her you're food. "Remember, Nicky? Your new boyfriend? The fabulous fuck?"

Monica stretched like a cat on top of her. "Nicky here soon."

"Yes, Monica. Nicky here soon. And Nicky won't be happy."

"Nicky mad?" she asked, her voice frighteningly deep.

"Yes. Get off, Monica. You're not thinking straight."

Monica rolled off her with a petulant sigh. And Emmy turned and sat on the floor, her eyes never leaving Monica's monstrous face.

Emmy looked over Monica's shoulder. "Is that Nicky coming now?"

Triumph suffused Monica's face, and she whirled toward the door.

Emmy jumped on her back. She had to subdue Monica long enough to get out of the apartment. If Nicky arrived before she could escape, she was a dead woman.

With Emmy holding on with all she had, Monica crashed into a wall, trying to dislodge her. Her hands reached behind her and she clawed at Emmy's clothes, snarling and howling.

Monica slammed back into another wall and bits of drywall crumbled around them. With the next slam, pictures slid from the wall, the glass shattering. Finding it difficult to draw a breath, Emmy released her grip on Monica's shoulders and slid to the floor.

Monica pounced, but Emmy was ready for her. She wrapped her thighs around Monica's neck and squeezed. Monica's hands clawed at Emmy's legs, shredding her khaki slacks and raising rivulets of blood on her thighs, but Emmy didn't let go.

Then Emmy realized she'd left two major arteries running down the inside of her thighs vulnerable to Monica's powerful jaws and teeth. Hoping Monica wouldn't figure it out too soon, Emmy decided to psych out her opponent with a little bravado.

"You may as well stop fighting me. These thighs are 'Sommersized'."

Monica's head continued to thrash.

"I can crack a walnut between them. You be careful, or I'll break your neck." Emmy squeezed tighter, growing more worried by the moment that Monica would ravage her with her mouth. She pulled hard on Monica's hair. "I'll snatch you bald if you don't stop moving."

Monica held her head perfectly still.

If Emmy hadn't been so frightened, she would have crowed over that little moment of victory. Monica might be a mighty vampire, but she was still not the sharpest tool in the shed. Emmy wondered how long her bluff would last. Monica should know her hair would grow back like a Beautiful Chrissie doll.

"What do you think she'll threaten her with next?" Quentin's amused voice drawled.

Emmy's head whirled toward the front door. Dylan and his stuffy friend stood in the entrance.

CHAPTER EIGHT

Monica's body stiffened between Emmy's legs.

"You can let go of her now, love," Dylan said.

Too shaken by the battle, Emmy realized her fingers were frozen in Monica's hair. "If it's all right with you, I'll just stay here for a minute or two."

Dylan approached and squatted next to the women. "Monica, tell Emmy you'll behave now."

Monica panted, then her body changed, softening. Her face reformed. Her round cheeks reddened with the pressure Emmy continued to apply. "You can let me go, Emmy. I won't hurt you."

Emmy drew a deep breath and let her thighs loosen their iron grip. "Am I ever glad to see you," she said to Dylan.

Dylan helped her to her feet, and she looked up, prepared to thank him, but his face was a tight mask of fury. She stepped back.

"Quentin, get her to the car." Dylan's voice was taut and hard.

Quentin grabbed her upper arm to lead her out, but Emmy resisted. "You aren't going to hurt her."

Monica rested on her elbows on the floor and smirked.

Emmy wished she still had an extra shoe to throw at her. Didn't she know better than to piss off Dylan?

"Get up," Dylan commanded.

Monica rose slowly, dusting plaster off her clothing, mocking Dylan with her nonchalance.

Dylan grabbed her by the neck and backed her up to the wall.

Monica's eyes rounded, and her hands pulled at his, but she couldn't dislodge his grip.

Emmy stepped toward them, but was stopped by Quentin's long-fingered shackle.

Quentin pulled her to him and slipped an arm around her waist, anchoring her to his side. "Wait," he whispered in her ear.

"I'll spare you tonight," Dylan said, his voice low and deadly calm. "You were Emmy's friend, but you'll stay clear of her now or I'll kill you. Do you understand?"

Monica nodded, her eyes wild.

"And take a message to your boyfriend."

"Yes," she replied, sounding breathless. "What shall I tell him?"

"*Run.*"

* * * * *

As she followed Dylan into his house, Emmy still trembled from the aftermath of her battle. She'd actually had the nerve to attack a vampire with a shoe!

Quentin followed close behind and drew her into the living room, pressing her down into one of the sumptuous leather chairs on either side of a large, pale marble fireplace. He flipped on a wrought iron floor lamp and golden light spilled into the dark corners of the room.

Feeling measurably safer, Emmy waited quietly while Quentin lit the fire.

"You have nothing to fear from Dylan," he said quietly.

"I'm not afraid," she said, and then realized she truly wasn't.

"Would you like a drink?" he asked.

Emmy shook her head. She raised her hands toward the fire to warm them and saw they still shook.

A tumbler was held in front her eyes, a finger of brown liquid sloshing in the glass. Rather than remind him she'd said no, she took it, but held it with both hands. She stared into the whiskey. She hated whiskey.

"It's scotch," he said, taking the seat opposite her.

"Smells like paint thinner," she mumbled.

"Be a good girl and throw it back — in your throat that is."

She glanced up.

He offered her a silent toast with his own glass, a small smile curving the corners of his mouth.

What the hell, she thought. Perhaps it would chase away the chilling fear she'd felt since leaving Monica's place. Or deaden the sting of the deep scratches on her thighs.

The liquor burned all the way to her belly, and she gasped. "That was awful."

He laughed softly. "You'll feel better in a moment."

Emmy's hands clamped harder around the empty glass and her lips trembled, so she pressed them tightly together. But the sob she'd held inside erupted, and she set aside the glass to cover her face. "I can't believe I attacked a vampire with a Manolo Blahnik pump."

She sobbed a second time. "I'm not usually such a wimp."

"You're not a wimp," Dylan's voice broke in.

Great! He'd think she was a crybaby too. She rubbed her hands over her face to quickly wipe away the tears and then looked at him.

He was kneeling beside her chair. His dark eyes filled with concern.

"I think this is where I find something better to do," Quentin murmured and left the room.

"Headstrong, stubborn—" Dylan said, his brows pulled together in a frown. "Lacking in common sense, perhaps, but not a wimp, my dear."

Emmy wanted to argue with him over a few of those adjectives, but realized what she wanted more was for him to hold her. She bit the inside of her lip, and wondered whether he'd offer his shoulder. If he didn't, she wasn't going to ask. Besides, going *there* was only going to lead to heartbreak.

"Emmy, you're thinking too much."

Her chin lifted. "Are you also saying my intellect is puny?"

"I'm saying, come here," he said, his voice firm.

"And I'm supposed to just fall into your arms?" A little resistance might convince him she wasn't desperate for his attentions.

"It's your choice, love." Something in his voice jangled her alarms.

"What am I choosing between?"

"Coming into my arms…or being dragged there."

Her body reacted instantly to the caveman vision that came to mind. "Oh."

"Emmy?" his voice held an edge of warning.

She didn't know where the courage came from, but she licked her lips, a slow circle that his gaze followed. There was more than one way to get his two arms around her. "Come and get me."

"Witch," he whispered, and then leaned forward to take her lips. His tongue swirled inside her mouth. "Mmmm. My favorite flavors."

"What? Tooth scum and paint thinner?"

His lips smiled against hers. "Whiskey and woman."

Her fingers combed through his hair and she pulled to seal their mouths. He kissed her, and then pushed her back.

Disappointed, she tried to follow.

He took her hands and placed them on the arms of the chair. "First, let me take care of your legs." He reached for the button at her waistband and slipped it open, then tugged down the zipper.

Emmy winced when he peeled the fabric from her thighs. How had she forgotten about the claw marks Monica had left in her flesh? Drying blood stuck in places, but Dylan was relentless.

Whimpering by the time he'd finished, Emmy dug her fingers into the chair.

His head lowered to the first set of wounds, and he licked them. Long wet strokes that soothed her flesh along the angry red scores. As she watched, the pain receded, and the scratches healed, and then disappeared altogether.

"Your tongue could earn millions," she said around a moan when his head bent over her other thigh.

He healed the last of Monica's scratches. Then his hands circled Emmy's hips and pulled her to the edge of the chair. She widened her legs, and he pulled her groin flush with his.

Emmy wrapped her thighs around his hips and rubbed her pussy along the long ridge of his desire. "Too many clothes," she complained.

Dylan grabbed her collar and pulled her shirt apart, popping buttons. A few clattered on the tile hearth.

Desperate to free her breasts, Emmy reached between them for the clasp of her bra and unhooked it.

His mouth descended on hers, and he skimmed her blouse and bra from her shoulders and let them fall. Her nipples pebbled instantly, and she scraped them over the fabric of his shirt.

Clumsy with frenzy, they ripped at the rest of their clothing until they knelt naked before the fire.

"I sure hope you have something my size in your closet," Emmy said, as Dylan's mouth skimmed over her collarbone and descended to her breast.

"When are you going to need clothes?" He tongued her nipple, and then sucked it between his teeth.

Emmy pressed his face harder against her breast. "Right, tomorrow's Sunday. No work. Play?"

He raised his head and took a breath, "Not play, loving you is a death sport." He pushed her back onto the carpet and lay over her body.

Her hands gripped his ears. "You should know all about it." Directing his mouth to the neglected nipple she contemplated a night and day of lovemaking. "Do you have real food in your fridge?"

"You mean," he said, his voice sounding somewhat garbled, "something other than organ meat or pig's blood?"

Emmy made a face. "Something vegetarian?"

"And if I say no?"

"The only organ meat I want is yours." To make sure he got the hint, she lifted her hips to nudge her bush against his...organ. "We'll order pizza. They deliver."

"So do I." His cock pressed into the entrance of her vagina.

Emmy winced, still sore from the previous night. "Perhaps, we should try a smorgasbord, instead. Cafeteria-style. No sausage. Little edibles."

"Emmy."

"Mmmm?"

"Stop talking."

"Ahem." The sound of someone clearing his throat sounded loudly in the room. She glanced toward the foyer and saw Quentin standing in the shadows with a bundle under his arm.

Emmy squealed and became aware that Dylan was lifting off her body. She wrapped her legs around him. "Where do you think you're going? I'm naked." Her hands rose to cover her breasts.

"Before you get too deeply into the pepperoni," Quentin said, with wry humor in his voice, "may I have a word with you, Dylan?" His gaze flickered over Emmy, assessing, almost clinical. "Doesn't she put you in mind of a Boticelli?"

Emmy removed her hands from her breasts and let her arms fall to her side on the floor. He was the one interrupting coitus. She didn't have a thing to feel ashamed of. Besides, if she was honest she enjoyed his perusal.

Dylan scowled. One of his sexiest looks, Emmy thought. As worthy as any Calvin Klein pout. "Quentin, is there a purpose to this interruption?" he said, his teeth gritted.

"I just wanted to remind you that you have a meeting to attend later." Quentin's smile fell short of innocent. "And to bring you pillows." He indicated to the bundle beneath his arm.

Dylan raised a hand and caught the pillows as they were tossed. "Now, get lost."

Quentin winked, then turned on his heels and left.

"Where were we?" Dylan asked, urging her with a hand to lift her hips.

Unclasping her thighs, she put her feet flat on the floor and pushed up. "Swallowing sausage?" she asked, grinning.

He slid one of the pillows beneath her hips. "No, going vegetarian." He pressed her knees apart.

Feeling overexposed, Emmy placed a hand over her pussy. "I'll take cucumber."

He raised a pointed finger. "I'm bringing the carrot."

She rolled her eyes. "I think this analogy is getting tired."

"I agree. Too much roughage." His gaze dropped to her open thighs. "I'm up for something…creamier."

"Potatoes?"

He lifted one eyebrow.

"All right, I promise to shut up. If you put your tongue to better use as well."

Dylan bent and kissed her inner thigh, nipping gently toward her core.

Emmy groaned, eager for the lash of his rough tongue.

He didn't disappoint. He stroked long laps over her outer lips, alternating with short darts between that fluttered against her clitoris.

Liquid seeped from inside her, bathing her vagina, and her legs turned to jelly, falling farther apart.

He dipped inside. "Ambrosia." He moaned, and the sound vibrated on her sensitive flesh. His tongue delved deeper.

Her hips rose. "I like carrots. Diced, sliced, puréed." His finger pushed inside and swirled.

"Raw. Whole. I love them whole!" She reached between her legs and spread her labia, pulling up to expose her clit. "Did I mention cucumbers?"

He lifted his head, his gaze spearing her. "I thought you were going to be quiet."

"It's not something I can help. I get excited and my mouth can't stop. Oh!" Emmy arched her back when a second finger joined the first. She squeezed her inner muscles. Nothing like a little girly calisthenics to entice a man to do the dirty.

Her hips pumped, shallow pulses as she concentrated on the sensation of his fingers deep inside. "You know a little tongue action would go a long way here."

"You've no patience, dear. Good things come—"

"To she who waits. I know, I know. But I was thinking of a new Confucianism."

He nipped her inner thigh again. "Is that even a word?"

"Pay attention. I think 'A good cum comes to she who does it herself!'" She reached with her other hand and touched a finger to her clit.

"Uh uh." His hand closed over hers and pushed it away. "No cheating. You see, I think three carrots beat a cucumber any day." He slid three fingers into her.

Her eyes closed and her mouth rounded around a breathless 'O'. "Are you raising me?" she asked, her voice held a plaintive note.

"Are we switching from vegetables to poker?"

She raised and rested on her elbows. "I'm just hoping for more poke." She raised an eyebrow. A direct challenge.

"To hell with vegetables." He withdrew his fingers. "Just turn over."

Emmy's heart pounded in her chest. Now! He'd cram every incredibly edible inch of himself inside her now. She turned onto her stomach, and then rose up on her hands and knees.

"Hold onto the edge of the fireplace."

She braced herself, gripping the marble hard.

Dylan slid his cock inside her.

A twinge of soreness gave way to pleasure so intense she clamped her jaw closed rather than cry out. Why give his immense ego a boost? Keep him humble.

"Breathe, Emmy," he whispered next to her ear.

His hips drove forward, stretching her, filling her. Her bottom wriggled as she accommodated his push through her tight channel.

Finally, sheathing him to the hilt, Emmy's back arched. "Fuck me, Dylan. Fuck me—hard."

Dylan had been right about her ass the first time he saw her. A man could die pumping against her soft, fleshy bottom. His palms curved around the milky-white globes and he spread them. He dropped spit into the crease.

"I don't think—" Emmy squirmed.

"That's right. Don't." He traced a finger between her cheeks, gliding lower until he touched the soft, puckered lips.

Emmy gave a cry, half-dismay, half-delight, and bucked.

Dylan pumped his hips and drove deeper, at the same time sliding a finger inside her ass.

"Dylan?" she asked, her voice sounding thin. She rocked, her cunt pushing and pulling on his cock.

"Emmy, slow down," he said. He wanted this time to be for her, but he could already feel the change coming over him, stretching his skin, expanding him.

Her warm, moist heat beckoned him deeper, and he slammed his hips into her, pounding so hard her buttocks jiggled. Her soft, round buttocks. Buttocks he'd die to pump against the way he wanted, hard and deep.

"Dylan, harder. Give it to me, harder."

"Damn," he muttered, feeling the tingle in his gums a second before his teeth slid into place. He growled, low in his throat. The muscles of his thighs and ass hardened like steel, driving harder, faster.

Her breath came in harsh grunts as he pummeled her hips, keeping rhythm with the slap of his balls and belly against her flesh.

Emmy stiffened, and cried out.

Then he was hurtling, crashing his hips into hers, following her over the precipice.

CHAPTER NINE

"That thing you did…" Emmy began.

"Thing?" Dylan stirred beside her on the carpet, still trying to catch his breath. Spooned together, Dylan realized this position was perfect for him to toy with both her breasts. So he squeezed them.

"Pay attention."

"You're a bossy, wench." His open palms circled on her distended nipples, round and hard as pencil erasers.

"I liked it."

Something he should pay attention to. "Which thing?"

"When your finger was inside me," she said, her voice small.

Male pride burst in his chest. "You mean, when I fingered your asshole?"

"Dylan!" She slapped his thigh.

He smiled against her hair. Bossy as hell when they were in the middle of a coupling, she was still a prissy little thing. "Well, I did."

"Never mind." Her breath huffed.

"Did you like it well enough to try something like it, again?"

She sucked in a breath and her blood thrummed in her veins.

Her body betrayed her every time.

Another thing he liked about Emmy Harris. *So she wants me to do it again.* "Seems like you're full of firsts, love. I thought you had a boyfriend."

A soft snort was her reply.

He squeezed her breasts, while nuzzling her delectable neck. "Must not have been much of a boyfriend, if he didn't take the time to discover what puts the kink in your hair."

"No. He wasn't much of a boyfriend. He was just convenient."

"Convenient? That's a bloody sorry excuse."

"Well. I didn't know it at the time."

"When did you discover this?"

No reply, but her heart beat faster.

"Emmy?"

"When you fucked me the first time," she said softly.

Fucked? Made love! He almost blurted that out. Dylan wanted to shake her. For whatever reason, Emmy was determined to keep a wall around her heart. *Is it because I'm a vampire?*

He smoothed a hand down her belly. *I'll bind her to me, somehow.* His fingers combed through her short, silky curls until he found the round button of her clitoris. He rubbed the pad of his thumb over the slippery nub.

Emmy hissed between her teeth, but widened her legs. "You came before. Without biting me."

"I told you it could be done. A lot of work, but an immensely satisfying job." He increased the pressure of his thumb as he rubbed in slow circles.

Emmy's ass pressed against his groin. "Does your company offer any perks?"

"Generous fucks." He drew the delicate lobe of her ear between his teeth.

"I'll have to apply." Her leg inched atop his, widening the gap between her thighs, allowing just enough room for his cock.

His cock glided into the well-oiled passage. "I can put in a good word for you," he said.

"Dylan?"

"Yes, Emmy?"

"Did anyone ever tell you that you talk too much?"

Dylan smiled. "You're the first."

"Shall we get *down* to business?" Her hand crept between her legs, and her fingers lightly grasped his balls.

Lying side by side was not conducive to the energetic thrusting he intended to give her. "Would you be terribly bored if we did this much the same fashion as the last time?"

"If it gets you deeper into the merger, I'm game."

They arranged themselves before the fire, her hands once again braced on the warm marble hearth.

Dylan spent long moments pleasuring her breasts and clitoris while he glided in and out, to an ever-increasing tempo.

Emmy was nearing completion, perspiring lightly, her hair sticking to her shoulders, her back arching, dipping, and rearing back to meet his thrusts. From her guttural moans, he determined she was "well-tenderized" for another initiation.

He nipped the back of her neck. "Emmy?" He slammed forward as far as he could go.

"Huh?"

"I think you're ready." He halted the motion of his hips and withdrew his cock.

"Don't stop, now!" she wailed.

He rubbed spit on the head of his penis. "We're going to do a little exploration. A little drilling, love."

"Just get back inside me quick. The mother lode is ready to gush."

Dylan parted her buttocks and guided his cock to her anus. He pressed the round head against it and met tight resistance.

Emmy whimpered, but didn't ask him to stop.

Slowly, the tight mouth gave way and he slid the crown of his cock inside.

"Ooooh," Emmy said, and her shoulders dipped to the hearth, her head lolling on folded arms.

He pulled out a little way, and then pressed inside, until the tip was buried. "What do you think, Emmy? Does it hurt too much?"

"I don't know. You're stretching me. Just don't go changing to the masked man in the middle of this—I won't be able to take it."

"I'll go slow." He dropped more spit and spread it around his cock, then pressed a little deeper.

Emmy's legs trembled, but still she didn't ask him to stop.

In, out—he fought his need to push deeper inside. Her rear entrance was a tight, hot, ring of torture that squeezed his cock like a fist. He increased the tempo of his shallow thrusts.

Emmy emitted a sob. "More. It's happening, give me more."

Dylan deepened the glides, carefully gauging the little murmurs and groans she made to ensure he didn't cause her pain. Then he wet his fingertips and reached around to bury his fingers in her cunt.

Emmy screamed and bucked, shoving backward to take his cock deeper into her ass.

"Come on, baby," he whispered in to her ear. "Come with me."

With his fingers drenched in her pussy juice, he noted the moment her vagina began to pulse with her orgasm.

Emmy keened, loud and long. "Ohmygod!"

Dylan closed his eyes and savored the ever-constricting band that circled his shaft, and controlled his transformation, halting before his body expanded. It was enough. He flung back his head and roared as a long stream of cum exploded from his cock.

After carefully withdrawing, Dylan pulled up Emmy to sit, cradled by his thighs. He kissed her shoulders and neck.

Smoothed his hands over her breasts and belly as her shudders quieted.

With a deep sigh, she rested her head on his shoulder. He pressed a kiss to her forehead, and Emmy looked up. His head descended and their tongues entangled, lapping without their mouths pressing together.

Their tongues parted and they stared into each other's eyes.

Emmy wrinkled her nose. "I think we need baths."

"Love is in the air."

She grimaced. "If you break into the Love Boat song, I'll lose all respect for you. I've created a monster."

"You didn't think vampires had a sense of humor? You inspire the comedic monster in me." He bussed her lips. "We'll shower. Then I'll have to leave for a little while."

Her eyelids dropped. "Can I come with you?"

"No, but you'll be safe. Quentin will be here."

"And your demon dogs. Maybe, I'll take a nap. Promise to wake me up when you come home?"

"I promise." He slapped her thigh lightly. "Now get up."

Together, they rose. Emmy's hands curled into little fists at her sides, and she didn't look at him. She knelt to pick up her ruined blouse.

"Emmy, are you embarrassed?"

"Um, is there anything for me to wear?"

"Into the shower?"

Her blush colored the tops of her breasts. "Well, I'm not like you."

"Not like me how?"

"Perfect. Do you always answer a question with a question?"

"You're deliberately changing the subject. Emmy, don't you know you're beautiful?"

She looked disappointed in his answer. "You don't have to say that. I know what I am."

"And what might that be?"

This time she glared at him, but he wanted to know what was in her mind.

"Fat," she said, and her chin raised a notch, daring him to declare otherwise.

"Come with me." He walked past her, his hand snagging hers to pull her into the foyer and up the stairs.

Emmy hoped Quentin stayed wherever Quentin was, or he'd get an eyeful of her ass as she jogged upstairs.

Dylan led her straight into his bathroom and halted them in front of his counter-to-ceiling mirror.

She took a deep breath and looked around the room—at the towel rack, the silver toilet paper dispenser—anywhere, but at her own reflection.

His hand gripped the top of her head and pointed her face toward the mirror. "Emmy, what do you see when you look at yourself in the mirror?"

He wasn't going to let her off. So she started at the top. "I see frizzy blonde hair."

He shook his head. "A golden halo of wavy hair."

"Fat boobs."

"Lush, firm breasts with rosy areolas, and nipples like eraser-tips."

She wrinkled her nose at him.

Dylan shrugged. "Only the truth, however unpoetic. I like erasers. Go on."

"A poochy tummy."

"I see a rounded, womanly belly. Soft, where a woman should be soft."

Moisture gathered at the edges of her eyes, and she batted her lids to keep the tears at bay. "A wide, J-Lo ass."

He slid his hand over her hips to close over a generous cheek. "An ass that cushions a man's belly."

Scarlet stained her cheeks. *He's going to make me cry. Time for a joke.* "You probably need glasses. You're what? Older than Methuselah. They say the eyes go first."

Dylan pulled her in front of him and ran his hands from her shoulders, down her belly, and then between her thighs. "You're soft where a man is hard to complement him. You're not fat— you're voluptuous, womanly. Incredibly sexy." His finger found her clit and he rubbed. "Do you believe me?" His gaze bored into hers.

"I believe you see me that way."

"Does anybody's else opinion matter?"

Her smile started slowly, then spread to warm her heart. Dylan found her ass sexy. "No."

"Now, wash my back."

* * * * *

Dylan pulled the covers over her nude body. She smelled of talcum and fresh sex.

"This has been wonderful," she murmured, her eyes already drifting shut. "Beyond my dreams."

He sat on the edge of the bed. "You sound as though you don't think it will last."

"I don't know what "it" is, yet. But I can't stay here forever." She yawned and rolled on her side. "I do have a job."

"You could stay here. I could take care of you." Not usually given to impulse in his dealings with the opposite sex, nevertheless his offer felt right.

"As in live together?"

"Yes." More sure by the second.

"Let's wait and see what happens. I don't want to make a mistake." She grinned. "And we've only known each other for twenty-four hours. You don't even know whether I snore or not."

"Fair enough. The offer is on the table. Get some sleep."

Dylan leaned down to kiss her, expecting to give her lips a quick buss, but Emmy's tongue sneaked out to lick his lower lip. He crushed his mouth to hers for another of their tongue-dueling matches.

Finally, he pulled back, disengaging her hands, which were twisting in his hair. He rose from the bed.

"Promise you'll wake me," she said.

"I will."

* * * * *

As he drove to the estate of the council member he'd petitioned, Dylan held the pleasant thought of waking Emmy from her sleep. Would he wake her slowly with gentle kisses and soothing glides of his hands, or would he come inside her, fast and hard? Both choices offered delicious possibilities.

Navarro's estate wasn't far from Dylan's place. As Dylan's rented car climbed the slopes of the exclusive neighborhood roads, the lights of the city below flickered like a thousand stars.

Dylan stopped at the tall brick and wrought iron gate and typed the password into the keypad. While the gates swung open on quiet hinges, he girded himself for a frustrating evening.

Navarro met him at the front steps and led him through his house to the study. Navarro had always had money—ever since his human boyhood in Spain. And he was a collector. His furnishings—heavy dark oak furniture, plush Middle Eastern carpets, Italian and Dutch paintings—had taken centuries to accumulate.

Candlelight illuminated the dark-paneled study. One of Navarro's many eccentricities was an aversion to the harsh glare of electrical lighting. He invited Dylan to have a seat before the fire and poured them drinks.

While Navarro swirled his brandy, Dylan watched his narrow, European features for any sense of where the conversation might lead. Navarro was typically cryptic in his communication, giving away nothing.

Of course, he'd had centuries longer than Dylan to cloak his emotions.

Finally, Navarro glanced up. "Son, what is it you wish to speak to me about?" His hand passed through the air in a diffident wave, granting permission for their conversation to begin.

Dylan shifted in his seat. "Father," he replied, addressing his sire formally. "I believe one of our inner circle is siring an army."

Navarro's thin lips curved only slightly at the corners. "Is there to be a war?"

Dylan simmered with resentment at Navarro's subtle mockery. "Nicky is turning young people at a frightening rate. Our human friends in the police force can't keep up the fiction they're gang-related killings for long."

"Nicky has acted imprudently. My emissary will speak to him." Navarro's words were measured and spoken in an even tone.

Irritated, Dylan bit back his temper. "It's not enough. He won't stop."

"Is the situation truly unsalvageable, Dylan?" Navarro's sloe-shaped brown eyes met his gaze directly. "This wouldn't have anything to do with the woman you harbor in your home?"

Of course, Navarro would know he had a houseguest.

Dylan drew in a deep breath. "I've marked her as mine." Once proclaimed, there was no going back. "Nicky isn't honoring my right of possession."

Navarro nodded. "Congratulations. It has been long since you've mated."

"I won't let her be harmed."

"Has he attacked you or your woman directly?"

Dylan's back stiffened. "No."

"Then how are you certain his children aren't taking matters into their own hands? The newly reborn are often over-zealous in their devotion," he said, his chiding words reminding Dylan of an episode in his own "apprenticeship".

An episode Dylan would sooner forget. It was another stain on his soul. "They're not acting on impulse. They're acting on orders."

Navarro raised a single brow.

"I know it to be true." Dylan's chest expanded with anger.

"I will not go to the council without proof. We are after all talking about sanctioning the death of one of our own."

Dylan had come on a fool's errand. There would be no support from the council. "I won't wait for her to die to give you your proof."

"Which is why we permit the extinction of newborns without consequence to the Master responsible." Navarro pinned him with stare. "You've been busy lately, amassing your own statistics."

Rankled his dustings had been questioned, Dylan replied, "Every killing was needed. Newborns can't turn a human until they've learned to rein in their lust."

The older Master waved his hand. "We are not concerned with your nightly patrols. I have every confidence your purges have been warranted."

Fighting his rising frustration, Dylan gripped the arms of his chair. "Can we come back to the issue of Nicky's activities?"

"We will not interfere with your right to protect your possession."

Dylan relaxed. He had permission to kill Nicky himself.

CHAPTER TEN

To his disappointment, Emmy wasn't asleep when he returned. Instead, Dylan followed the sound of muffled laughter to the kitchen. Quentin and Emmy were inside, seated at the table.

She was dressed in his robe, the dark blue a foil for her rosy cheeks and sunshine-colored hair. Her gaze swung to the door and her eyes lit up like Christmas lights when she saw Dylan. His heart swelled in his chest—grateful he could produce such a look of joy.

Quentin raised a slice of pizza, loaded with pepperoni and sausage from the savory aroma, and waved it at Dylan. "Join us. Emmy was just telling me she has a distinct preference for organ meats."

Dylan's gaze narrowed as he stared at the gap at the top of *his* robe. It exposed more cleavage than he wanted to share, even with his best friend. "Only mine, I hope."

"That's not what I said." Emmy blushed scarlet. "And for your information, Dylan, *that* wasn't what we were discussing."

"Better not be," he growled, feeling grumpy. How many ways could he say 'get lost' to his buddy? Dylan strode past the counter littered with open pizza boxes to the table, and hooked his foot around the leg of chair, pulling it close to Emmy. He straddled it backwards.

"Didn't go well, hmmm?" Quentin asked.

Dylan's gaze didn't leave Emmys' face. "About what we thought."

"Damn. We're on our own then."

Emmy took a bite of pizza and darted a glance at Dylan. "Do I have tomato sauce on my nose?"

"No, love. And it's not your fight, Quentin."

"And leave me out of the party?" Quentin drawled. "This little intrigue is more fun than I've had in a long time."

Emmy set her pizza on her plate. "Okay, I'm just a little bit tired of being left out of the conversation, when I feel like I *am* the topic of the conversation."

Gratified he'd brought her temper to peak, if not her body, Dylan clutched the back of her head and brought her forward for a kiss.

She shoved at his chest. "I have pizza breath," she warned.

"My favorite."

"Thought it was whiskey and woman," she murmured, her eyes drifting closed.

"It was." He kissed her full on the lips. He hoped Quentin took notes.

Emmy pushed him away. "You changed the subject. I hate when you do that."

"Because it's so easy to do?" he asked, teasing her into a temper.

She rolled her eyes. "I swear I'm going to scream."

"Not again, my ears are still ringing," Quentin drawled.

Dylan leveled a killing glare at his former best friend. "So what was this about organ meats?"

Emmy's blush deepened. "Dylan! Drop the subject."

"I thought *that* wasn't what you were talking about," he said, feeling the tension in his shoulders roll away. Teasing Emmy was fast becoming his favorite pastime.

"Organ meats on pizza," Quentin said with a smirk. "Will you get your mind out of Emmy's gutter?"

"Quentin!" Emmy's frown was seriously shy of ominous. She turned to Dylan. "I just wondered why they never make pizza with liver or hearts. There'd probably be a market for it with so many vampires walking the streets — now that I know you guys eat things other than pig's blood." She drew a deep breath. "I'm rambling again, aren't I?"

"Yes!" he and Quentin responded, sharing a look of male commiseration.

"So why do you need blood, if you can eat real food?" Emmy asked, her eyes wide and curious as a child's.

"We need the nutrients," Dylan replied. "Our stomachs don't digest other foods well."

"So you still need calories? Or what? You get skinny? Lose your gorgeous hair?"

"Our skin dries like a mummy's," Quentin said.

Dylan pressed his lips together to prevent a bark of laughter. Emmy looked so appalled, he took pity on her. "I experience hunger the same way you do. If I don't feed, my stomach feels like it's gnawing on itself. Makes me grumpy."

"I can so relate," Emmy said, taking another bite of pizza. "And I'm relieved about the mummy thing."

"Regular food is like roughage." Dylan couldn't resist another oblique reminder of their previous conversation about vegetables. "Passes right through."

"I say," Quentin said. "That was rather indelicate in mixed company."

"No, no," Emmy broke in. "It explains a lot. So is it just human blood and body parts?"

Dylan wished the conversation would come to an unnatural end. "No. Human blood is the tastiest, but any mammal's will do in a pinch."

"You'd better eat some pizza, or I won't kiss you again," Emmy said.

Dylan grabbed her hand and directed her slice to his mouth. He took a large bite all the way to her fingers, making sure he brushed her with his lips before biting.

Emmy drew her bottom lip between her teeth and set the remainder of the slice on her plate. "I think I'm full."

"Clean up the kitchen, will you Quentin?" Dylan drew Emmy from her chair.

"What else am I here for?" Quentin grumbled.

* * * * *

Dylan's heart slowed its pounding and he stretched, careful not to dislodge Emmy. The fading pleasure of a moment ago was already giving away to a slow reawakening. He'd have her once more before the sun rose.

"So, how does one become a vampire?" Emmy asked, her chin rested on his chest and her gaze was fastened on his face.

Dylan knew she'd be relentless until he satisfied her with an answer. Emmy's curiosity was proving as insatiable as her sex drive. "By your expression, you expect something ghoulish?"

"Is it?" she asked, excitement making her eyes shine. "I mean, I've watched vampire movies. In some, you get bit on three consecutive nights. On the third, you die. By the time you wake up in the morgue you're a bloodsucker. Sometimes, you get partially eaten and come back the next night looking like you've been partially eaten. And then there was this one movie with a voodoo priestess—"

"Em! One must be drained nigh unto death, then fed a vampire's blood to replace it."

"Oh." She looked disappointed. "Sounds simple enough."

"Well, it's not," he replied curtly. "More often than not, the person dies before she can be turned."

"She?"

He didn't answer.

Emmy laid her cheek flat on his chest and smoothed her hands over his chest. "I'm glad you didn't die."

Dylan waited.

"Are you very old?"

With a wry smile, he replied, "I'm one hundred and eighty-six."

"Wow! That's old enough to be my great, great, great—"

"Old enough. Let's leave it at that."

"How did it happen for you, Dylan?" she asked quietly.

Miss Twenty Questions would drive him mad. But he supposed he'd have to tell his story sooner or later.

"My wife and I were starving to death," Dylan began.

Emmy raised her head, her eyes full of questions.

Dylan plucked a strand of hair from her cheek and rubbed it between his fingers. "First we lost the potatoes—the only crop we were permitted to keep. Then our rent was increased. When I couldn't pay it, we were forced out of our home by the magistrate, our cottage burned to the ground.

I looked for work, but there were so many people who were displaced—just like we were. Everyone starving. I stole food when I could find it. Took charity when it was offered.

Then we heard the Brits were offering free passage to America—a chance for a new start. Breda's health was already failing. She was a wraith. But we had to try."

Dylan closed his eyes. The picture he'd carried in his heart for so long was finally fading. Red hair, soft brown eyes. "She suffered terribly from seasickness. Many did. We were housed in the hold of the ship. Bunks four-deep. Stacked like cords of wood. The smell of vomit and the dying was often more than I could bear. At night, I'd escape to the deck. The captain didn't mind, because his paying passengers were usually in their cabins."

Emmy touched his face. "You don't have to go on, if you don't want to."

Dylan opened his eyes and shook his head. "One night, I met a man walking near the railing. A storm was picking up, the sea was battering against the hull. I could barely keep my footing and had decided to go below. Then I saw his face. He was staring at me. His eyes were glowing in the dark. I thought I was seeing things. He introduced himself. His name was Navarro.

He asked me if my woman was dying. I wondered how he knew. I'd never seen him before. How could he know my circumstance? He said he could smell her on me.

Then he told me there was a way to save her. But there must be a sacrifice. I told him, whatever it was, I'd gladly pay."

"He was a vampire," Emmy breathed.

"Yes. I gave him my life's blood. When I awoke, I lay on the deck. I felt powerful, strong. I could see in the dark. Every darkened shadow was bright as daylight. My sense of smell placed every deckhand. But my hunger was incredible.

Navarro warned me not to act on it. That he would guide me, but first I must bring him my wife.

I carried her to his cabin. She was delirious, but I followed his instructions. While I drank from her, sating my hunger, I felt her life passing, ebbing like a wave away from me. When it was time to feed her with my blood, she was too weak to drink." Dylan paused, his voice feeling rusty, his tongue thick. "She died in my arms. I killed her."

Emmy's arms spread across his chest, hugging him tightly.

Dylan drew her up, his arms encircling her, and he pressed his face into the corner of her shoulder. "I'll not attempt to turn another," he said, his words muffled against her neck.

Emmy's shoulders shook. Her tears wet his chest. She cried while he couldn't. "I don't think you killed her, Dylan. She was already gone. You acted with love." Her head raised and her eyes were bright with tears. "So tell me how you came to have a Brit for a best friend."

Dylan laughed, a joyous, freeing laugh, and he rolled Emmy beneath him. "That is a tale for another day. For now, let me come inside you."

Immediately, Emmy's legs parted, her knees rising to either side of his hips. Her tentative smile turned to a gasp as he pushed deep inside.

"Stay with me, Emmy." He drove into her, long powerful thrusts, bathing his cock in her creamy channel, seeking absolution for his sins in the goodness of her human soul. "Be mine, Emmy."

Emmy's hand clutched his hips, her fingers digging into his buttocks, encouraging him to propel faster, deeper. "I'll stay," she said. "I'll stay."

Dylan slowed his pace and leaned back to hook his hands beneath her knees, lifting her buttocks off the bed. "I won't let you change your mind."

He pumped into her, controlling the depth, pressing deep, then short, deep, short—until she writhed on the bed, her hands on her breasts, twisting her nipples, begging for release.

"Say it. Say you won't leave." He swirled his hips to rub the crisp hairs at the base of his cock against her clitoris.

Emmy's head thrashed upon the pillow. "I promise. I won't leave you. Just fuck me, Dylan. Fuck me!"

Dylan slammed into her, faster and faster, until his hips jackhammered into her tender flesh.

Emmy bucked, her legs straightening, rising higher, sobs erupting from her throat the closer she rose to the summit. Then her body stiffened, and she cried out.

Dylan continued to pound into her, and then his teeth glided down. He quickly withdrew and draped her knees over his shoulders and sank his teeth into her dripping cunt. Her orgasm pulsed against his mouth, around his teeth, trickling blood onto his tongue, and he roared as his cock pressed into the bedding beneath them and exploded.

Afterward, he drew her into his arms, her back to his chest. Their bodies slid together, slick with sweat. Lying on their sides, he drew her upper thigh over his and pressed his cock into her vagina to glove him while they slept.

Emmy murmured sleepily, "What will I do if I wake up horny, and you're sleeping like the dead?"

"Whatever your heart desires. Have you ever heard of morning wood?"

Emmy snickered. "Then you'll have a stake between your legs, just for me?"

Dylan grimaced. "A stake anywhere near my person doesn't engender pleasant thoughts."

"Even when you are the stake?" She looked over her shoulder and circled her lips with her tongue in a slow tease. "Then how about a pole?"

"I've got a bloody pole for you now, witch."

"But I want to have my wicked way with you while you sleep. I bet you won't even know it."

"I will. It'll be a wet dream."

* * * * *

Emmy woke well past noon. Her inner clock was quickly aligning with Dylan's, she mused. Stretching like a cat, she rubbed her buttocks against Dylan's groin. Sure enough, his cock had plenty of starch. She made a space between her thighs and tightened around him, flexing her hips to make him slide along her cunt.

Liquid pooled between her thighs. Her very own anatomically amazing Dyl-do. Emmy rolled over. Dylan laid on his side, fast asleep, his dark hair spilling across his face.

Her fingers smoothed the locks away, and she leaned close to kiss his lips. Not an eyelash fluttered. She sighed. It was so much more fun when he participated.

She pushed him on his back, and he rolled easily, settling with his legs spread wide.

"How convenient." He was all hers to explore. She reached for the lamp on the bedside table and flicked it on, tilting the shade to bathe his body in the golden glow.

She straddled his hips, teasing her cunt with a glide over his rigid pole and leaned down to begin her exploration.

The flat, brown disks on his chest drew her like a magnet. She tongued them, savoring the velvet skin, then drew the tips between her teeth. As she sucked, they hardened to tiny, beaded points. She wet her fingertips and glided them over the tips of her own breasts, tugging the nipples until they grew rigid, then she guided her breasts to rub her nipples against his.

Her breath quickened and her pussy moistened. She drew her bottom lip between her teeth, and flexed her hips for another, wetter glide over his cock.

Combing her fingers through the hair on his chest, she raked through it, enjoying its soft, silky texture. She followed the dark arrow of hair down his belly and scooted further down his hips. His cock sprang skyward, fuller, redder than before.

She tapped the swollen head. "You'd better be dreaming of me."

Wrapping her hand around him, she was thrilled her fingers didn't meet. Then both hands encircled him and she squeezed, pushing down. Lowering her head, she licked down the length of him, then up the other side. His flesh was satiny-smooth and invited a more thorough examination.

Dylan's head rolled on the pillow, and he murmured. But still he slept.

"Oh Dylan," she whispered. "I'm going to be a very naughty girl."

And she'd give Dylan the sexiest, wettest dream he ever had.

Emmy spit into her hand and rubbed it over the head of his cock. Then she rose on her knees, and with one hand guiding him to her asshole, and the other spreading her cheeks, she sank down on him, gasping when the blunt round head breached her tight ring, and he glided inside.

At first, her tender, inner flesh resisted the intrusion, then she pushed down and levered up, then down again, reveling in the painful fullness. She wet her fingertips again and sought her clitoris, already swelling with arousal, and swirled her fingers over it, rubbing harder as she picked up the pace, pumping her ass on his cock.

Her climax built gradually, and she closed her eyes, arching her back as it burst over her. She groaned loudly, her hips jerking until she couldn't move again.

She collapsed onto his chest and rubbed her face in his hair. "Baby, if you only knew how bad I really am."

Emmy eased off him and retrieved a washcloth from the bathroom. As she cleansed his body, she admitted a possessive streak she'd never known. He was hers. Every sexy, rigid inch of him.

She reached to pull up the sheets. When she reached Dylan's shoulders, she realized his eyes were slitted. He was watching her.

"You are a naughty girl," he whispered.

"You were awake? The whole time?"

"Mmm-hmmm." He smiled — a wicked self-satisfied smirk. "A man would have to be dead to not notice when a beautiful girl is enthralled with his cock." He patted the bed beside him.

Emmy crawled over him, mortification heating her cheeks. Spooned together, Emmy waited for his breathing to quiet. Her heart finally stopped thumping in her chest. He'd never let her live this down. Her stomach growled loudly and she decided to go in search of leftovers. But first things first.

After showering, she found his robe lying in a heap on the floor and put it on, cinching it around her waist. Tonight, she'd have to make a trip to her apartment for some of her own clothing. It was positively decadent to walk around naked all the time.

Letting herself out of the bedroom, she closed the door and turned toward the stairs. She heard a creek on the staircase below and stiffened. Had one of the dogs gotten into the house? Come to think of it, she hadn't heard a single bark. Surely, she would have wakened earlier if she had. Senses on the alert, she walked slowly to the head of the stairs.

From the corner of her eye she saw a movement and gasped, but before she could call out, a hand closed over her mouth and she was drawn back against a long, tall body. Her head bumped against the hard shell of a helmet.

"Not a word…" a voice whispered in her ear, "…or I'll see Dylan dies before he clears the bed? Do you understand?"

She nodded, her heart pounding with fear.

"We're leaving now. Do as I say, and you won't be harmed."

Not believing a word Nicky spoke, nevertheless Emmy let herself be dragged down the stairs and out the front door.

CHAPTER ELEVEN

"There were two vamps," Dylan said, as he surveyed the bodies of his dogs, lying in a heap next to the side gate. Indentions from boot prints in the mud next to the dogs told the story.

"Nicky's doing?" Quentin asked.

"Of course, it was his doing." Dylan ran a hand through his hair. He had to keep it together. He could only imagine how frightened she must be now.

"He's mad. Surely, he realizes he's courting death."

"I have to hope that's exactly why he's doing it," Dylan said, stony resolve making his voice hard.

"To use her for leverage? And if he isn't?"

"Then we need to find her fast. He'll kill her." Dylan fought the panic that rose in his throat. Calm. He must be deliberate and calm.

The moment Dylan had woken at dusk, he'd known she was gone. He smelled engine oil and leather inside the house—but so far outside, only the dogs' blood.

"But where?" Quentin asked, raising his stark gaze to Dylan's.

"I know where. To Hell."

* * * * *

Emmy fought the rising terror that threatened to choke her. Flickering candlelight distorted the shadows the vampires cast as they moved around the cramped room, making them appear larger, darker. She already knew they were dangerous as hell—and crazy to be fucking with her boyfriend.

Nicky had tossed her robe to a dark corner of the room as soon as they'd entered, and she was naked.

Naked and spread-eagle on the soiled mattress—in the back room of the Viper's Den.

The smell of stale sex, urine, and a few unidentifiable odors emanated from the mattress. The cockroaches and mice she heard skittering from the room were the least of her worries.

Nicky's gleaming gaze sent warning signals clambering to her brain. He'd prepared well. Spikes had been driven into the floor and walls, to which chains fitted with manacles were attached.

Emmy struggled against the chains to free herself, but only managed to further injure the tender flesh around her wrists and ankles. She gave up hope of rescuing herself. Instead, she prayed for Dylan to find her soon.

"Leave us," Nicky said to the male vamp that had remained silent throughout Emmy's kidnapping.

He'd driven the second motorcycle, while Emmy had clung to the back of Nicky's, sitting on the edges of her robe to keep it from flapping away. Her stomach had tightened to a knot when she'd recognized their destination. Nicky didn't intend to ever let her go. She'd die in Hell.

After one last covetous stare, the male vamp shuffled from the room.

Relieved his unblinking stare was no longer on her skin, all her attention focused on Nicky.

The apartment outside the small, stifling room was quiet. Emptied at Nicky's order, no doubt. Still dressed in the leather biker gear, he had removed his helmet and gloves. His long, tousled dark hair framed a symmetrically perfect face that was marred with a twisted sneer.

He bent to pull one of her chains, stretching her legs wider. "Now you look—perfect." His hand skimmed over her calf and up her thigh, pausing inches from her core. "This will be the first thing he sees," he said, and then cupped her mound. "I can see why your flesh fascinates him. You're so responsive. I've raised gooseflesh, even here."

Emmy fought the urge to cringe from his hand. She refused to give him the satisfaction of her fear.

"Never doubt. You'll be mine, tonight."

Emmy glared, for once at a loss for a snappy comeback. She hoped like hell rape wasn't part of his agenda.

"All this lovely white skin," he said, smoothing over her belly, and then up to cup one breast. "Very pretty. Monica didn't do you justice. Said you were a lumpy little thing." He twisted her nipple.

She fought the urge to cry out, knowing any response would incite a reprisal. Time was her friend. Dylan was on the way. She knew it. She could feel him drawing closer.

"What will Dylan say when he sees you like this?" he said, echoing her own thoughts. "Will he care?"

Of course he'll care. He'll kill you, asshole! Unable to stop herself, she jerked when he knelt on the mattress and then climbed onto her, straddling her hips. "You know, I'd be very worried if I were you. Very worried, indeed."

"Speaking of Monica. I'm surprised she isn't here for this," Emmy said, trying to prolong the conversation. "After all, she introduced us."

Nicky's hand caressed her jaw, and then turned her head to the side, exposing her neck. "Monica suffered a severe case of sunburn. She won't be joining us — ever."

Emmy closed her eyes. The Monica who had been her friend had died days ago. "So this little party's just for me? I mean, it seems you went to an awful lot of trouble for one lumpy girl."

"You're just the appetizer, sweetheart. And the bait. Sweet bait." With a low growl, Nicky bared his teeth.

As she watched his fangs slide over his teeth, her heart beat so loudly she could hear its pounding in her ears.

He stepped his knees between her legs and ground his leather-clad crotch against her pussy. "He's coming," Nicky said. "But he'll be too late." Planting his hands on either side of her chest, he leaned forward and sank his teeth into her neck.

Emmy cried out against the pain—he hadn't prepared her tender skin as Dylan always did. And he bit deeply into her. Blood left her face and mind, racing to the two small wounds in her neck as he suctioned.

She had a fleeting thought that perhaps it would be better for Dylan if she were never found.

* * * * *

Dylan turned the door handle to the entrance of The Viper's Den, and let it creak open a couple of inches. What he already knew was confirmed. A single vamp lurked inside the living room.

He drew back and flattened himself against the wall.

To Quentin, flanking the other side of the door, he raised one finger and pointed at him.

Quentin nodded, then stood in front of the door. With a powerful thrust, he kicked the door the rest of the way open, making it bounce against the wall loudly and charged into the room.

Already in full bloodlust, the vamp within roared and leaped at Quentin. Quentin feinted to the side and the vamp hit the wall. Hunkering on his haunches, he sprang at Quentin, taking him to the floor.

Now that Quentin had one of them well in hand, Dylan took advantage of the vamp's preoccupation and skirted around the combatants and into the hallway beyond. His heart pounded heavy in his chest as he approached the small dreary bedroom at the end.

The door swung open and Nicky stepped into the opening, clothed only in leather pants, the snap at the top open, and the zipper halfway down. Dylan smelled Emmy's blood on him, along with her perfume — and Emmy's own musk.

Dylan roared his agony, his face reforming, and his teeth sliding down, ready to take Nicky apart. He raised his hands, letting the bloodlust transform his hands into claws to swipe the self-satisfied gloat from his enemy's face.

Then he heard a soft mewling like a weakened kitten from within the room.

"What will you do, Dylan?" Nicky taunted him. "You have only a few moments to save her — if you can. Or are you so far gone you have to take me?"

Fighting the bloodlust, Dylan bellowed again and stepped inside the room.

Emmy lay on the bed, her pale skin nearly translucent, blue-tinged. A dark crimson ribbon of blood stained her neck and the tops of her breasts. But Dylan could hear her thready pulse and see her chest struggle to rise.

Brushing past Nicky, his armor melted away as he hurried to the mattress. Nicky's mocking laughter trailed down the hallway, but Dylan cared only that Emmy still lived, still had a chance. But there wasn't much time.

He knelt on the mattress beside her. "Em. It's Dylan. I'm here."

Her lids fluttered, but didn't open.

"I'll turn you, love. You can stay with me, if that's what you want."

"Dylan…" she whispered.

He leaned closer, his ear to her lips.

"Will I have…this ass for eternity?" she asked, a feeble smile lifting the corners of her lips.

"Yes, love."

"Then do it. Don't want to leave you. Promised."

Dylan's jaw clenched. "First, I have to take more of your blood."

"I know…"

Dylan closed his eyes and murmured a quick prayer, and then bit into the unmarked side of her throat. Her blood entered his mouth, sluggish and cooling by the moment.

When her breath rattled one last time in her chest, he stopped and tore his wrist with his teeth, then held it to her mouth, trickling blood onto her tongue. "Drink, Emmy. For God's sake, drink."

Her throat didn't move to swallow. He leaned back and massaged her neck, until he felt a feeble gulp, and then pressed his wrist to her mouth again. This time, she latched onto it, her tongue working against the edges of his flesh. She inhaled, her lungs gasping for air.

Tears streaked down Dylan's face. Emmy would make it.

"Dylan, Nicky set a fire," Quentin yelled from down the hallway.

"Bastard!" Dylan continued to let Emmy feed, needing the extra minutes to make sure she was strong before he moved her.

Behind him, Quentin closed the door. "We'll have to take her through the window." Quentin shoved aside the curtain and cursed. "He installed bars. We're trapped."

"We haven't a choice, then. We have to go through the fire. Help me with the chains." Dylan pulled his wrist away from Emmy.

Her eyes, hollow but shining in the dark, offered him her trust.

Together, he and Quentin wrapped the chains in the floor around their wrists and pulled with all their might, working the stakes free. They lost precious minutes tugging on the chains in the wall, breaking chunks of plaster to free Emmy's arms.

Dylan helped her to her feet, and then dipped down to drape her over his shoulder. "Get the mattress. We'll use it as a shield to walk through the fire."

With Quentin in the lead, Dylan followed down the hallway, which was filled with a roiling cloud of black smoke. When they reached the entrance to the living room, Quentin laid the mattress on the floor, and then lifted it, damping down the next few feet of flames that ate at the wood flooring.

"We'll have to run for it," Quentin shouted over his shoulder, then with a roar, he held the mattress in front of them and charged toward the door.

Without breaking stride, Quentin pushed the mattress through the door, splintering the wood. Dylan, gripping Emmy tightly, was at his back and the two men stumbled through, landing on the smoldering mattress in the hallway beyond the apartment.

The flames had traveled through the ceiling and cinders rained down on them from above. "Run!" Quentin shouted and pushed Dylan in front of him.

Filled with smoke and the crackling roar of the fire above, the hallway seemed to stretch endlessly in front of Dylan. Unable to see beyond a few inches in front of his face, he rushed forward, praying he had the strength and breath to make it to the door.

Hold on, Emmy. Almost there. He slammed into the wooden door at the entrance, and wasn't the least surprised to discover that the door handle had been removed. "Quentin!" he shouted above the roar of the fire.

Quentin shoved him aside and rammed his shoulder into the door. It didn't budge. He backed up and hammered into it again. A crack in the center sucked air into the foyer. Another blow, and the doorway gave, and the fire roared toward them, fed by oxygen sucked through the gaping hole.

Dylan leapt through the gap and cleared the steps beyond. Quentin slammed into his back, and together with Emmy, they rolled clear of the ball of flame that followed them toward the street.

Coughing, Dylan crawled, dragging Emmy across the grassy weeds to the sidewalk. He rose on his knees to strip the shirt from his back and draped it across Emmy's naked body.

"Emmy? Are you alright?" he asked, afraid of her pallor and her stillness.

Her chest raised and she expelled a ragged breath that caught. She curled on her side as a series of coughs racked her body. Dylan lay down beside her, stroking her hair, kissing her shoulders, knowing that she'd recover soon. She was a vampire now and the injury to her lungs would heal in moments.

"I'll bring the car around," Quentin said, standing over the couple. His soot-covered face cast a worried glance at Emmy before he walked away.

As her coughing quieted, Dylan crooned into her ear and wrapped his arms around her. The danger was past. Now he was left to wonder whether her soul was intact.

CHAPTER TWELVE

Emmy sat quietly in the leather armchair as the locksmith sawed at the remaining cuff on her ankle with a thin, wire blade. She shivered at the chill the fire was slow to dispel. Her hair, still wet from her shower, dampened the shoulders of her robe.

She leaned toward the locksmith, alert to the aroma of his cheap aftershave—and the resonant thrum of his heart pushing blood through his veins. The beats were as clear as the crackle of the fire, the ticking of the clock above the mantle, and the metallic scrape of his saw.

She rimmed her mouth with her tongue, which was already tingling with anticipation of a meal.

The man looked up at her, his gaze falling to her wet lips, and he stiffened. He darted a glance over his shoulder at Dylan and Quentin, before continuing the seesaw movement of the wire blade beneath her cuff.

Emmy smiled when he adjusted his thigh alongside her foot. *He thinks I want to fuck him.* That would never happen. The duo who stood watch to ensure her good behavior would prevent any playing with her food. *Spoilsports!*

Not that she truly wanted to fuck him, but she'd give him better—a bite to send his heart fluttering and his dick gushing in his pants.

Instinctively, she knew she had the power to orchestrate the man's response, physically and mentally. The only problem was she wasn't sure once she tasted him, she'd be able to stop—drinking and pleasuring, that is.

The urge to experiment with this man was fast becoming impossible to ignore. Her breasts tingled, the nipples sharpening to hard peaks against Dylan's navy, silk robe. And her tongue massaged her gums and the roof of her mouth, which itched unbearably. Her body was slowly changing, and it thrilled her, awakening hunger that made her teeth ache and power that tensed her muscles.

What would Dylan do, if I drew this man between my hard thighs and pressed my breasts against his chest while I drink?

Emmy gripped the armchair tighter.

The man's forehead glistened with sweat, and the crotch of his coverall tented over his erection.

Can he smell my arousal just as I can smell his?

One last scrape, and the blade passed the rest of the way through the metal cuff. The locksmith set aside the blade and reached for another tool with handles and a vice-like snout.

Murmuring a husky apology, he carefully placed her foot between his thighs, so that her toes touched his erection, and then slipped the nose of the tool around one edge of the break in the cuff. He twisted upward, bending the metal—and sliding her foot along his cock. Doing the same to the other side of the break, he finally removed her last restraint.

Emmy patted him with her toes, before sliding her foot to the ground. "Thanks," she said her voice a husky purr.

"Next time, make sure you have the key," he said, his gaze conveying a message that no doubt meant, "I'm available for a fuck, anytime."

"Emmy…" Dylan's voice growled a warning.

Emmy's gaze left the locksmith, and she scowled at Dylan.

But Dylan's face remained implacable.

"Dylan, she does need to feed," Quentin said.

"Perhaps," she said, "I could offer this kind man a kiss?"

"That's not necessary," the locksmith said, looking a little uneasy now that his flirtation was acknowledged.

"A kiss," Dylan said. "But it ends when I say."

Emmy smiled at Dylan, and then grabbed the locksmith's collar in both hands, bringing his kneeling frame in alignment with her thighs. "I'll be the best kiss you ever had."

Her lips covered his, and his tongue shoved inside hers with a groan. Peppermint and cigarettes flavored his tongue. Nice, but not what she wanted to taste. Emmy traced her lips along his jaw and nudged him with her nose to raise his chin. The tanned column of his throat was bared, his skin growing steamy — hot with lust.

Her fingers touched the vein at the side of his throat and gasped when his warm blood — millimeters beneath his skin — beckoned her closer.

"Remember to prepare him, love," Dylan said, nearer to her now.

She licked the man's throat, alternately laving the skin and suctioning with her lips.

His cock scraped against her thigh, and Emmy gave him what he needed, caressing him with her inner thigh.

"Now, Emmy," Dylan said.

Emmy positioned her mouth over the pulsing vein and her vampire's fangs automatically slid down to pierce his neck.

The man gasped, but Emmy continued to massage his cock, until he surrendered to her tender attack, his arms circling her waist to clutch her tightly.

Emmy's mouth filled with blood, setting fire to her senses. Rich, warm, pulsing — it glided past her tongue and down her throat. Her body warmed, her pussy moistened.

And then it wasn't enough that his blood spilled into her mouth, she wanted to bathe in his blood, be filled with his sex.

"Enough, Emmy," Dylan broke through the haze of desire that clouded her mind. He was squeezing her shoulders.

She disengaged her teeth and licked closed the wounds she'd made. She rubbed her face on the back of her hand, ensuring her face was its human form again, then raised her head to smile at the locksmith.

"You've done a fine job tonight," she intoned. "We paid you well, but you can't recall much about the evening. You need a beer."

"I need a beer," he repeated.

Quentin helped him to his feet and shoved his toolbox into his arms. "Time to head home."

"Time to go home."

As Quentin lead the locksmith away, Emmy leaned back in the chair and breathed deeply. "That was the most amazing thing."

Dylan grunted and walked toward the bar. He poured a drink and knocked it back. When he turned to look at her, the scowl he'd worn froze.

Emmy had opened the robe and raised both thighs to drape over the arms of the chair. Her smile widened when she saw his gaze dip to her cunt, open and swollen with unrequited desire.

"I'm not sure I'm flattered," he bit out.

His jealous anger fueled her fire. "C'mon, Dylan. I was only hot because you watched." She wet the tip of two fingers in her mouth and lowered her hand to her pussy. Finding the hard kernel of nerve endings, she rubbed her fingers in circles on her clit, and deliberately squeezed and released the walls of her vagina to tease him.

His chest rose sharply. "I'll not watch you fuck another man," he said. "That I won't share."

She raised a single eyebrow, mocking his anger. "It's our nature to answer our bloodlust with sexual lust," she said.

"Baby, you're such an expert," he scoffed. "You've been a vampire for all of two hours."

"Some things you're just born knowing." *Like pushing your sexual buttons.*

"In the future, you'll let the lust build while you feed, but save the fucking for me."

"Will you always be there when I'm done with a meal?" she said, with a lazy glide of her fingers inside her juicy cunt.

"Always," he ground out the words.

"There's so much you didn't tell me. About how powerful this hunger is. Have you taken men as well as women?"

The corners of his lips curled. "Already asking questions, Emmy?"

"I haven't changed all that much." She let her head fall back against the cushion and arched her back, lifting the taut points of her breasts. Anything to entice him to take her.

Dylan stepped towards her. "I've taken men as well as women." His hands pushed his pants down his thighs and he stepped out of them. Proof of his desire for her rising straight and engorged between his legs, a pearl of cream glistening at the tip. He knelt before her chair.

She scooted her rear to the edge of the seat. "Did you...do it...with them?"

"Sometimes," he answered honestly. His tongue stabbed into her vagina, coating his tongue with her cream, then circling to spread the moisture on the thin lips that framed her opening. "The lust can be overpowering, without a partner to hold you in check."

"Or a fuck-buddy to take the edge off?" she asked, knowing her coarse words would incite him to lose his restraint. She needed his violence.

"You do have a way with words, love," he said, his breath gusting against her pussy.

He tongued her clitoris—sharp, quick jabs that left her gasping. Her hands gripped his head, but he resisted coming closer, delivering a long swipe of his tongue along her quivering flesh. Then he licked lower, tonguing her nether mouth. Dipping the tip of his tongue inside then fluttering lightly around her asshole.

Emmy wanted to kill him for teasing her, instead she shrieked, bucking her hips to encourage him deeper.

His palms cupped her buttocks and held her still for his plundering, as he alternated stabbing into her cunt and her asshole.

Emmy's belly tightened, her pussy releasing a gush of cream. Dylan groaned against her core, the vibration engorging her clitoris, so taut that each teasing flutter was exquisitely painful. Abruptly, he sat back on his heels.

Left gasping, Emmy stared at him. Willing him with her gaze to take her.

"What do you want, Emmy?"

"You," she breathed.

His jaw tensed. "Tell me."

"Your cock in my cunt," she said between gritted teeth.

His face grimaced as he pushed his engorged penis down to press at her opening. "Not good enough, Em."

"Fuck me, Dylan."

His mouth opened, about to say something. Inexplicably, he looked disappointed. Then shook his head and slammed into her—all the way to the mouth of her womb.

Emmy let loose another shriek, and drew back her knees to her chest, giving him greater access to move unimpeded.

Dylan pulled out, and then rammed forward again. "Promise, I'll be the only man you invite inside you, Em."

"You're all I need. All I want."

"Promise."

"I promise. Only you. Just move, Dylan. I'll die if you don't move."

Dylan leaned over, ramming into her, pressing her deeper into the chair with each hard thrust.

Then he halted, buried so deeply, Emmy could swear he'd feel her heartbeat against the head of his dick. She hadn't thought about it before, but she was glad she had a heartbeat—and then she couldn't think because his hands cupped her buttocks and moved her up and down on his cock, grinding her pussy against his pubic hair. His dick was a hard steel shaft, shoved so deep inside its thickness expanded the walls of her vagina.

And he was changing—which triggered Emmy's metamorphosis. The plates rose beneath her cheeks and forehead, her teeth slid from the roof of her mouth, and her body filled with power. She shoved him to his back on the floor and leapt on top of him, securing his hands on the ground next to his head.

He snarled, a signal of his approval.

She reached between their bodies and clasped his cock in her hand, pushing it toward the mouth of her pussy.

The round, blunt head slipped into her. And she shoved her hips down hard to take him all the way inside her. His hands pushed on her hips to make her rise, and soon she bounced on his cock, a rigorous contest of wills as she forced down and he pushed back.

Faster, and faster, her thighs smacking his hips, levering, forcing, pounding.

His hands rose to her breasts and he squeezed hard, twisting. The harder he squeezed the more exquisite the pain. She leaned into his hands to encourage him.

Then he caressed her cheek, and her nose nuzzled his wrist. Too tempting to ignore, she bit into him, sucking deeply, her belly drawing taut, as she flexed her thighs a final time and drove downward, cramming her cunt over his dick as hard and deep as she could.

She felt as though her head exploded. Her body was wracked with shudders of completion. Finally, she went slack, folding over him like a blanket.

Her head rested over his heart. Its rapid beat, a reassuring measure that they both lived and breathed. They'd come too close to losing each other in the fire.

Slowly, she became aware that he changed, relaxing into his human self. She rather liked the beast and smiled at the thought of coaxing him out of hiding again. She turned her face to lick his salty skin.

"Are you preparing to make another meal of me?" he asked. "I'll have to replenish my blood soon, or I'll be sucked dry as a mummy."

"Would you like that?" she asked. "For me to suck you dry?"

His arms tightened around her. "Are you ready for round two, so soon?"

"It is a vampire's blessing—this rapid recovery." She flexed her hips producing a slurpy sound that made her giggle. "I think we're probably soaking the carpet beneath us," she said.

"You did blow a geyser."

"Me? And none of this dripping goo is yours?"

"What can I say? You inspire me."

She licked around one flat, brown areole. "Your daytime staff will think we peed on the rug."

"And how do you know I have any staff?"

Emmy lifted her nose to the air and inhaled. "Because I can smell them here."

His hands glided over her sweat-slicked back, and she rose up to let her nipples graze his chest. They had an eternity of loving to explore, but she wanted it all, now.

"You're a greedy witch." His hands swept lower to close over the globes of her ass, pressing down, driving his cock deeper.

"Aren't you glad?" she asked.

"Anybody for pizza?" Quentin said from the foyer. Then he blew out a loud breath. "I say. I see what you meant when you said she had an ass to die for."

CHAPTER THIRTEEN

"Now that you embarrassed her half to death—" Dylan began, hands on his hips.

"Embarrassed? Em?" Quentin raised both brows. "I'm half-certain the girl likes being caught in *flagrante dilecto*. It happens too often for mere circumstance."

Dylan scowled, shoving his feet into his pants. "Man, you sound pompous!"

"I practice," Quentin said, with a Cheshire grin, picking up the navy robe.

Dylan grabbed the robe and rolled it in a ball. Emmy had forgotten it during her long screech and lope up the stairs. "Care for a drink, before you leave?" he asked, pointedly.

"A scotch, please."

Dylan poured their drinks, and then joined Quentin, seated before the fire. "All right, there was a point to your interruption?"

"Yes. I spoke with Navarro while you two were playing hide the sausage."

Dylan narrowed his eyes. "And?"

"Navarro's seeking a sanction against Nicky from the council. He's to be killed on sight."

Grim satisfaction filled Dylan. "Now, we only have to find him."

Quentin's face grew uncharacteristically serious. "Dylan, don't you think Em has had enough excitement for a while?"

"I'm not taking her with us. But I can't let him get away. He must be hunted. Emmy won't be safe until he's dead."

"He almost killed me, too," Quentin said. "It's personal now."

"You mean, let you go on your own?" The thought would never have occurred to Dylan. They were a team.

"You need time with her to tutor her properly in our ways. Not that she isn't a quick study—a natural, actually. And you need time by yourselves. You haven't known each other that long."

Dylan contemplated the wet spot on the rug. It really did look like one of them had peed.

"You aren't worried about her, are you?" Quentin said.

"No." Dylan answered too quickly.

"What is it?"

Dylan sighed. "Would she have stopped in time with the locksmith, if I hadn't intervened? Or would she have killed him?"

"She was just overcome with the bloodlust. It was her first time. Are you worried that she's lost her soul?"

Dylan lifted his glass and let the whiskey slide down his throat. "Wouldn't be the first time. But I'm about to find out." He set the glass on the fireplace ledge. "Where will you start looking? I know you, you've already got a lead or two."

"I'm thinking of catching a few waves. He has a vamp brother in Florida."

"Florida? So far? You'll be in unknown territory. We haven't developed council ties that far south. Don't go and get yourself dusted."

"Just keep that girl out of her clothes—and out of mischief. Oh, and you can sleep easy. The council's providing watchers until Nicky's found."

Dylan walked with him to the front door. They shared a glance up the stairs.

"You're one lucky Paddy."

"Bleedin' toff." Dylan smiled crookedly.

They shared an awkward embrace, before Quentin turned and let himself out the door.

* * * * *

Dylan slipped beneath covers that held a wintry chill. Emmy hugged the far side of the bed, her back to him, her shoulders stiff. "Emmy, we have to talk."

"You don't have to say a thing. I lied. You were right," Emmy said, her voice quiet. "I wanted to fuck that locksmith to death. Wanted to bathe in his blood."

Dylan held his breath. He'd let her speak. He needed to know the state of her soul—and whether he'd lost her forever. And if she wasn't whole, she was his responsibility—although ending her new life would likely kill him.

"Thanks for stopping me." She turned towards him, tears on her cheeks. "I couldn't have lived with myself, if I'd taken his life."

Dylan closed his eyes, relieved beyond words. Remorse was only possible if one still cared about human life.

Emmy's breath caught on a jagged sob, and she pushed back the covers to get up. Dylan couldn't bear to look at her.

"Where do you think you're going?" he asked.

Her gaze met his, but his face was closed, remote.

"Ho—ome," she wailed, her face and what was left of her composure, crumpling.

"Aren't you forgetting something?"

"I don't have anything to wear. I'll send back your robe," she paused to sniff. "Wherever it is." She hated when she cried. Her face puffed up like a blowfish. And she needed a Kleenex. Dylan's last sight of her would be of an enormous, snotty nose and eyes nearly swelled shut.

"I wasn't talking about my robe. Come here, Emmy."

That didn't sound like a goodbye. She squinted to see his face, but he still looked imposing. Afraid to read too much into his invitation, she figured he just wanted to offer her a little manly comfort—before he let her down easy.

"I know men hate tears. But I can't help it," she said, wiping her cheeks with the back of her hand. "I just keep thinking about it. He was there. His blood was such a temptation, and I just wanted a little bite—"

"Em," his voice lowered in warning. "Don't remind me."

Emmy's heart leapt. That particular tone in his voice usually preceded an intense sexual experience. He was jealous! "Ooooh!" She started crying a fresh spate of tears.

"For fuck's sake." Dylan's hand clamped over her arm and he jerked her toward him.

Emmy fell against him and buried her face in the soft fur of his chest.

Dylan stretched his arm to slide the drawer of the nightstand open and drew out a packet of tissues. "There," he said. "You've twenty of them to mop up the mess."

She hiccoughed and plucked at the plastic, but she couldn't open it.

Dylan cursed and took the packet from her. After a moment, he shoved a tissue into her hands. "You'll stop crying this instant."

Emmy took the tissue and blew her nose loudly. "I can't stop, just because you order it, you know. Once it starts," she shrugged, "I'm pretty much at its mercy…k-kinda like that po-poor man."

"Then how do you stop crying?"

"I think happy thoughts." Emmy blew again. When she finished she handed him the tissue.

Dylan tossed it on the floor and handed her another. "Happy thoughts?"

"Yes, like ice cream and pepperoni pizza thoughts."

"There's freshly cut steak in the refrigerator."

Emmy perked up at that thought. At least they wouldn't starve tonight. Although she had no intention of leaving the house any time in the near future to hunt. She couldn't trust herself. Her face crumpled again.

"I thought steak was a happy thought."

"It is." Her shoulders shook with the next bout of crying.

Dylan pushed her down onto the bed. Before she guessed his purpose, he was hovering over her, his cock pressed against her entrance. "Want a happy thought?"

"Is this a pity fuck?"

Dylan rolled his eyes. "Are you quite through feeling sorry for yourself? We've only an hour of darkness left and I'd intended to ride you all the way to dawn. And this isn't fucking." He pushed his hips forward, spearing into her.

Emmy's hands closed over his buttocks, "Then what is it?"

"Did you just stick your tissue to my ass?"

"Oh!" Emmy quickly pulled it off his skin and tossed it over the side of the bed. "You changed the subject again."

He drew all the way out of her, and then placed the head of his cock at her entrance again. "Tell me what you want, Emmy."

"I want you, Dylan."

He gritted his teeth against the urge to surge inside. "Be more specific."

"I want your cock inside me?" She was in pain and he wanted to play semantics?

He shook his head.

"I want you to fuck my brains out!" she shouted at him. What else did he want?

"*Not fuck!*"

Emmy's heart stilled. He wanted the truth. "I want you to…make love to me."

His breath gusted out. "Was that so hard to say?"

She nodded. "Yeah. It has certain connotations, you know."

Dylan circled the head of his penis around her opening. "Tell me more, Emmy. What connotations?"

Emmy's forehead scrunched into a frown. He wasn't going to leave her any pride left. "Such as, you must be in love to make love."

The head penetrated her opening, and she wriggled her hips to caress him with her inner muscles.

"And are you?" he asked. His face was taut. Heat stained his cheeks. But his eyes staked her to the bed.

"You're going to make me cry again."

"Oh no, you're not." He pushed deeper inside her. "Only happy thoughts. Fucking is a happy thing, right?"

"I thought you said we were making love?" she wailed. "Are you taking it back?"

Dylan flexed his hips, driving his cock inward until he was fully gloved. Then he lowered his body over hers and rested on his elbows. "Am I taking what back, Emmy?"

"That you love me."

He raised a hand to brush her hair back from her face, while his gaze held hers. "And do I?"

"You must love me."

"Why's that?"

"You're looking at my blowfish face, and you aren't throwing up."

His gaze narrowed. "No jokes now, Em. This is just you and I. Only the truth between our skins. Do you think I love you?"

She was afraid to say it, in case she wasn't right. And she said so. "I mean, you might just be obligated to love me. You sired me, right? You have to love your children."

His face grimaced. "You make it sound like incest."

"I like this kind of incest. Will you fuck me, now?"

"Only if you say the magic words."

Emmy held perfectly still.

"Em?"

"I'm thinking. If I say it, you'll feel obligated to say it back. And then I'll never know the truth until you're packing a suitcase to run away with the maid."

"Bloody hell. Just say you love me."

She drew in a deep, ragged breath. "I love you," she blurted.

He nodded. "Fine. That's all I asked." He pulled back and drilled back inside her.

Emmy couldn't help rolling her hips in response to his deepening plunges. But she really wished he'd stop, so she could think. "Well? Aren't you supposed to say something?"

"What?" he asked, closing his eyes and groaning as he picked up the pace.

Emmy's hips slammed upward to meet his thrusts, even as her face screwed up, ready to wail.

His eyes opened. "Not again. I love you, Em. I wasn't going to give it to you so easily. You don't deserve it. I've loved you longer, and frankly, you've put me through hell."

"Dylan…" she said, her voice lowered in warning.

"What?"

"Shut up and fuck me. You're starting to sound like me."

"Good God!" He leaned back, and hooked his arms beneath her legs. "I know one way to make certain neither of us has the strength left to talk."

Emmy's hands fisted in the bedding. He was as good as his word. In minutes, she was breathless and grunting with each hard stroke he delivered. His glorious face, red and glistening with sweat. His body was taut as a bowstring as he pounded at her cunt.

And looking down her body, she saw what he saw for the first time, her body cushioned his thrusts, her belly shivering and rolling, her nipples peaking—beckoning him to suckle.

The parts of them that moved together were wet and lightly furred. His cock a strong, straight sword speared into her warm, wet scabbard.

They were made for each other. Beautiful together.

"You're getting that look again," Dylan said, his breaths coming in short pants.

Emmy sniffed. "I'm not going to cry. I'm going to come."

"Then hurry it along," he said. "I won't last another minute."

"But you haven't changed."

"I told you. It's not required. I simply…have to be…completely…" His arms jerked her hips up, snug against his groin. Shorter, sharper thrusts, faster than before.

Emmy's back arched off the bed, her shoulders grinding into the mattress to press her hips higher. Then she was flying, screaming as she hurtled toward the stars.

When she grew aware of herself again, she looked up to find Dylan staring at her. And no wonder, she'd thrown her ankles around his neck, and her body was suspended on his cock.

Feeling a little sheepish, she unwrapped her ankles, but Dylan continued to hold her hips flush against his groin. "Sorry. Did I put off your orgasm?"

Dylan slid out of her slowly and dropped her hips on the mattress. His cock was bathed in come.

"Is that you?"

"It's us, Em."

"But you're still—"

"Hard as a stake?"

She shivered. "A pole. Stakes anywhere near my person—"

"Yeah, gives me the willies too." He grinned and sat back on his haunches. "Do you think we can do that thing, again?"

Emmy's eyelids lowered and she drew her bottom lip between her teeth. "What thing, Dylan?"

His hand closed around his cock and he caressed it. "You know."

Emmy's hand slipped between her legs. "Drill for a gusher? Come on, Dylan. Say it."

"Turn over and get on you knees."

Emmy was there in under a second, her ass pushing back to meet his cock. Her chest on the mattress, she reached back to spread her cheeks. "Come to mama."

He pushed inside, hard and straight, driving forward without pausing to let her tender flesh adjust.

Emmy groaned and pressed her cheeks together to give him as much friction and resistance as her body could bear.

"Bloody hell! You've no idea what your ass does to me." He leaned over her back, his teeth scraping the top of her shoulders.

Emmy pushed up from the mattress and shoved her hips back to take him the rest of the way inside. "It's an ass to die for, isn't it love?"

Dylan licked her shoulder, then bit her to hold her still.

Emmy wiggled her ass from side to side, grinning. Dylan wouldn't be able to resist for long.

"Witch!" He licked her neck, then pulled her up so that she sat on his thighs, impaled on his cock. "Now, I get to touch all of you. Who do you think will come first—and loudest?" His hands closed over her breasts and squeezed.

Emmy giggled, then pushed one of his hands down her belly, to her sopping pussy. "I planned this. I get all the attention, now."

His fingers plucked her clitoris and a nipple. "Think you're smart? I can make this last forever."

"You'll last a minute at most." She bounced on his lap, intending to show him he couldn't possibly resist. "Oh!" She hadn't expected that to feel so good.

His fingers pushed inside her cunt, and he swirled and dug, and swirled and pressed three of his long fingers as far as they could reach.

"Ohmygod!" She bounced faster, her ass stretched and impossibly full, her pussy dripping with another wash of cream.

"Say it again, Em," he whispered into her ear.

"I love you, Dylan."

He withdrew his fingers and flattened his hand over her belly, holding her still. "Say it again."

"I love you," she groaned. "Now finish it."

"Bossy little witch." Another hand joined the one pressing into her belly. "Tell me what you want."

"Bastard! You know damn well, I want your cock fucking my ass."

He tsked in her ear. "Such language. And I thought you were a shy little thing."

"You created this monster," she reminded him and struggled to move on his cock, but he held her firm. "I was minding my own business, wasn't looking for any vampire-man—"

"Aren't you glad I whisked you off your feet and had my way with you?" He kissed her shoulder, and Emmy's head fell to the side to let him stroke her neck with his rough tongue.

Her hands rose to her breasts and she rolled her nipples between her fingers, tugging them hard. "Bite me, baby," she begged.

Fingers combed through the hair of her mons, then pulled back the hood of flesh to expose her clitoris. "Pleasure yourself, Emmy."

Her head fell back to let him watch over her shoulder. She rubbed her clit, gasping as the hypersensitive nub swelled beneath her fingertips.

His hands gripped her ass and lifted her, and she sobbed because her climax swept over her breasts, tightened her belly, and centered on her clit as he levered her hips on his cock.

"This is incredibly happy thoughts," she said. "Cataclysmic, orgasmic—"

Her vagina convulsed, and the deep pulses shuddered around his dick. She felt his thighs tense before an endless stream of cum shot into her.

"Promise me, you'll love me forever," she said, when she'd finally found her breath again.

"I will," he said, his voice roughened, his monster face rubbing on her shoulder. His arms hugged her tight to his body.

"Promise me, we'll go after Quentin."

Dylan stilled.

"I know he's gone after Nicky, alone. I don't have a good feeling about that."

"I won't let you anywhere near Nicky again. We're staying here."

Emmy pulled away from Dylan and turned to face him. "Nicky touched me, Dylan. He stripped me, shamed me, and then tried to kill me."

Dylan bared his teeth, his fearsome face contorted with rage.

Emmy reached up to smooth her a hand over his forehead. "He marked me. But you made me a part of this. I have to be there."

Dylan shook his head, beyond words.

"Promise me?" she asked.

His face reformed slowly, his breath evening. "I promise. But you will rest and gain strength before we leave."

Emmy blinked away the moisture that pooled in her eyes. "All right. We'll leave when the time is right." Feeling very tired all of sudden, Emmy stretched out on the bed. "Can we sleep now?"

Dylan crawled over her and laid his head on her breast. "I'll wake you with kisses."

Emmy combed her fingers through his hair, soothing him to sleep. Her dark, immortal knight had saved her life and her soul. As she held him, she made a final vow to keep his heart safe.

When the dawn's light peeked around the edges of the curtains, Emmy's arms wound tightly around Dylan's shoulders, and she held him to her heart.

LOVE BITES
MY IMMORTAL KNIGHT II

CHAPTER ONE

"He's coming in. Get ready," Joe's voice jerked Darcy Henry to wakefulness.

Berating herself for dozing off during a stakeout, she fumbled for the switch on her night vision goggles. Instantly, the landscape before her was awash in shades of luminescent green. She scanned the water's edge. The crests of the ebbing tides rolled onto the beach, unbroken by any sign of "Bat-boy." Had she already missed her opportunity?

"Where do you see him?" she whispered into the mike on her headset, glad the roar of the incoming surf masked their voices.

"Ten o'clock. Get cocked."

She reached for her crossbow and drew back the linen cord with both hands and latched it in the spring clip. Then she slid a steel-tipped arrow onto the track. Sighting down the shaft of the arrow, she braced the bow in her left palm and dug her elbow into the sand. With the stock snug against her shoulder, her right forefinger slid around the trigger and she turned her sights back to the water's edge—just in time to see a tall figure stride out of the surf.

He fit the description of the new vamp in town she'd purchased from the barman at the "blood bank." Only the barman hadn't filled in all the details. Darcy stiffened against her body's sudden surge of attraction and firmly reminded herself the vamp's body was like any other man's. *Yeah, right.*

Her gaze flickered over him, inventorying his characteristics—for her *After Action Report*. Broad-shouldered, leanly muscled, just over six feet tall. Blond, she could tell, despite the fact his hair was plastered to his head. Handsome, too. With broad prominent cheekbones, a longish straight nose, and lips that appeared permanently curved in a smirk.

Unable to resist the temptation, she adjusted the lenses of her goggles to zoom, and her gaze slipped lower. His package was as fine arriving as his ass had been going into the water. His long, uncircumcised cock dangled between his legs. Something not mentioned in the barman's description—and definitely not something that would make it into her AAR.

"Cease!" Joe said, impatience clipping his words. "A civilian's in your line of sight."

Darcy lowered the bow, cursing under her breath. "Where? And how the hell did we miss that?" she whispered angrily.

"She had to have been here when we arrived," Joe replied. "If I hadn't seen her hand rise above the dune..."

Nothing was ever as simple as it seemed. A vampire spotted on Vero Beach just happened to meet the description of a suspected killer they'd circulated that day.

This night's stakeout might be a bust after all. They'd have to track him to his lair and try to take him out while he slept. Dusting a sleeping vampire never sat well with Darcy. Too unsportsmanlike. Asleep, even a probable serial killer like this one wore a face like an innocent.

She burrowed deeper into the wet sand at the bottom of her shallow foxhole, prepared to wait it out. This time she wouldn't doze, no matter how balmy this November night grew. Too many late nights and too little sleep, were taking their toll on the whole team. Instead, she concentrated on how uncomfortable she was with damp sand working its way into her clothing and the smell of rotting seaweed all around her.

Having a target to observe helped. Hopefully, the vamp wouldn't make a meal of his host or Darcy would be forced to intervene. Hand-to-hand with a vamp was a last resort. Humans almost always lost to their superior strength. No matter how many degrees of black belt one had earned.

Joe let out a low whistle. "Damn! How'd a ghoul like that get a such a fine piece of ass?"

A woman sat up near the top of a dune, her arms outstretched, revealing a slender back, rounded hips and a cascade of long, dark hair.

The male vamp went down on his knees and leaned over her.

Darcy tensed, ready to spring to the woman's rescue at the first sign of fangs.

Instead, the woman's back arched to offer her breasts to her lover. His mouth closed over a beaded tip and the woman's loud groan of approval was discernable over the rumble of the incoming tide.

Joe's soft laughter sounded in Darcy's ear. "Better take notes, Darc. See what you're missing?"

Darcy knew better than to answer her partner. Any response would only add fodder to the ribbing she'd receive at the Special Unit's outbrief in the morning. Her lack of a social life was already a favorite topic.

As it was, she was glad the guys weren't "wired in" to her goggles. Joe's fed the monitor in the van parked further down the beach.

Maybe she'd get even luckier and the vamp would move his tryst indoors.

Instead, he released the woman's breast. With his hands braced on either side of her, the tops of his shoulders rippled as he "walked" down her body, his head circling as he kissed a path across her belly. Then he moved lower.

Darcy squirmed. When was the last time a man had buried his face in her pussy? God, had it really been three years since Manny had transferred to Miami-Dade?

The woman's hips lifted and her hands dug into the sand. When his face reached the juncture of her thighs, she shouted and her head thrashed from side to side.

Darcy wished she could roll to her back and give the couple their moments of privacy—and herself a reprieve from an unwanted rush of desire. Tight as a spring, it wound inside her belly. She was helpless to stop the flush of heat that swept from her face to her breasts. And thankful for the darkness so no one on her team would see her blushing.

When the vampire rose to kneel between the woman's legs, Darcy's heart thudded dully in her chest and increased in tempo. His cock fell onto the woman's belly, engorged and enormous, just before he hooked his arms beneath her knees and lifted her buttocks off the sand. The woman reached for his cock and guided it to her pussy. Then his hips slammed forward, hard.

The woman arched into the sand and shouted again.

No man had ever made Darcy shout, a thought that niggled her feminine pride while it aroused her curiosity. Although with his super-sized hardware, the shout might not have been one of ecstasy. The thought cheered her for the moment, and then she noted the woman slamming her hips upward to meet the vamp's thrusts.

From Darcy's angle, she had a perfect view of the long gliding action of his hips as he pumped into the woman's body. Darcy's legs widened and she dug her knees into the sand, shifting her hips to relieve the itch between her legs.

"I'll bet you twenty she comes before he does," Max's voice broke in.

"You're on," said Joe. "What man wouldn't come all over a woman like that?"

"Ahem. Just a little reminder, guys," Darcy said, hoping to dampen this particular line of conversation. "Captain will be reviewing this feed, too. Joe, you better not have your zoom on."

Soft chuckles sounded from the guys, but they soon quieted and hunkered down to wait—and watch.

Darcy's attention returned to the couple further down the beach. The woman's legs straightened, her toes pointing toward the moon, and her long moans indicated she was fast approaching the big 'O'. The vampire ground his hips into hers, and the woman screeched.

Joe groaned.

"You owe me twenty," Max said.

"Damn," Phil whispered. "Wonder if the wifey will be up for a little tickle in the morning."

"I'm telling Bets you called her that," Darcy said, her mouth so dry the words almost cracked.

The woman's legs jerked up and down, and the vamp flung back his head and thrust faster.

Suddenly, he stopped, his nose lifting into the breeze.

Realizing the wind had shifted, Darcy hugged the sand and held her breath.

The vamp opened his eyes and stared straight at her.

Darcy froze, hoping he hadn't really seen her. But a grin stretched across his face.

"Fuck, Darcy!" Joe shouted into her headset. "You're made. Get out."

Darcy couldn't risk a shot with the woman downrange. She ditched her crossbow, ripped off her goggles, and sprang from the foxhole. Running straight for the road a hundred yards in front of her, Darcy felt the world slow. Her feet mired in the sand. Her heart drummed loudly in her ears.

Then she heard bare feet pounding in the sand and knew he was gaining.

"I'll try to get off a shot," Joe said, his breaths coming short and fast, "but he's moving in on you. Pick up your feet. You're running like a girl."

Anger and a spurt of adrenaline increased her pace. She leapt over a hummock of tall sawgrass and hoped it scraped his balls. The road was fifty yards away. The headlights of the approaching van swept the beach in front of her.

"He's too close. I can't get off a shot," Joe said. "Hold him off, I'm coming."

Twenty-five yards and uphill, now. Her boots sank ankle-deep as she climbed a dune. She reached the top, and then her feet left the ground as a heavy weight knocked her through the air.

They rolled in a jumble of twisting limbs to the bottom of the dune. When they stopped, his long, hard body stretched over hers, anchoring her limbs to the ground.

Darcy opened her eyes, expecting a vampire's mask and a row of jagged teeth. Instead, the vamp's handsome face hovered inches from her own.

"Well, well, well," he said, his voice a low, rumbling purr. "A she-cop. A dangerous species, indeed."

"You're English," she blurted. Something else not in the report. Was he even a vampire?

Despite the layer of clothing separating their skins, Darcy burned from his heat. She struggled against his restraint.

He stretched and hooked his ankles around hers and his hands held hers easily to the ground.

Finally, she let her head fall back in the sand. "So, how'd you know I was there?" she asked, already knowing the truth, but needing to distract him.

His face lowered, and he sniffed along her neck and the collar of her shirt. "I could smell your arousal."

Darcy jerked, that hadn't been quite the answer she'd expected, and then noted that up close he smelled of the sea and the other woman's perfume.

Noise from a half a dozen pairs of booted feet hurtling down the dune filled the air around them. When the sand settled, the clicks of rounds chambering in pistols sounded loudly.

The blinding glare of multiple flashlights trained on Darcy and the vampire lying in the trough of the dune fully illuminating his features. His wary gaze held Darcy's.

"Get off her now!" Joe shouted.

"Now, gentlemen," the vamp responded, his voice calm, "why would I give up my only advantage?"

He leaned close and Darcy forced herself not to flinch. *Christ, he's going to bite me.* Expecting teeth to sink into her neck, she was surprised when his warm, rough tongue lapped her instead. *So that's what their tongues feel like!*

"Just in case," he whispered.

When she could organize her scattered thoughts she realized he'd prepared her skin—used saliva from the special glands in the back of his throat to deaden the nerves. *Why bother?*

"I give you my word. We won't harm you if you let her go," Joe continued.

"And our long standing relationship assures me your word to a vampire is your bond?" Wry humor laced his words. "No thank you. I think I'll stay right where I am. Besides it seems a fair trade. I have an interesting bit of woman-flesh beneath me to replace the bit you chased off."

Joe cursed softly.

The vamp's gaze drilled her into the sand. "I'm sure you've wondered what it's like. From where I'm sitting...er, laying...it's pretty damn sweet."

Which reminded her his sex nestled between her legs. Awareness stiffened her belly and thighs. Darcy glared at him—vampire or not—she was getting pretty mad.

"You son of a bitch," her partner growled.

"Joe," Darcy said, trying not to strangle on her words, "Let's not piss him off. Remember, I'm the one with a naked vampire squashing the breath out of me."

"Yeah. Captain's gonna have your ass," Max said.

"Somehow, I think that's the least of my worries," she murmured.

"Well folks, it looks like we got ourselves an old-fashioned Mexican standoff," Joe said, disgust in his voice.

"You're fucking Cuban," Max pointed out.

As a smile stretched across his face, the corners of the vamp's eyes wrinkled. "Is this what you have to put up with every day? Poor girl."

Darcy's breath hitched. He'd been handsome before, but smiling, his attraction was lethal. Even with a crowd of her buddies standing with fully loaded weapons trained on them, Darcy's body responded to the vampire's sensual pull. Her breasts tightened and her nipples pressed painfully against her sports bra.

"We should probably put this to a swift end," he said, lowering his head to nuzzle her neck.

That wasn't what she wanted to hear. Bracing for violence, she was unnerved when he raised his head. He still smiled.

In fact, his smile was so broad she could detect the state of every one of his pearly whites. Darcy stilled, her mind racing. He wanted her to know he was in control. Not the action of a blood-crazed vampire.

But still a vampire.

With her mouth dry as a desert, Darcy said, "If you keep your mouth next to my neck, we could sit up and talk with the guys about what to do next."

His gaze flickered to her lips and back up. "Do you really want your friends to see what you do to me?"

Confused, she felt something nudge her inner thigh and remembered his erection. Heat rushed to her cheeks. The whole crew would know a horny vampire pinned her to the ground.

"Shy?" he whispered.

Her eyes narrowed. "Performance problems? Couldn't get it off before?"

"She bites!" Louder this time, "I'm going to move behind her slowly. So that we can talk." He winked.

This was a big joke to him. In that moment, she knew he wasn't the killer. Vamp or not, he wasn't going to harm her.

With his mouth against her neck, he lifted his body off hers, and she followed him up, sitting in the sand. He slid around her, until she was between him and six raised weapons. When he settled, his long bare legs stretched alongside hers and an arm held her back against his belly, his cock snug between them.

"Our little secret," he whispered.

She was getting damned annoyed with the whispers that raised the hairs on the side of her neck. "Not so damn little. And definitely not a secret."

"Glad you noticed."

Darcy glared straight ahead.

"You're the Special Unit, aren't you?" the vampire asked, his voice pitched for the group to hear.

Darcy wished she could see the expressions of her team, but the lights trained on her kept them in shadow. *How the hell did he know that?*

"I've been looking for an opportunity to approach you regarding a delicate matter."

"You have our full attention now," Joe said.

"There's a serial killer in your midst."

Darcy heard a snort of disbelief and shuffling of feet.

"Yeah, and we're looking at him," Joe said.

This male posturing wasn't getting the vampire's cock off her back. "Joe, shut up. This isn't getting us anywhere." Glancing over her shoulder, she said, "My name's Darcy."

"A pleasure to meet you," he murmured in her ear. "Call me Quentin."

Quentin. Now it would be harder to kill him. He had a human name to go with his human face. "There's more you want to tell us?"

"I believe we have a mutual foe. I, too, am hunting."

"The way I see it," Joe said, "the killing started about the same time you showed up."

Quentin's hand tightened on her belly. "I followed it here. From Seattle. My friends aren't any more pleased with the attention his actions bring on our community than you are cleaning up his messes."

Before Joe could issue another challenging remark, Darcy broke in, "What are you suggesting?"

"That we partner."

"Our unit partner with a vampire?" It was unheard of. Their unit killed vampires—all vampires.

"There would be advantages to us both. You know the area. I have a vampire's perspective and special skills."

"We don't need you to help us find a vampire," Joe said. "We do just fine on our own."

"And when you catch him? He's not going to go into escape mode like most. He won't panic. And you won't find him by accident."

His words sent a chill through Darcy.

"He's a calculated killer." The vamp's words were becoming clipped.

An impatient vampire wouldn't be good for her health.

"Think guys," Darcy said. "The killer has left remnants of his meals in plain sight, taunting us."

"Are you suggesting we should take this vampire on?" Joe asked.

"No." *I just want him off my back.* "I'm saying this isn't our decision."

"We'll bring you to the Captain," Joe said, sounding disgusted.

"If you help us," Darcy said, "What's in it for you?"

"I need a place to stay. I choose yours."

The air whooshed from her lungs at the thoughts his remark invoked.

"Let's get this guy some pants before Darcy hyperventilates." Max said.

CHAPTER TWO

The guys were crowded around the bathroom door at the station house when Darcy returned with a cup of steaming coffee. "What gives?" she asked. "Doesn't the uniform fit?"

"Seems when a vampire gets it up, he has to do something with it." Max shrugged. "You asked."

Darcy's face burned. "Sorry I did."

A roar echoed from inside the bathroom, and Darcy turned on her heels. Head down, she carried her cup to the conference room table to wait for the rest of the crew to file in and take their seats. She hated to admit, even to herself, that she was eager to see the vamp again. Her fascination horrified her.

Or so she wanted to believe.

Finally, he strode into the room looking irritated and wearing prison orange. Despite the unfortunate color, he was devastatingly handsome. Darcy had seen him in luminescent green and in shadow, but bright fluorescent light revealed his eyes were a startling blue and his hair, finally dry and combed, fell in silver-blonde waves to the tops of his broad shoulders.

Darcy cleared her throat, hoping no one had noticed her staring. "What's the matter," she asked him. "Not your color?"

He shivered in disgust. "It's vile." He took an empty seat beside her.

Never having been this close to a vampire without ramming a stake through its chest, Darcy's senses were ringing all alarms.

Joe slipped into the chair on the other side of her, his brown-eyed gaze glaring at them both.

"Your boyfriend?" Quentin asked, his voice silky.

"My partner," she said, between stiff lips.

Feeling awkward sandwiched between the two of them, Darcy was supremely aware of the silent testosterone war going on between the two men — one glowering, one smiling. Darcy straightened in her chair, blocking their staring war. Immediately, she recognized her mistake. Now, they were both looking at her.

Another of the team, Phil Carstairs, entered carrying Darcy's bow and quiver. "I retrieved this from the beach." He held the crossbow in front of Quentin and sneered at him.

Darcy murmured her thanks, accepted her gear, and laid the items on the table.

The vampire reached past her and drew an arrow from the quiver. "Not silver?" he asked, with a single raised eyebrow while he fingered the tip.

"I wanted to be sure it would pierce your chest," she said with a smile that didn't reach her eyes.

"You prefer an arrow to drive deep?" he asked in his sexy purring voice, his expression innocent.

Darcy's cheeks turned pink.

The door of the conference room swung open and Captain Springer entered, looking strangely pleased. He approached the vampire, his hand extended. "I'm Captain Leon Springer."

The vamp stood and accepted the handshake. "Quentin Albermarle."

"I'm pleased to meet you. And I apologize for the inconvenience."

Darcy sat stunned. The Captain was apologizing to a vamp? She'd half expected him to ream their asses for bringing him here in the first place. She looked around the table and saw that the rest of the team was similarly shocked by their ferocious frowns.

"You must understand our concerns," the Captain continued, "Everyone's a little on edge. The reports of random murders out of Seattle, and then murders following the same M.O. begin here, shortly after you arrive. My guys jumped to conclusions."

"Understandable, given the circumstances," Quentin replied. His smug expression made Darcy want to plant her fist in the middle of it.

"Can you believe this?" Joe muttered.

"I've verified your story with the police there," the Captain said. "You come highly recommended."

Quentin nodded and watched while the Captain took his seat at the head of the table, his crew of black-uniformed officers taking the remaining chairs.

All were prime specimens of human males — well able to take him in a battle to the death. His gaze fell on the one exception — the woman sitting beside him. Her slender backbone was as straight as one of her deadly sharp arrows. But he knew better than to take her outthrust jaw and angry expression as anything other than a mask. Her body had melted beneath his on the beach, her ripening arousal a pungent betrayal of her hard-fought battle for composure.

Beneath her prickly exterior beat the heart of a wanton.

How delightful it was going to be to break through her resistance. With barely a woman's curve evident beneath her uniform, he wasn't fooled. Her boyishly slender hips held a subtle feminine flair that had cradled his sex nicely. The gentle curve of her taut waist had quivered when he'd stretched his body over hers. And her small, soft breasts were tipped with sensitive nipples that had pebbled to hardened points when his chest met hers.

She didn't know it, but her eyes had grown wide as saucers when she'd realized his cock pressed into her thigh. Without a hint of makeup, her gaze framed by dark thick lashes had betrayed her excitement. Her expressive brown eyes, glittering with heat, had also told him she was curious.

Careful where his thoughts lingered, lest he find the need to seek out the WC again, Quentin widened his legs in the hard plastic chair and turned his attention back to the details of the outbrief.

"Folks, I'll admit I was skeptical when I first heard Quentin's proposal. We've been fighting vampires for over four years. We see the darker side of their interaction with humans — the violence and harm they can do. We're the ones who are called out when they step over the line.

"But the fact is, we haven't been doing so well in this war. And I think it's time we rethink our strategies. Time to consider a partnership. Vampires live among us. For the most part, we can't tell them from us."

"At least not until they show us their teeth," the one who'd introduced himself as Max Weir replied angrily, his hard-eyed glare letting everyone in the room know of his objection to the offer.

The Captain leveled a glare of his own at the large man. "I've considered Quentin's offer and I accept. I think he'll be an invaluable asset to the team while we're hunting our killer. He has personal knowledge of this vampire and understands his habits."

The Captain held up a hand to quiet the murmured protests from the team. "It'll be dawn soon. We need to get Quentin to a safe place to wait out the day, and the team needs to rest up as well."

"I have a place," Quentin said, smiling. "Hers." He nodded to the woman beside him whose face was reddening with anger.

"Fuck no," her partner growled.

"That's out of the question," she said, her back bristling.

"Darcy, it would solve several problems if you would." The Captain's ruddy complexion grew darker. "We wouldn't have to draw attention to our 'arrangement' with expense reports we'd have to justify. But you needn't worry — he checks out with

Seattle PD. Seems Quentin, here, has helped on several major investigations. He's considered a trustworthy sort."

"A trustworthy vampire?" The woman's partner, Joe Garcia, snorted.

"Having him assimilated with the team is an excellent idea, actually," the Captain said. "Darcy, I'm assigning you and Joe to be his shadows during this investigation. In the meantime, Joe, I think you'd better stay at Darcy's place, too. She's got the room."

Quentin grinned.

"As soon as he wakes tonight, we'll start picking his brain. I'll send an artist around to get a sketch of the vamp we're looking for."

Darcy's arms folded over her chest, her expression pure bulldog obstinance. "I don't trust him, Captain."

"Well, now you can keep an eye on me," Quentin said. "And if I step out of line, you can use one of your toothpicks to turn my black heart to dust."

Finally, she looked at him. "I will be watching you. Have no doubt about that."

"All right, then," the Captain said. "It goes without saying that this little arrangement is strictly need to know. This is an unprecedented step the department is taking. I want it to work. Now, get out of here."

* * * * *

Darcy entered her house quietly and set the bags she'd retrieved from Quentin's hotel room on the floor. He could carry them the rest of the way to his bedroom when he woke. *His bedroom.* Already, the house felt alien. *Invaded.* As soon as she'd deposited Quentin and Joe on her front doorstep earlier, she'd hotfooted it out of the house. Retrieving his things had only been an excuse to put some distance between the vamp and her raging hormones. *Why him?* Why did her body come alive at just the sight of him?

Sunshine poured into the large open space of her Florida room, and she grinned. Joe was a devious man. He'd opened every blind and shutter to ensure the vamp remained trapped behind the guest bedroom door. Joe was on the couch sleeping, a tangle of covers knotted around his waist. His chest bare. With his arms flung above his head, she had an excellent view of his washboard abs and the arrow of black hair that stretched from nipple to nipple and down below the edge of the sheet.

Cursing herself for noticing, Darcy tiptoed past him. Her sexual libido had rotten timing. The vamp had awakened feelings she'd tamped down for three years.

Thankful she had Joe around to save her from herself, Darcy headed to her bedroom. Inside, she stripped off her clothes and padded on bare feet into her bathroom, intent on showering away the sand she was sure had worked itself into every crevice.

Reaching behind the shower curtain, she turned on the water. She brushed her teeth, and rummaged beneath the cabinet for the scented soap her mother had given her at Christmas. The raspberry-perfumed soap would be her secret indulgence. No matter she normally used only plain bar soap for a quick scrub. She wondered if the vampire's keen sense of smell would detect her change of routine.

She reached in to lift the stopper and stepped beneath the shower's spray.

"I thought you'd decided to find yourself another place to stay."

Darcy nearly screeched at Quentin's husky whisper. She whirled and then remembered she hadn't a stitch of clothing on. Her hands covered her breasts, but she quickly realized she had to look ridiculous. The rest of her was bare, and his hot gaze devoured every exposed inch.

"What do you think you're doing?" she hissed, keeping her gaze glued on his face.

"Availing myself of my hostess's amenities?" he said, a smirk tilting one corner of his mouth.

One glance down and she'd be toast. She was already having problems breathing after noting the way the water ran in rivulets from the ends of his hair and down his broad, hairy chest. "Well, you can just waltz right out of here and go use the guest bathroom. I'm not sharing."

"Your boyfriend's made that impossible for me to do." He folded his arms over his chest. "You're stuck with me until dark."

"Not my problem. And his name's Joe. How the hell did you get past him?"

Quentin's smile stretched and he shrugged.

Darcy wished the rose-colored tile behind him would make him seem less...manly. "I'll scream, and Joe will come running. He'll kill you if he finds you here—and I won't be happy to clean up the mud you leave behind." She jerked when he reached over her shoulder for the shampoo.

His long, muscled forearm grazed her shoulder, and Darcy held herself stiff as a statue to keep a shudder from racking her body. His large, broad frame crowded her, sucking the air from the steam-filled stall. When he calmly squeezed a glob of shampoo into his palm and raised his hands to lather his hair, her breath hitched.

She didn't know why she didn't make good on her threat to scream for help, except she'd be embarrassed as hell if she were found naked with the vamp. Her reticence couldn't have a thing to do with all that golden skin and the tufts of dark hair beneath his arms—and certainly not the cock lifting from its bed of wiry brown hair.

Ah hell! She'd looked.

Darcy spun away and grabbed the washcloth. Scrubbing her arms and breasts, she abraded her skin to remind herself this was a dangerous man—whom she probably shouldn't turn her back on.

When his soapy hands slid around her waist and pulled her back snug against his chest and abdomen, the only thought that didn't blow her mind was that his cock rested in the crease of her ass.

"I'll offer you a trade," he said, his mouth next to her ear.

Darcy fought her body's inclination to lean into his embrace. If she were going to be weak, she'd lay all the blame at his doorstep.

"I need blood — about half a pint to stave off grumpiness…" He licked her ear then sucked her lobe between his teeth.

A frisson of desire shuddered through her body, unwanted, but so strong her head fell to the side, exposing her neck.

"… and I can give you an orgasm unlike anything you've ever known."

Mention of the "O" word tightened her belly to a hard knot. He'd stirred an ache when he'd first strode out of the waves. Nothing less than a wild fucking would do to get him out her system.

His hands smoothed up her stomach to cup her breasts.

Darcy tried to push his hands down. Not because she didn't crave his touch there, but because she knew her small breasts didn't stack up well against the globes on the woman he'd been with earlier. Her traitorous nipples constricted instantly.

She eased her legs apart and let his cock slide between them.

Quentin groaned and tongued her neck. All the while his hands caressed her, smoothing over her breasts, across her belly, and down to her pussy.

Darcy swayed on her feet as pliant as a rag doll in his arms, biting her lips to keep the moans that threatened to tear from her throat. His fingers separated her labia and stroked between. Her hands reached behind to grasp his thighs, otherwise she'd have melted to the floor of the shower in a puddle.

He licked behind her ear, then tsked. "We'll have to do something about this sand first."

Again, he reached for the shampoo. When his fingers massaged her scalp, Darcy swore someone purred. His strong fingers worked in the suds and kept right on kneading and shaping. When he drew her under the water to rinse her hair, Darcy's eyes were closed and she followed him, docile as a lamb.

"Give me your soap," he said.

Her eyes slowly blinked open. "Soap?"

"The bar you're clutching in your hand."

Darcy looked down her arm and realized she still held her mother's soap in her hand. She held it up for him.

Leaning down, he sniffed, then took the bar. "Raspberries. My favorite. Now come here." He drew her away from the water and sat on the ledge at the far end of the stall, pulling her to stand between his open thighs. With a twirl of his finger, he indicated that she should turn around.

She shot one last meaningless glare, then turned away.

He worked the lather between his hands then glided his soapy hands over her skin from shoulders to buttocks and all the sensitive points in between. When he reached her ass, Darcy's heart beat loudly. His hands parted her buttocks and his finger trailed down the crevice. "No sand here," he said, gravel in his voice.

In the creases between her legs and buttocks, he found a trace of grit, so he lifted her cheeks and spent minutes soaping and smoothing to ensure not a granule was missed. By the time he'd finished, Darcy's legs wobbled and she was ready to scream.

When he turned her to wash her front, Darcy's gaze fell on his face. His nose was flared, his cheeks reddened and the smirk was now a tight line of tension. Gratified he was every bit as overcome with desire as she was, Darcy gave herself over to his touch. *Just this once.*

He lathered his hands and reached for her breasts. Already tight and puckered, her nipples caught the soap bubbles he smoothed there. His large hands dwarfed her breasts, but despite her earlier doubts, he played with them, apparently fascinated.

His fingers rolled her nipples, tugged and squeezed until they stretched, engorged. She nearly protested when he left them to glide his hands down her belly. He swirled a finger inside her belly button and Darcy's abdomen jumped and quivered, her legs once again turning to jelly. Then he reached lower.

She parted her legs to make room for his hands and he swept them between, rubbing over her outer labia, then parted them to finger her tender inner lips.

Darcy reached for his shoulders to steady herself, then leaned to rest her head on his shoulder as his fingers rimmed her cunt, circling, rubbing. He found her clitoris and plucked it. "Lift your leg over mine," he said.

He didn't want mere compliance—he demanded her knowing participation. Darcy was beyond any pretense of defiance. She lifted one leg and draped it over his. The space between her legs was wide open for his marauding fingers to explore. Her nails bit into his shoulders.

Looking down the space between their bodies, Darcy's breath grew shallow and raspy. Their differences, human to vampire, weren't important now. How their bodies complimented each other's, feminine to masculine, assumed precedence. Something deep inside her soft core yearned to yield to his mastery.

His erection stood straight up, veins crisscrossing beneath golden skin tinged with red. The wide, plump head looked soft and purplish. She couldn't resist smoothing a fingertip over it.

"No touching. Not yet," he said, his words clipped.

He rolled the bar of soap between his palms working up lather, then set it aside. When his hands descended to her crotch, Darcy closed her eyes and let her head fall back.

His fingers rubbed over the hair on her mons, tugging, massaging, and then he reached lower to follow the lines where her thighs met her pussy, his fingers smoothing, yet creating an ache that drew her belly taut.

She widened her legs and sank slightly on one knee to rock against his hand. *Hurry!* She wanted to shout at him, she needed him to be inside her now.

He traced a finger between her labia and Darcy gasped, sure that now he would dip inside. "Open your eyes," he said.

He removed one of his hands from her and circled his cock. "This is vampire cock, sweetheart," he said, his voice roughening.

"What? You think, once I've had vamp, I'll never go back?" As soon as the words were spoken, she regretted her quip. It was something she tended to do when she was nervous.

Quentin's face broke into grin. "I can guarantee any *man* who comes after me will be found wanting."

"You think highly of yourself, don't you?"

"I've over a hundred fifty years of practical experience, love. I'm just stating facts."

A hundred fifty years of fucking? She wet her lips with her tongue. "From where I'm standing, I'm not seeing anything that special." *Liar!*

His hand glided up and down himself. "This is only one piece of the equipment, love. But I'm getting ahead of myself. I want to describe the process, so there will be no surprises. I don't want to frighten you."

"I'm not scared." Her skittering heartbeat made a liar out of her.

One brow rose, mocking her assertion. "Well, then let's get on with it." The hand between her legs, rubbed over her hips, then clasped one buttock to force her closer. He lowered the head of his cock to her pussy and pushed between her legs.

Darcy's nails bit harder into his shoulders, but she refused to betray her excitement in her expression. She pressed her lips tightly together and dared him with her eyes to take her.

Instead, he leaned forward and kissed her lips. Darcy gasped and he took advantage, sliding his tongue into her mouth. She angled her head and deepened the kiss. When her own tongue swept inside his mouth, she encountered sharp barriers. His incisors.

She tried to jerk away, but his hand on her ass anchored her against his hard, lean body. Her skin noted changes there, too.

"I wanted to prepare you." His voice was deeper, rougher. Quentin was losing his veneer of humanity, changing into his vampire self. He pressed her ass closer, causing his cock to rub against her aching cunt. His gaze pinned her like a butterfly to a mounting board. "Tell me you don't want this."

Darcy shivered in his embrace, her nipples constricting tightly. "Just this once," she whispered, not recognizing the husky tone of her voice.

The corners of his lips curved and the tips of his fangs appeared. He stood, his cock pushing unerringly inside her cunt, higher, deeper, until his hips lifted her from the floor.

Darcy gasped loudly. She'd known he was large, but knowing and *knowing* were two different things entirely. She was stretched to the limit. The walls of her vagina eased around him, softening to accept his intrusion.

In two steps, he pushed her beneath the shower's spray, pressing her back against the tiled wall. Darcy closed her eyes as water sheeted over her face. Her legs rose to wrap tightly around his hips, and her arms clutched his shoulders. Instantly, her focus became the rigid pole of his sex, driving impossibly deep inside her. His hips rolled. Darcy's back rose and fell against the wall and her legs squeezed to draw him closer, deeper.

His hands grasped her buttocks and he lifted and shoved her hips down, causing a friction between her vagina and his cock that threatened to sweep over her like a wildfire.

"Give me your neck," he growled.

Now! Now she'd find out what a true vamp-induced orgasm felt like. She rolled her head to the side and offered her neck for their pleasure.

His tongue lapped at her skin and Darcy trembled. Then his fangs bit into her, and her breath hissed between her teeth. A short, sharp pain was followed by an indescribable euphoria as his mouth suctioned against her neck.

Darcy grew still in his arms, sensation overpowering her limbs. Her passion-drugged senses noted his body was hardening, muscles expanding. His cock thickened and lengthened, and Darcy's hips lurched. She whimpered.

His teeth pulled away. "Wait. Will ease." His chest and hips shook.

Darcy opened her eyes and saw his savage mask. Plates of bony armor pushed his forehead out, altering his gaze into a sinister, hooded leer. His mouth dripped with her blood.

"I don't want you to stop." She bit her lips and moaned when his hips jerked beneath her. "Move! Move now!"

He lowered his head and sank his teeth into her neck again, anchoring her in place as his hips resumed their deep, upward thrusts.

Darcy mewled like a kitten, one hand fisting in his hair, the other scraping his back with her nails.

Quentin pounded harder, driving her higher against the wall—faster and faster.

Then she was writhing in his arms—a wild thing, clawing his back to reach the summit. Her orgasm slammed through her, stiffening her legs, arching her back. She cried out.

Quentin's answering howl reverberated on the tiled walls.

Still panting, Darcy's gaze rose to meet Quentin's. As she watched, his face reformed but his gaze was wary. "You can let me down now," she said.

His lips tightened, but he nodded.

Suddenly, the door to the bathroom slammed open and the shower curtain was jerked back. Joe took in their compromising position with a single searing glance.

He raised a sharpened stake in his fist.

CHAPTER THREE

"No! Joe, don't do it." Darcy cried out, her hand reaching beyond Quentin's back to stave off the blow.

"You god-damned bastard!" Joe spat. "What did you do—use your vamp hypnotism on her?"

Quentin remained where he was—deep inside Darcy's still-pulsating channel. Despite the interruption, he wasn't ready to withdraw from the sweet flesh that fisted around his cock.

Joe raised the stake higher. "Get off her!" he said, his jaw clenched.

"Unless you care to join us," Quentin said, his tone even, "I'd suggest—"

"We're finished," Darcy said, and pushed against his shoulders.

Reluctantly, Quentin backed away from the wall and eased his cock from inside her. Her legs slid to the floor, but he was gratified when she clutched his waist to steady herself.

He turned to face his adversary, unconcerned his cock gleamed with their combined cum.

Joe's face darkened, his body taut. When his gaze swept over Darcy's naked body, his stance grew more rigid. "Bastard!"

Quentin realized Darcy's blood still trickled from the punctures in her neck. He held up both hands. "I'll close the wounds." Keeping an eye on the man holding the stake, Quentin drew Darcy close to him.

Darcy flinched, but allowed him to lick her neck to seal the small punctures. When Quentin lifted his head, he glared a challenge at Joe.

Joe's gaze darted to Darcy. "Go get some clothes on," he said curtly.

Darcy's arms wrapped around her waist and she stepped toward Joe. "You can't hurt him."

Quentin hoped Joe didn't see her backside or he'd be dust. His fingers had left bruises, which were quickly turning blue.

"Were you willing?" Joe asked.

"Yes," she whispered.

He closed his eyes for a moment and lowered his stake. "How could you?"

Darcy's face was ashen, and a sheen of moisture glazed her eyes. "I don't know. I was curious, I guess."

Curious? Anger bristled through Quentin, but he held his tongue. She'd been a hell of lot more than curious. Hotter than a bitch in heat was a more apt description.

Joe's gaze swept over her again, and a muscle tensed in his jaw. "Fuck you, Darcy."

Darcy blanched and turned her face away.

Quentin's hands fisted. He resisted the urge to tear the man's head from his body. He recognized jealousy and desire when he saw them. And Joe was eaten up with bitterness borne of both emotions.

"Get dressed," Joe repeated.

Darcy left the room without a backward glance.

Quentin would have liked to follow her out, to soothe the hurt he'd seen in her eyes.

But Joe loomed over him, his chest rising and falling rapidly. Finally, his face twisted into a sneer and he tossed the stake at Quentin's feet. "Stay away from her, or I swear I'll kill you." He turned on his heels and followed Darcy into the bedroom.

Quentin pulled the shower curtain closed and turned the water a notch hotter. Then he reached for the raspberry soap.

When his lathered hands encircled his cock, he murmured, "This is going to be more interesting than I thought."

* * * * *

"Darcy!"

Ignoring Joe's angry voice, Darcy shrugged into her robe and belted it tightly around her waist. When his hand clamped onto her shoulder, she stiffened.

"Did…Did he hurt you?" Joe asked, his voice softer now.

"No." The word strangled in her throat. She was sore and she wouldn't be at all surprised if her tender inner flesh was slightly torn. The vampire's cock had almost been more than she could take.

"Dammit, Darc, don't lie to me."

Darcy whirled, fighting tears and embarrassment. "Joe, this is none of your business. I'm fine."

"Then why are you lying?" Joe's gaze pinned her.

Darcy fought to remain immobile and not give him a clue concerning her conflicting emotions.

He must have seen something anyway, because his lips twisted and he grabbed her arm. Pulling her behind him, he entered the living room, then dragged her down the hallway to the guest bedroom.

When the door closed behind them, she shook off his hold. "I'm tired. I want to rest."

"After you've satisfied me," Joe said, his jaw set.

Darcy jerked. "What did you say?"

"Just take off that robe."

"I will not. Get out."

Joe's hard-eyed gaze narrowed, and Darcy felt a moment's uncertainty.

"I said, take it off." His voice was low and menacing.

Her gaze swept over his bare chest to the top of his jeans. The snap at the waist was undone, but she detected no bulge of sexual arousal.

"Stubborn..." he said, stepping close to her. His hands landed on the collar of her robe and he pushed the lapels wide. "...foolish..."

So shocked she could only stand there while he stripped the robe from her body, Darcy didn't realize she was naked again until the cool, conditioned air hit her moist skin.

"...stunning..." Joe's hands hovered just above her breasts. His brown-eyed gaze stared at her nipples, which were drawing to painful, rigid points.

It was the cool air, she told herself. Not the heat that flushed his cheeks, nor the muscle that clenched his jaw. One palm lowered to cover her breast and she gasped. Already abraded from Quentin's play, her breasts were sensitive, tuned to the powerful, sensual pull of Joe's rigid posture and the deep breaths that billowed his broad chest.

His gaze rose to her face. "I'm sorry, Darc," he voice raw. "I meant only to see if he'd harmed you." Still, he stepped closer.

Darcy didn't step back. Their chests met and her head fell back. Their mouths were inches apart. When his arms closed around her, she whimpered and widened her legs to let him nestle between her thighs.

"I won't hurt you, I swear," he said, then his lips closed over hers.

Too lost in his kiss and the confusing maelstrom of her awakened desire, she didn't protest when he walked her backward to the bed. Her mouth latched onto his and she sat on the edge then allowed him to follow, dragging her into the soft center. His body blanketed her cooling skin, and she welcomed him, opening her thighs wide around his hips.

His kiss deepened, his tongue swirling into her mouth. Not wanting to surrender, but helpless against his sensual assault, Darcy reciprocated, murmuring unintelligible protests until his mouth lifted from hers. His expression was still angry, but the hurt lingered in the stark clarity of his gaze. "Tell me to stop."

His command echoed Quentin's—jarring and direct. But she knew she wouldn't ask him to stop. He'd been her partner, her best friend. And she wanted him every bit as much as she had the big, bad vamp. Clasping his face with her hands she pulled his face to her breast and cried out when his mouth closed around her nipple.

He shifted to the side and his hand glided over her belly and below. His strong fingers delved between her swollen flesh. Darcy widened her legs and pushed her hips up to take him deeper.

But she flinched when a second finger joined the first. She was too sore to take him.

He withdrew.

Afraid he'd reject her after being reminded of why she was sore, she was surprised when his mouth continued to suckle her breast—softer now, his tongue sliding over the tip.

Darcy's hips lifted off the bed again, and Joe slid a jeans-covered thigh between hers, pressing gently into her soft core. The gentle abrasion was almost too much, but she rode his thigh.

Needing him closer, Darcy smoothed her hands over his bare back, then down to slide her hands beneath his waistband, cupping his firm buttocks.

Joe's buttocks tensed and he murmured, and then pulled away. Without breaking with her gaze, he stripped his pants down his long, lean thighs and kicked them to the floor.

Darcy's chest constricted. She'd seen him in gym, wrestled him to the floor during workouts, but she hadn't any idea how beautiful his male flesh was—like warm, creamy cocoa. His cock was a shade darker, springing high and tight from a nest of black curls.

"I won't come into you," he whispered, his brown eyes soft and caring. "You're too tender. But let me love you."

Darcy let her legs fall apart, splayed wide for his hot gaze. Joe's hands cupped her knees and glided along her inner thighs, pausing inches from her pussy. He leaned down and blew on her heated flesh. His fingertips rubbed briefly around her opening, and then he raised them. His expression grew dark. "You're bleeding."

"Not much," she answered quickly. "It's just...it's been a long time."

"He hurt you. Why did you lie for him?"

This was the one person in the world who deserved the truth from her. "Because I liked it."

"Why him?"

Darcy looked away. His disappointment burned a hole in her stomach. "I don't know. Watching him with that other woman..."

"If you were horny, why didn't you turn to me?"

Crassly put, but honest. Darcy couldn't give him anything less. "I didn't know you wanted this. With me."

"Who's watched your back for three years?" His voice rose. "Who held you when you cried your eyes out after Manny left?"

"We're friends, Joe. It's what friends do. I thought that was all you wanted us to be." Darcy sighed deeply. "It isn't like you haven't had other women. You told me all about them."

"Maybe, I wanted to see whether it bothered you."

"You were testing me?"

He raked a hand through his hair—the gesture evidence of his frustration. "If you'd given me any indication you cared..."

"I do."

"Not the way I want you to. Hell, you'd let me fuck you, now."

"Aren't you going to?"

He glanced down at his cock, a look of disgust twisting his mouth. "You may not want me the way I want you to, but I won't refuse what you offer."

Regret tore at her heart. "I'm sorry Joe."

"For fuck's sake. Don't apologize. I'll really feel pathetic."

"You don't look pathetic from where I'm laying. And this isn't a pity fuck. We're friends. I love you."

"Don't look at me that way. I was just…surprised. When I heard you in there… with him…I thought he'd forced you."

"Well, he didn't."

Joe's eyes closed briefly. "Why a vampire? We kill them. Was it his cock? Did his size fascinate you?"

"It wasn't…just that. I wanted *him*. He makes me insanely angry, but at the same time I've never been so…turned on by a man."

"And now? You want me?"

Darcy blinked. Stated baldly, she sounded like a whore. "Yes."

"Will you have him, again?"

She shook her head. "I shouldn't. I know that. But I don't know. He pulls me."

Joe took a deep breath and his gaze raked over her body, coming to rest on her open legs. "You've got a gorgeous cunt, Darc. Especially now—pink and wet." His hands clasped her knees again, but he pushed them closed.

"What are you doing?"

"Being a friend. Get some sleep, Darcy."

* * * * *

Quentin woke to the rumble of male voices outside Darcy's bedroom door. The SU team had arrived. He stretched and then turned to his stomach, rolling his face in her flower-sprigged, pink pillowcase. The sweet scent of her shampoo and natural musk filled his nostrils.

Darcy had been quite a surprise. As surprising as the feminine décor of her bedroom, which contrasted with the spare iron bed that dominated the center.

He'd expected tensile strength and endurance to match his. But her lithe, spare body had been unexpectedly feminine. Nor had he expected her passion—his back still bore the marks her fingernails had scored in his skin.

Just this once. She'd said it with her eyes clouding with desire. Quentin hadn't a doubt in the world she'd be back in his bed before morning—unless her partner put a spanner in the works.

He regretted her humiliation. A super-cop caught with the enemy. That wouldn't go down well with a straight arrow like Joe Garcia. And Quentin hadn't missed the hot look the other man had swept over her naked body.

Well, he could look all he wanted. Quentin wasn't going to share this one. Although, he wouldn't mind if Joe watched. He'd rather enjoy rubbing the other man's nose in his jealousy.

Quentin's stomach growled and he recognized the aroma of streaks frying on a grill. He rolled out of bed, intent on halting the group from cooking the essence out of a perfectly bloody steak.

But there was the problem of a lack of clothing. He refused to contemplate donning the rumpled orange uniform he's tossed in the corner of her closet. And there wasn't any sign of his bags. He grabbed a towel from the bathroom, knotted it around his waist, and headed for the door.

As soon as he swung the door wide, all eyes turned to him.

"Now that's your color," the large, beefy man named Max said, biting the side of his lip.

Quentin swept the room with a glare and hitched the pink bath towel higher. He spotted his bags next to the door. As he retrieved one, chuckles followed him. Quentin stalked toward the privacy of the bedroom to change when the door to the kitchen swung outward and Darcy strode into the room.

Her gaze raked over him, and her cheeks flushed.

Joe followed her out, and his arm curved around her waist. By the interested stares from the rest of the team, his gesture wasn't a common occurrence. Joe intended to mark her as off limits to Quentin.

Quentin smiled and let go of the towel.

Darcy froze, but her gaze dropped to his cock.

Quentin took his time unzipping his bag. He pulled out a cotton shirt and blue jeans and dressed.

Darcy glanced away and folded her arms over her chest. Her mouth drew into a tight line. If not for the spots of bright color on her cheeks, Quentin would have thought she'd been unmoved by the sight of his naked body.

"We don't hold with vampires flashing their privates in our homes," Max said, his rough-hewn features hardening to stone.

"Since, *my privates* have been a subject of some scrutiny by this group, I didn't think you'd mind," Quentin replied to Max, but his gaze didn't leave Darcy.

Max cleared his throat. "We're having steak and potatoes before we head out for the night. That artist will be over here shortly to get your description of our perp."

"Yummy," Quentin replied.

"The steak or the artist?" Darcy asked, her chin lifting.

"Neither." His gaze swept over her, telling anyone who looked he'd much rather have her.

Every male back in the room stiffened.

Darcy turned to the door and opened it wide. "Come choose your steak," she said between gritted teeth.

Quentin moved to follow, but Joe stepped into his path.

"The lady invited me," Quentin said.

Joe's gaze narrowed. "I'm in charge of the fire. I'll be right behind you."

"Going to make sure I fall on a stake?"

Following Darcy's straight back through the kitchen and into the back yard, Quentin knew the two had a bone to chew. His hopes for a rollicking night between the sheets with the lady cop were dwindling.

When the outside door closed behind Joe, Darcy rounded on Quentin. "I'd appreciate it if you'd keep your sexual innuendoes to yourself."

Quentin stepped close to her. "Why so bothered, Darcy?"

Her glower could have scorched the sun. "I have to work with these guys. If they knew—"

Quentin caught a whiff of an aroma other than steak coming from Darcy's person. He stepped closer and inhaled. "If they knew what? That I fucked you senseless in the shower, and then you crawled in bed with your partner?"

Her eyes widened. "I didn't—"

Quentin raged. She'd turned to another as soon as she'd left him. *A human male, at that!* "In case you didn't know, vampires can't impregnate a human. We have other means of procreation. We also don't carry disease. The ultimate safe sex, wouldn't you agree?"

"What the hell does that have to do with any of this?"

"I'm just reminding you there are certain advantages to a vampire lover." Quentin's face hardened to stone. "How could you go to him with the scent of me still on you skin? And my cum dripping from you?"

"That's enough," Joe said, shoving Quentin away from Darcy.

"Joe." Darcy's stricken gaze held her partner's for a long moment.

Disgust was written in the sour curl of his lips. "I'll be in the kitchen. Yell if he needs killing." Without a backward glance, Joe left Quentin and Darcy alone in the back yard.

Darcy's eyes narrowed and she pointed her finger at him. "Now, look here. We fucked. That doesn't give you any hold over me. I could screw an entire football team, and it wouldn't be any of your damn business."

Quentin drew in a deep breath to let loose on her, then realized he was angry—over a woman. He's shared dozens, no hundreds, of women in his lifetime. Why not this one? Then he realized what she'd just said. "While I share your bed, there will be no footballers anywhere near you."

"Footballers? Football *players*, jerk. And I didn't say I was going to share your bed."

Quentin stepped closer and caught her by the waist, pressing his lower body hard against hers. "Aren't you?"

"You arrogant ass—"

"Such language! Must'nt let your temper fly, love."

She wriggled to escape his hold, but he held her fast. "That's it! I'm gonna take you down. You and the batwings you flew in on!"

Quentin kissed her. Her hands pushed at his chest, but her lips told a different story. They melted beneath his.

He lifted his head. "Are we having our first row?"

"You bet your ass!" Her hands tugged at his hair and pulled him down for a second kiss. Her lips parted beneath his and her tongue lapped the tip of his.

Quentin grabbed her arms and held her away from his rapidly hardening body. "I won't share you with your partner."

Darcy's gaze fell from his. "Nothing happened." She looked up. "Nothing."

He raised one eyebrow. His sense of smell never let him down.

"Not really," she said quietly. "He stopped it."

Disturbed that she hadn't been the one to halt the love play, Quentin's hands tightened around her arms. "You'll share my bed."

"Only until the investigation is over. And the bed's mine, by the way."

Satisfied she'd surrendered to his will, he said, "Not while I occupy it. I'm in charge of that particular fire."

CHAPTER FOUR

Later, armed with the sketch of Nicholas Powell, their serial-killing target, the SU team hit the known vampire haunts—the "blood bank" bars and the streetwalkers' corners. Joe, Quentin, and Darcy however, were headed to the seedier destinations—accessed by invitation only—vampire escorts required.

Places the team had only dreamed of going before Quentin provided entry.

The first was a nondescript house in a subdivision. Passing swing sets and manicured lawns, Darcy exchanged a glance with Joe. This could be her neighborhood. Suburban Vero Beach hid dark secrets.

"How'd you find this place?" Joe asked, as he turned onto a long gravel drive. The house wasn't visible from the road. Chain-link fencing surrounded the yard, which was overgrown with vines and the occasional palm tree. The drive ended in a circle with vehicles parked bumper to bumper in a long row.

"Tessa told me where I could find a meal," Quentin said, quietly.

Darcy fumed. Tessa had been the blonde-haired vamp who rubbed her body all over Quentin's while they'd danced in a dark corner of the Piki Tiki bar.

"What do we need to know?" Joe asked, all business as he parked the car.

"Just follow my lead and do whatever I tell you." Quentin glared at Darcy for a moment.

She wondered what that glare meant.

The trio exited the car and approached the front door illuminated by a single naked bulb. A low thrumming rhythm sounded from within the small, square one-story house.

Quentin ignored the doorbell button and pushed opened the door. Joe raised his eyebrows and shrugged, and then indicated Darcy should precede him.

The smell within the house was pure sin.

Sickly-sweet opium, cannabis smoke, and stale sex hung in the warm air. Music with a heavy, grinding Latin beat emanated from deep within the house.

Darcy's fingers itched for her bow, but they had come weaponless.

A woman approached them. She wore a pareo, knotted at one hip and nothing else. Her gaze raked over Quentin and she flicked her long, bleached-blonde hair over her shoulder to expose her full breasts. "Hey stranger. Need a pick-me-up?"

"As a matter of fact, I brought my own," Quentin murmured with a nod to Darcy and Joe.

Her lips formed a moue. "Well, if you need a foursome..." Her fingers trailed across his chest as she passed them.

Darcy wanted to break her fingers, but Quentin's sardonic glance kept her expression neutral, even as her chin lifted in defiance. She couldn't really blame the girl. Dressed in a long-sleeved, cotton shirt, blue jeans and sandals, he was a sun god — golden-haired, golden-skinned. Too beautiful to believe.

They entered the living room, which was lit by a single table lamp. Most of the occupants were naked or in the process of losing their clothing. Wearing jeans and a halter, Darcy felt conspicuously overdressed. Most were also engaged in sexual acts. "Quentin?" she began, uneasy with the tableau.

His hand pressed the small of her back, urging her toward a plaid-upholstered couch in the dingy room. "Let's play," he whispered in her ear.

Darcy sat on the edge of the seat, her eyes darting to the darkened corners. The couple on the sofa opposite theirs disengaged their lips, and the woman knelt in front of the male vamp to take his cock in her mouth. Would he expect her to do *that* in front of everyone? "Quentin," she hissed. "If you expect me to—"

Quentin pressed a finger to her lips. "Do you know these people?"

She shook her head.

"Do you think they'll recognize you on the street?"

She shook her head again.

"Then hush." He sat down next to her and indicated that Joe should sit on her other side. He leaned behind her and said, "Start to undress her. We have to look 'engaged' or we won't be approached."

Darcy glared at Joe who shrugged, then reached for the clasp at the back of her neck. He leaned into her and whispered, "We have to play by his rules. I won't let this go too far."

She snorted. It was fine for him. He wasn't about to be exposed to a group of vampires and sluts with Double-D boobs. The straps of her top loosened. Her hands caught and held the material to her breasts for a panicked moment, and then she let it slide to her lap. "Why is it you vampires can't go to the drive-thru? Does everything come down to sex?"

"Our bloodlust feeds our sexual hunger and vice versa. It's just the way we're made. Relax," Quentin whispered, and he turned in his seat to kiss her, his hand gliding over the breast nearest him.

With her eyes opened, she saw him nod to Joe. "Don't enjoy this too much," Quentin warned.

Joe's hand cupped her other breast, and he kissed her shoulder. "This is gonna kill me."

Darcy wanted to protest. *She* was the one dying here. Both men's mouths worked on her flesh and mouth while their fingers tweaked her nipples.

Quentin glided his lips along her jaw. "I need blood," Quentin said, "or they won't believe I brought you here to feed."

Darcy pushed the hair from the side of her neck, but he shook his head. "It's too soon. Joe, give me your arm."

Joe knelt in front of her and lifted his arm to Quentin. Quentin licked once, and then pierced his wrist. "Fuck!" Joe hissed. Then his head sagged onto her shoulder. "Sweet Jesus."

Darcy understood the quickening of Joe's body. Her gaze locked with Quentin's as she pushed Joe's head down until his lips grazed her breast. His mouth latched onto her nipple and drew hard.

While she told herself this was just for the job, her body exulted. Her eyelids fluttered and her legs opened to let Joe press against her. Quentin's hand slid between their bodies and he cupped her sex through her jeans. *Mine!* his angry gaze said.

Joe moaned and burrowed his head into her breast, alternately nipping her swollen flesh and licking to soothe. His thighs straddled her leg, and he pumped his erection against her.

Darcy grew alarmed as tension built in her belly. Coming for the two of them wasn't in her job description. And who the hell would she give the credit? Knowing Quentin, he'd demand it.

Surrounded by both men's scent and warm skin, she was overwhelmed. Sweat broke on her forehead and upper lip. Her abdomen trembled as Quentin ground the heel of his palm into her cunt.

Darcy's hand curled around Joe's head to encourage him to suckle. Joe drew her nipple between his teeth and suctioned hard.

The snap to her jeans popped open and the zipper eased down. Quentin's hand slid inside, and his fingers found her clitoris.

Darcy moaned and her head fell back against the cushion. Forgotten were the mission and the other occupants of the den.

With her free hand, she pushed her jeans further down her hips to expose her pussy.

Joe's mouth left her nipple and licked a path down her belly. He stopped suddenly, and Darcy opened her eyes, ready to issue a protest.

Quentin's hand was fisted in Joe's hair.

"All right," Joe growled.

Quentin disengaged his teeth from Joe's wrist and let blood trickle down his chin. "Someone's coming. If I leave you, you're to play — only!"

Joe lifted an eyebrow. "Of course."

Darcy rolled her eyes. An inch from orgasm, her body screamed for release and the two of them were dividing territory. "You started this."

Quentin grasped the back of her head. "And I'll finish it." He kissed her hard then stood to greet a tall, slim black man whose avid stare made Darcy want to crawl into a hole and hide.

Joe's arms encircled her hips, and he drew her flush with his body, covering her from breast to hip. She wrapped her legs around his waist and hugged him tightly. "Quentin's leaving with him," she whispered.

"Then let's continue with the game plan."

"I think you need to lose some clothing too," she grumbled.

Joe grinned. "It is hot in here. Will that make you feel better?"

Looking at his broad shoulders, she murmured, "Probably not."

Joe pulled his T-shirt over his head. His deeply tanned skin was shiny with perspiration. "I see now why you were so blown away." He grimaced. "He's a guy, but I was ready to come all over you when he was sucking on my arm."

Darcy smiled at his look of disgust. "Mind-blowing, isn't it?"

"I still have a hard-on that could pierce steel," he said with a crooked smile.

Darcy knew. It was pressed to the juncture of her thighs. Like a kid with her nose pressed to the candy store window, she eyed the wide expanse of muscle that spanned his chest. Her body was primed and well oiled—desperate for release. "He said we could play."

His expression looked troubled, a frown creasing his forehead. "Not the way I want to."

Her hands caressed the tops of shoulders. "The team's not wired in, and Quentin told us to play. Betcha we can find a place to melt your metal."

Joe chuckled. "I didn't know you were such a nasty girl." He leaned toward her and licked her lips. "Is it just coitus that's strictly against Quentin's rules?"

She sucked his tongue between her lips and bit gently. "You're starting to sound like him."

"God forbid." He shuddered.

Darcy laughed and framed his face with her hands. "I think it's fucking he has a problem with. He seems very possessive of my cunt."

"Don't blame him," he muttered.

"But there's so much else we could do." She kissed his lips. "I'm so hot now, I can't wait."

A smile curved his lips. "We're undercover. Have to play like the natives, don't we?"

Darcy groaned. "Like I said, he started this." *Will I be able to face Joe in the morning like nothing happened between us? Will our friendship change?*

Joe's grasp tightened on her hips. "Put your hands inside my pants, Darcy."

She liked the baldness of his command. "Okay. You first." She unsnapped his jeans and slid down the zipper. His sex sprang into her hands. His cock was fully engorged and hot to her touch. The skin stretching over it was smooth like satin. "Did I tell you how beautiful your cock is?" she whispered.

Joe's eyes closed for a moment. When he opened them again, his gaze was stark with longing. "Did I tell you, you have the prettiest tits I've ever seen?"

Thrilled by the compliment, she blushed. "You're full of shit. You just want to fuck me."

His cheeks flushed red, and his jaw tightened. "Hell, yeah. But it's true. Your nipples are dark pink, like your pretty cunt."

Darcy's heart raced, and her hands squeezed his cock.

Joe leaned forward to kiss her lips, and she glided her hands over him, up and down. Squeezing, twisting.

He leaned his forehead against hers and closed his eyes. "I'm already there, baby. I'm gonna come all over you."

Darcy took his lips in a deep, grinding kiss and thrust her tongue inside while she pumped her hands faster.

He pulled his mouth from hers and gasped. "Shit!" Spurts of white pearlescent cum striped her bare belly.

"There are limits to my largesse."

Darcy gasped and released Joe's cock at Quentin's curt tone. She looked up to see him standing over them, his hands fisted at his sides.

Chest still heaving, Joe reached for his T-shirt and wiped Darcy's belly clean. "Sorry about that, old man." Only he didn't look sorry at all.

"It's time to go." After Joe stood, Quentin's hand grasped Darcy's and he hauled her up into his arms. "You don't seem to take instruction very well, my dear."

With her jeans sagging mid-thigh, Darcy summoned what was left of her pride. "I make my own choices."

"That's where you're wrong. You haven't any choices. I'm making them for you. And by God, you will be mine." His hands slid over her buttocks and he tugged up her pants.

Darcy fumbled with the zipper and snap, and then gasped again when he spun her and reached for the halves of her halter. His hands smoothed the fabric over her breasts, and then he fastened the clasp at the back of her neck. Trembling, Darcy didn't resist when one hand grasped her crotch and the other palmed her breast.

"Mine, Darcy," he whispered in her ear.

* * * * *

Quentin followed close on Darcy's heels as she sped to her front door. All night long he'd simmered. The sight of her hands wrapped around Joe Garcia's cock as the other man gained his satisfaction had boiled like an ulcer in his gut.

After two more fruitless stops at vampire dens, he finally had her to himself. He'd toyed with her breasts and sweet cunt at each of the *hells* until her fevered gaze and the aroma of her arousal had nearly driven him mad.

Joe had watched Quentin's seduction, impotent, his fists on his thighs, his gaze bleak. When he'd finally dropped them at the curb in front of her house, he'd mumbled something about making reports and gunned the engine as he left.

This time Quentin would have her to himself. No interruptions—and a bed beneath her back while he ravaged her senses. After tonight, she'd have no doubts about which man she preferred between her legs.

Quentin didn't heed the voice in the back of his mind, warning him to woo her. He would take her.

Darcy fumbled with the keys and dropped them.

Quentin smiled, grim satisfaction filling him. She had reason to be nervous. He was going to eat her up. Wring every drop of sweet cream from her she had to give. After he taught her a lesson.

He stepped beside her and snatched the keys from the ground. Holding them out for her to take from him, he relished the tremor he detected when her hands accepted the keys.

This time she opened the door and shoved it wide. "I'm tired. Goodnight," she said over her shoulder, heading straight for her bedroom.

When she slammed her door closed, his hand stopped it, and he shoved it open and advanced into the room, stalking her.

"You're angry. And I suppose—from your viewpoint—you have reason to be."

His smile grew as she babbled and took a step backward for each he advanced.

He admired the stubborn tilt of her chin. She didn't lack courage. "But you haven't any right to your anger. You don't own me."

When her thighs met the side of the mattress, she tried to sidestep him, but his hands grasped the edges of her miniscule top and he tore it down the middle, halving the slender strips of fabric. Perfect for what he had in mind.

She backed onto the mattress and then crawled on all fours away from him.

Quentin leapt onto the bed and straddled her back. His hand smoothed over her bare skin and cupped her shoulders.

She shuddered beneath him, the quaking raising his already rock-hard cock. "All right. You win. I want to fuck just as much as you do. You've been driving me crazy all night."

He traced her spine with a finger. "I'm not going to give you what you want. Not until you beg. And then, I'll make you wait some more before I let you cream."

"What are you going to do?"

"Why? Don't you trust me?"

"You have me pinned to the bed. Why should I?"

He leaned down to whisper in her ear. "Because I'm about to become your whole world." Her answering shiver of delight was all he'd hoped to arouse.

He stretched his hand along her arm until he reached her wrist. Her arm tensed, but she didn't resist when he tied the fabric strip around her wrist in a knot. She was curious. More curious than afraid. *Foolish girl!*

He eased off her and dragged her closer to the headboard, and then looped the fabric around one iron bar and tied it. He did the same with her other wrist. "Now, get on your knees."

Darcy's breath was harsh and coming faster. She struggled against her bonds and pulled herself into a kneeling position.

He reached around her body to the snap of her jeans and opened them, then smoothed the rough fabric over her hips and down her legs.

Raising one knee at a time, she helped him remove the pants.

He tossed them to the floor. "Do I have to tie your legs?"

"No," she replied, her voice small.

Having subdued her, Quentin was ready to begin his campaign. "What do you want, Darcy?"

Her back quivered. "For you to touch me."

With his hands on the soft skin of her buttocks, he almost lost his resolve. He parted her cheeks and pressed his thumb against her asshole. "Like this?"

"Quentin?" her voice rose on a plaintive note.

"No?" He leaned down and tongued the rosy ring. "Like this?"

"Quentin!" Her breath caught.

"Is that all you want me to do?"

"No. I want you to fuck me."

He kissed each cheek. "Well, we all have our disappointments."

He left the bed and walked out of the bedroom, closing the door behind him.

"Quentin? Quentin!"

With her angry curses ringing in his ears, he strode into her kitchen and found a bottle of lousy Scotch. Pouring two fingers into a tumbler, he savored the bite of the liquor and willed his flesh to obey his command.

He wasn't one to ponder over the deeper emotions, so he didn't question why this particular woman raised his possessive hackles. He just accepted that she was his. It was time he took a mate.

He imagined her still perched with her shapely ass in the air, fighting her restraints. She'd spit nails at him right about now.

It was going to be a long night, but she would learn who was the master.

* * * * *

Darcy woke to an incredible sensation. A hot, wet cloth swirled over her ass and in between her legs. She moaned and widened the gap between them. The cloth dipped to circle her cunt and she lifted her hips. An invitation her tormentor couldn't miss.

"You're awake," Quentin said, his tone matter-of-fact.

In an instant she recalled everything. Her hands tugged against the headboard, but her restraints held. "What are you doing?"

"Preparing you, love. I don't want Joe's scent on you when I take you."

Darcy bit her lip. Her body remembered even better where they'd left off. She still ached for completion after his diabolical seduction. He'd promised to make her cream.

Instead, she'd been left to scrunch the bedding between her thighs in an attempt to masturbate herself.

"Get on your knees." His voice held a self-satisfied tone. He was enjoying her torment.

She glowered, but complied immediately.

"Good girl." His naked skin blanketed her back and his cock slipped between her legs.

Darcy tilted her hips, hoping he'd slide right in.

"Not yet."

She was afraid of that. Her legs trembled and her cunt wept.

He brought the cloth to her neck, rubbed over her breasts, paying special attention to her aching nipples. Then he scrubbed her stomach. "That's better."

"I'm not going to beg," Darcy said, hoping to incite an argument and break through his icy control.

He chuckled, a mirthless sound that worried her more. "Your legs are shaking. I'll make you more comfortable." He reached past her and snagged a pillow, then placed it beneath her belly. "Lie down on this. "

Darcy lowered herself, disturbed to find the pillow raised her ass. She was positioned for his pleasure.

His hands cupped a buttock each, then glided to her thighs. "Open your legs." He arranged her thighs and knelt between them, encouraging her to widen the gap with nudges from his knees. "Just right."

Just right for what? A warm gust of air blew over the heated flesh between her legs.

"Tell me what you want," he commanded.

Darcy hesitated. The last time he's asked that question her answer hadn't done the trick.

"You have to tell me, or I won't help you." His words gusted over her quivering flesh.

"I want you to fuck me."

He slapped one side of her ass. A stinging, sharp blow. "Wrong answer."

"Did...did you just spank me?" she asked, her voice incredulous.

Smack! "You don't ask the questions. I do."

"You arrogant —"

Smack! "Don't raise your voice to me. Not unless it's to plead."

Darcy gritted her teeth, seething, but holding onto the thought that eventually she'd get an opportunity to give him some retribution. In the meantime...

"Now tell me."

"I want to please you," she said between clenched teeth.

He shifted on the bed and his rough tongue lapped her pussy. "That wasn't so hard, was it?"

"No." The word was a moan.

"What do you think pleases me?"

Control, you fucking asshole! "Being inside me?"

Smack! He spanked the other cheek.

"What the hell did I say wrong that time?"

Smack!

Darcy pressed her hot face into the bedding. Her ass was warming up and she couldn't help wriggling on the pillow. If he'd just lick her cunt one more time, she was sure to pop.

She needed one right answer.

His hands kneaded her buttocks, and Darcy moaned.

"What will please me, Darcy?"

"For me to beg," she said, her words muffled in the comforter.

"Will you?"

"Yes."

"Beg sweetly, love." His tongue fluttered on her cheeks, then moved to the crease and descended. When he reached her anus, he paused.

"Please," she blurted, hearing her rebellious inflection.

He gave her a single flicker.

She got the point. He wanted a constant stream of supplications. *Shit!* Darcy's chest heaved. Anger warred with need. "Please, Quentin. I need you inside me. Oh please."

He bit her ass. "Try to sound a little more convincing," he said, a wry note of humor in his voice.

"What do you want?" she asked, angry with this humbling, but unable to deny what would satisfy her body. "I ache. I've been hurting for hours. I need you to deep inside me." She took a deep breath. "Please, come inside me."

"Better." The point of his tongue pushed into her ass and fluttered.

"Oh God. Please, take my pussy." Her words this time were sincere. "I need your cock, deep inside me." Her moan ended on a higher note, when his finger replaced his tongue.

"You're tight here, love. Don't guess my cock will be playing in here for a while." His finger pushed and pulled, in and out.

Darcy sucked air into her starving lungs.

"Don't forget to beg, love," Quentin warned.

"Can't even think, you bastard."

He swatted her ass, part of his palm slapping her cunt.

The sting ignited her. "Oooh. Fuck me. Fuck me, please," she pleased hoarsely.

"Then raise up to meet me."

Eager to comply, she knelt, her hands twisting in the fabric that bound her to the headboard. The head of his cock pushed into her cunt.

She needed no further prodding. "Please, yes! Give it to me."

He thrust his hips forward, and Darcy whimpered. He didn't go very far, her vagina was tight and resisted his thick cock. She wriggled her hips to accommodate him, and he plunged deeper this time. Her gasps were loud as each successive thrust shoved him deeper inside until he was fully seated.

It was embarrassing how easily she came. He didn't have to move again—her cunt did all the work. Deep, spiraling spasms gripped his cock and squeezed, pulsing around him. Darcy hung on her ties. His strong shaft was the only thing that kept her from crumpling to the bed.

When her heart slowed, she realized he was still buried to the hilt inside her. There'd be more.

CHAPTER FIVE

The ties loosened and Darcy's arms fell limp as noodles to the bed. Quentin pulled her up until she was sitting in his lap, their bodies still connected.

So overwhelmed was she by her response to his lovemaking, she trembled in the aftermath. His arms circled her belly, and Darcy felt strangely comforted.

She closed her eyes and rested her head on his shoulder. "No one's ever filled me like you do."

Quentin nuzzled her until her head tilted. He tongued the lobe of her ear. "Am I hurting you?" he murmured.

Her hands closed over his, and she brought them to her breasts. "I like this pain."

"Can you take more?" He squeezed her breasts.

Her breath caught. Exquisitely tuned to his touch, her nipples flowered again. "Do I have to beg?"

He gently bit her ear. "My turn to ask. I want to transform to find release."

"That didn't sound like a request," she grumbled.

His shoulders shrugged. "I haven't mastered begging."

"Can I watch you change again?"

"You won't be frightened?"

"Maybe," she answered honestly. "I still want to see it."

He kissed the top of her shoulder. "Then turn around and straddle me."

She turned and looked at him for the first time in hours. Even in his human form, he frightened her. Bathed in soft lamplight, he overwhelmed her with his size and golden beauty — and the things he made her want.

His arms opened in invitation.

She'd take him this time. She climbed onto his lap, her legs spread wide across his hips. With her hands anchored on his shoulders, she looked to where their bodies strained to join. He held his cock, and she centered her pussy over it. Taking a deep breath she lowered herself. This time his intrusion was easier to take.

Darcy hissed as she sank partway down, and then lifted. Her eyes drifted closed and she concentrated on the feel of his large, rigid cock as she rose and fell, taking him deeper each time. Her pussy, awash in her cream, lubricated each slow slide.

His hands lowered to her buttocks, and he gripped her tightly, forcing her to move faster. Darcy smiled, recognizing his rising passion by the deep growl from the back of his throat and the increased tempo of his breaths. She smoothed the hair from his face and leaned forward to kiss him.

"It's okay," she told him. "I can handle it."

His jaw strained, and he seemed to fight an inward battle for control, but finally the monster in him won. His eyes gleamed golden and reflected the lamplight like an animal's. His head fell back, his mouth gaping to reveal long incisors.

Darcy bounced faster on his lap, already carried along by the excitement of his quickening. His body was changing. The shoulders she gripped were harder — the definition of each muscle more articulated. His hips pumped like steel pistons, driving his expanding cock deeper with each opposing thrust of her hips.

Afraid she'd blow first and miss the show, she bit the inside of her lip to distract herself from the tight coil twisting inside her belly. Then his face changed, the bones beneath his cheeks and forehead pushing forward into a sinister mask. Alarmed and thrilled, Darcy noted only the smirk that curved the corner of his lips remained to tell her he was still inside the monster she rode.

His nostrils flared and his hands pulled her closer until her chest flattened against his. His mouth hovered over her neck. "Tell me what you want," he growled, his voice a deep, raw slash that cut straight through her sex-primed soul.

Darcy was glad he couldn't see her face. She needed him desperately. "Bite me."

His arms encircled her, and she gripped his hair hard. Their thrusts grew shorter, harder, and he groaned when his teeth entered her neck.

This time he didn't prepare her skin, but she was so hot for it the pain only increased her escalating passion. When he started to suction her skin, the blood rushed from her head and points below, and she stopped moving for a moment to savor the sensations.

Then she had to move or go insane. Her skin felt tight and hot. Her nipples tingled, and she rubbed them wildly on his chest. Her cunt was pliant, the interior walls hot with friction between their opposing movements.

He was growling against her neck, and she was falling — the ground rushing at her so fast, she couldn't catch a breath. She screamed.

Quentin held her shuddering body close and rubbed his face on her shoulder, ensuring his human mask was once more in place.

He bore her back onto the bed and stretched over her body, still embedded deep inside her warmth. He licked her neck to close the punctures, and then lapped at her skin to wash away the trace of blood that smeared her flesh.

"Mmmm," she moaned and writhed beneath him. "Do you think we have time for one more?"

He glanced at the window and saw the light filtering around the edges of the curtains. "Insatiable hussy," he murmured, and ground his hips against hers.

"You owe me." She wrapped her arms around his neck to pull him closer. "I still ache. You left me too long."

"You needed punishing, minx."

A frown drew her dark brows together. "I'm not yours to punish. How archaic is that?"

He circled his hips. "Primitive, love. A law of nature—man to mate. I won't have you sharing your sweet cunt with another."

"I haven't made you any promises. This thing between us is just sex—and convenient. Further, you're not a man and I'm certainly not your mate." She gasped when he jerked his hips.

You're wrong sweetheart. In time, you'll recognize you're mine. All these hours later, jealousy still ate at him. The sight of Darcy's hands clutching Joe's shuddering climax had enraged him. Worse, had been seeing her taut belly glistening with the other man's cum and her eyes glittering with sensual excitement. *You belong to me!*

He gripped her thighs and pressed them up and wide, and circled again, rubbing the crisp hairs at his groin into her clitoris. The color of her cheeks grew brighter as her passion escalated. He could feel her heart beat faster in her chest. She liked his mastering. "Has your curiosity with vampire fucking been satisfied?" he drawled.

Her eyes widened. "You heard?"

"Every wretched word you uttered to your besotted partner."

"He's not 'besotted.' We're just—"

"Friends? I don't buy it." Anger fueled him. He raised on his arms, which were still hooked beneath her thighs and pumped his hips hard, lifting hers with each short, sharp stroke.

Darcy's breath quickened and her hands clutched the bedding. "You shouldn't have eavesdropped. This is confusing for me."

"What? Wanting a vampire?" His hot glare pinned her to the mattress. "Or having two lovers to choose from?"

"Yes! Wanting you. Wanting him. It had been so long."

"A drought, now you have a deluge. You can't help but drink?" His thrusts came faster, sweat broke on his chest and belly.

"Why do I have to choose?"

Quentin halted. "You don't. I told you before. You're *my* choice."

Darcy arched her back and squeezed her inner muscles around him. "Christ, don't stop now!"

Unable to resist her plea, Quentin surged forward, burying himself as deeply as he could.

Darcy groaned and squeezed him tighter, her teeth bared in a grimace as she strained.

Quentin slammed back inside, and his hips pumped, faster and faster, finding a rhythm that edged him closer to the precipice. He held nothing back, all his energy and strength focused on the clenching muscles of his ass, driving him harder and deeper, propelling her off the bed.

Sweat from both their bodies aided his momentum. The only sounds that filled the room were her harsh grunts and the slap of his thighs and balls against the backs of her thighs and ass.

Darcy reached for the bars of her headboard to brace herself and held his gaze as her orgasm rolled over her, tightening her muscles and leaving her gasping for air.

Quentin followed, his orgasm rising from his toes, tightening his thighs and balls, slamming through his cock. With one last thrust into her rippling sheath, he roared as a stream of cum shot into her womb.

When the haze receded, he was still staring down at her, and her vagina milked his cock with one last, deep caress. He released her thighs to slide along his hips to the bed, but he lay, draped over her body, reluctant to break their connection.

"I want to get up," she said.

Quentin laid his hand on her breast. "I thought we might stay like this. Sleep for awhile."

Darcy dropped her gaze. "I need to do some things."

He opened his mouth to cajole her, and then thought better of it. Why did it matter to him? If she didn't want to remain in his embrace, what of it? "Sure." He withdrew his cock from her slowly, noting her slight wince. Poor thing was sore. He had ridden her hard. The thought pleased him immensely. She'd have a physical reminder of his prowess.

The purr of an engine pulling in front of the house drew both their attention away. "Your partner's returned from his sulk. I wonder if he found company."

Darcy pushed at his shoulders.

Quentin rolled onto his back. "I guess you'd better speak to him to assure him I haven't bitten your head off."

She was already headed to the shower without a backward glance.

"But no exchange of bodily fluids! Do you understand me?" he called after her.

Darcy lifted her hand and shot him the bird. He grinned. The woman was a hard case. A stubborn minx who was proving a delight to master. She hadn't worked it all out yet, but she'd come round. He didn't believe for a minute that she had actually conceded. But he still hadn't unleashed his full arsenal of tricks.

He yawned and was asleep in moments.

* * * * *

Darcy shut the door quietly behind her, leaving Quentin sleeping like the dead. Wondering what self-immolating demon possessed her, she padded to the guest room and rapped lightly on the door. "Joe?"

"Go away, Darcy." He sounded irritated.

She bit her lip. The smart thing to do would be to walk away and let them both have some distance and get rest. But she wasn't accustomed to letting problems lie. She wouldn't be able to sleep until things were right between her and Joe. Quentin had to be wrong. Joe wasn't in love with her. He'd been as carried away by the moment at the vampire's den as she'd been. That's all.

There was no good reason for this chasm to stretch between them. They'd been friends too long.

She knocked again.

The door swung open and Joe's wide, naked chest filled her view. Her mouth went dry and she cleared her throat. "I thought we might talk."

He looked beyond her into the living room, his face set in a cold mask. "Boyfriend let you off the leash?"

"He's not my boyfriend."

"That's supposed to make me feel better? You fuck him. What should I call him?"

"Look, just forget it." She turned to retreat.

Joe's hand stopped her. He grabbed her shoulder, his fingers softening to caress her. "Sorry, I bit your head off. I don't have the right to reprimand you."

Darcy glanced back at him and dropped her gaze, afraid of what she'd read in his expression. Disappointment might break her heart. But looking down turned out to be a bad move.

The crisp dark hairs that arrowed beneath the waist of his sweatpants drew her gaze to his erection, which tented beneath the soft gray fabric. She cleared her throat.

"Yeah. I've been like this all night," his voice rumbled.

"Why?" She nearly strangled on the word, her mouth had gone so dry.

"You don't get it, do you?" He stalked her into the hallway like a panther until her back met the opposite wall. He braced both hands against the wall, enclosing her in wall of muscle without touching her. "Every time I close my eyes, I see you with your hands wrapped around my cock. Then I imagine what that sweet pink mouth of yours would feel like when it opens for me to come inside. "

Darcy remembered his beautiful, creamy-cocoa cock and fought the wave of heat that swept over her. "Why are you telling me this now, Joe?"

"Because you're slipping through my fingers. I gave you time to get over Manny. Time to see *me*. I thought I had plenty of it." He tugged a lock of her hair. "I guess I'm just not the right species, am I?"

Darcy jerked. "Don't be an asshole about this."

His hand curved around her breast and it pebbled, drawing deliciously tight. Joe grunted. "Huh. Has he been neglecting these little wonders?" He knelt in front of her and opened his mouth over the tip, wetting her T-shirt, sucking so hard Darcy's toes curled into the cream-colored carpet.

"Stop it, Joe."

"I just want a taste." His hands reached beneath her T-shirt and he grew still. He glanced up at her. "No panties? What were you thinking?"

"I wasn't."

"Liar." He gathered the edges of her shirt and lifted it to bare her pussy to his gaze. "Are you dripping with his cum?"

He inserted a finger and Darcy's head hit the wall behind her. He brought it to his mouth. "Sweet. You must have bathed first. Good thinking." He opened her with his fingers, exposing her clitoris and leaned forward.

Darcy nearly leapt out of her skin at the first flutter of his tongue. She braced her hands on his shoulders, sure she would slide into a puddle at any moment. Too much stimulation—too soon after being with Quentin. The sight of his dark head moving between her legs swept away the last protest she could utter.

His tongue swirled on her clit and her knees grew weak. He substituted the pad of his thumb and increased the pressure. Then his tongue dove into her cunt and lapped.

"You're so hot here, Darc, swollen. That bastard." His tongue returned to torture her some more.

A gush of liquid anticipation greeted his tongue and he groaned. "Christ, you're sweet. Will you come for me?"

She sobbed when he finger-fucked her—three long fingers thrust as far as he could reach. Her hips ground down on his hand.

"Baby, this is for you." His mouth latched onto her clit and he suctioned hard, at the same time rotating his fingers, twisting so his knuckles scraped her tender channel.

She was coming apart. The intensity of her passion frightened her. How could she want this after a night spent in her vampire's arms? "Joe. You have to stop." She pulled his hair hard and he halted, his chest heaving. He turned his face into her belly.

God help me. How can I deny him? I love him, too!

Joe stood, his shoulders slumped. Darcy couldn't bear to see his dejection. She was lying to herself and to him. She wanted him every bit as much as she had wanted Quentin. Both men called to her newly awakened sensuality. She wished she could squelch it as quickly as it had arisen, but there it was. She desired them both with a longing that made her knees weak and her pussy weep. How could any emotion so powerful be wrong?

She reached for the waist of his sweatpants and tugged them down his hips. He stopped breathing and closed his eyes.

From one moment to the next, she stared at him, her heart in her throat, and then she was winding her arms around his neck and her legs around his taut waist.

He pushed his cock inside her and murmured in her ear, "I love you, Darcy!" He backed her hard against the wall and ground his cock into her, lifting her up then withdrawing to let her slide down the wall, then up again.

Darcy held him tight. "Jooooe!" She splintered into a thousand pieces.

His face pressed into her shoulder, muffling his cry of release.

They slid to the floor in each other's arms.

"Sshhh. It's okay. I have you," he crooned.

Darcy realized she was shaking and turned her face into his shoulder and cried.

"Shhh. Please don't cry." He took her to the floor, blanketing her with his warmth. He framed her face with his hands and kissed her. "I never wanted to hurt you."

His sweet entreaty and undemanding kiss contrasted sharply with his burgeoning arousal. He trembled and she wrapped her arms around him.

"It's not enough, Darc. I'm sorry," he whispered. "I have to have you, again."

Impossibly, she felt her body respond. Although she ached from use, she allowed him to push her thighs upward until her ankles hugged his neck. He pushed up on his arms and angled his hips for maximum penetration and began to rock.

Darcy dug her fingers into the carpet and gasped with each strong, deep stroke.

His face reddened, the skin of his cheeks and jaw tightening as he increased his pace. He turned his face and kissed her ankles. "Darc, tell me you don't want this as much I do."

"I can't. Please, faster," she whispered hoarsely.

It was all the encouragement he needed. His thrusts grew shorter, faster, until their skin slapped and moist, sucking sounds emanated from her drenched vagina. His breath caught and she felt the spurt of his cum wash inside her, but he kept moving, faster, harder—and then she fragmented, her cry echoing in the hall.

* * * * *

The SU team was once again assembled in her living room, reviewing what they'd learned the previous evening. Dressed in casual clothing, they prepared for another night's hunt.

Darcy was subdued, trying not to jump at every creak or bark of laughter. The sun had set an hour ago and Quentin had yet to make an appearance. She wondered whether he'd noticed she never came back to her bed. After making love with Joe, she'd opted for the couch despite his invitation to sleep with him. Darcy was starting to feel like salt-water taffy, pulled in two different directions.

She'd taken a seat on the buff-colored sectional sofa on the far end, opposite Joe. She felt his gaze on her, knew he had questions and wanted to talk about what happened between them, but she wasn't ready to acknowledge how she felt.

Logically, there wasn't any real choice. Quentin was here only as long as the operation lasted. Joe was here for the long haul. Quentin wasn't human. Joe was definitely all man. She risked her reputation and her place on the team by consorting with a vampire—however helpful his expertise was turning out to be. A relationship with Joe wouldn't be without its implications to the team, but wouldn't prove divisive.

Quentin was a charming, but conceited, ass. Joe was a considerate, straight-arrow kind of guy. So why was she torn? Why couldn't she just turn her back on Quentin and mark the whole misadventure as just an aberration? A sexual experiment?

Her bedroom door opened and the group fell silent. Quentin's steps drew near and the hair on the back of her neck rose. He was coming straight for her.

Darcy straightened and darted a glance at Joe. His face remained impassive, but she saw his fists clench.

Quentin's hand fell on her shoulder. "Missed you when I woke up, love."

Darcy closed her eyes. She didn't need to look at the faces of the men she worked with to know their reaction to his little bombshell.

"That's enough," Joe's voice cut through the silence like a knife.

Quentin walked around the sofa and took the seat beside her.

Did he not know how close he was to being dusted? Darcy willed him to shut up, but Quentin stretched his arm along the back of the sofa and tugged on her hair. "What's for supper?" he asked his expression guileless.

"Phil's wife, Bets, made enchiladas. I'll check the oven," Max said quietly and left the room.

"I better help," Darcy said and rose to follow him out.

Quentin's hand fell to the small of her back. "This isn't finished."

She didn't reply and headed for the kitchen. As soon as the door swung closed behind her, she let out a deep breath.

Max's angry gaze sliced her to the bone. Normally easy-going with her, his expression was hard-eyed and accusing. "What the hell were you thinking, Darc? If you needed nailing, why didn't you turn to Joe? He's been in love with you for years."

Max's disappointment made Darcy feel about a foot tall. "I didn't know how Joe felt. I didn't see it."

"Is it just about the sex?"

She felt shame wash over her cheeks. What would he say if he knew she'd screwed both of them? "Maybe, at first."

Max raked a hand through his dark brown hair. "It's none of my business, but we're like family. This isn't gonna sit well with the rest of the guys. You do what you have to, but just remember: Interspecies relationships don't work." He hit the swinging door with his knuckles and left the room.

Darcy busied herself removing the pan of enchiladas from the oven and the salad Phil had brought from the fridge. Although her back was to the door, she knew who stepped into the kitchen next. The rumble of voices in the living room grew louder.

"I hope you have something other than that mess in the pan to feed me," Quentin said.

She opened a utensil drawer and extracted a spatula, then slammed the drawer shut. "There's a couple steaks, nice and bloody, in the fridge. Help yourself." She turned to face him. "Are you trying to get yourself exterminated?"

"I warned you." His voice radiated quiet fury. "You've bathed, but his scent is still all over you."

"It won't work between us, Quentin," she said quietly.

"Because the guys are mad as hell at me?"

"No. Because there's no future for us."

Quentin crossed his arms over his chest. "As long as you remain human, there certainly isn't."

Her eyes widened. "Are you saying what I think you are?"

"I can give you eternity."

"To spend it with you?" she asked incredulous. "How arrogant you sound. Do you think all humans aspire to immortality?"

"Don't you? And don't tell me you haven't ever considered it." His gaze narrowed. "I won't believe you."

Darcy stopped herself from denying it. It was true. Especially, since she'd met him. "That wouldn't change how I feel. Would it?"

"It's a risky process, I admit. More humans die than make the change. And some aren't the same after they turn. Some lose their souls."

"Doesn't sound like much of a choice." She didn't know why, but she felt close to tears. His argument only strengthened her belief that their relationship wasn't meant to be. She turned and opened a drawer to pull out the silverware.

Quentin's arms circled her waist and pulled her close to his body. "I'll make you want me more than him."

Darcy fought the urge to surrender to his embrace.

"You can't deny your attraction to me and the dark and dirty things I do to you. Did he make you scream?" He grabbed her ass and squeezed. "Did you wriggle your little ass for him because you wanted it so bad you felt like you'd die of want?"

Darcy's breath grew ragged but she refused to answer him. Her body was doing all the talking. Her breasts grew heavy and pointed, and her pussy was damp with her desire.

"Well darling, you begged for my touch. Think about it, tonight. Remember what I can make you feel. You'll crave my touch and my cock. Before the sun rises, you'll be mine."

CHAPTER SIX

Two nights later the team hit pay dirt.

The weather had turned stormy. High winds from the Atlantic whipped up six-foot whitecaps that had the most devout surfers heading north to Cocoa to catch the waves despite the chilly air.

Just after dusk, Phil radioed in that a group of young vamps were trashing a nightclub along the boardwalk.

Joe drove with Darcy in the front seat. If Quentin was chafing at the distance Darcy had kept since the team discovered their dalliance, at least he had the satisfaction of knowing Joe hadn't enjoyed the woman's favors either. They'd both been shut out in the cold.

No matter how hard he'd tried to break through the icy barrier she'd erected, Darcy had repelled every advance. She slept alone on the sofa, although he'd offered to return the use of her bed. He was secretly glad when she refused. Although he was tortured surrounded by her scent, he wanted her to imagine him there—sleeping on her pink pillows, stretched across the mattress where they'd shared wicked delights. He hoped like hell she got as little sleep as he did.

They barely spoke except to discuss the evening's business. Something had to give soon. Quentin planned to be the man nearest when Darcy broke.

Joe, Darcy, and Quentin arrived outside the bar just as a man was tossed through the plate glass window. Quentin didn't have to look closely to know the man had been drained dry first.

"Perhaps, I should go in by myself," Quentin said, his hand on Darcy's arm.

"Do you think we haven't faced a real rave before?" she asked.

Quentin bristled. Those were the most words she'd spoken directly to him all evening. "You want information, don't you? If you go in with your bows cocked, they won't be in the mood to talk."

A scream rent the air and Quentin stepped ahead of Joe and Darcy to cut them off. The rest of the team was arriving for clean up. He had to be quick. Letting his incisors slide into place, he entered the bar.

There were four young vamps inside. Their T-shirts with the Ron Jon surfer logos looked incongruous with their armored faces. They'd paired off and were dining on their newest victims. The bodies strewn between the tables were evidence of their rampaging bloodlust.

Quentin lifted his head and snarled, his deep growl alerting the vamps of his presence.

One of them, a lean, blond-haired teenager, lifted his head from the gaping wound of a woman who looked more dead than alive. "You're on our turf. Move out," he said.

"You're attracting undue attention, children. Did your sire not mentor you in the need for discretion?" Quentin said, with a sniff. "You lack finesse."

The young vamp's lips lifted in a snarl. "Don't need it. This is a lot more fun. Now move out, old man."

Quentin raised an eyebrow. "I'll let you live for another minute or two if you answer one question."

The others raised their heads from their meals, their deep thirst forgotten in the challenge he had issued.

The blond, who must be their leader, dropped the woman and stalked toward Quentin. When he was half a dozen paces away, he launched himself at Quentin in a single impressive leap.

Quentin sidestepped the boy who landed against a table, overturning it and several chairs. Before he could extricate himself from the tangle, Quentin reached down and staked him through the chest. He disintegrated into dust, leaving only his rumpled jeans, T-shirt, and tennis shoes.

Quentin turned back to the remaining three. "Now, about that question…"

The three looked at each other and raised their hands.

"What the hell do you want to know?" Another sun-bleached blond youth asked.

"Where can I find your sire?"

"The Master?"

Quentin snorted. Nicky really was reaching. "Nicky. Where do I find him? We're old friends." He took a step toward them, and they backed away.

"He has his own place now. If you're a friend, how come you don't know?"

"I just arrived in town." Displeased with their lack of candor, Quentin let his armor reform his face to indicate his impatience.

"All right, man. He's got a place near here. In South Beach Park." His face morphed. He couldn't be more than sixteen and beardless. "You aren't going to tell him we left a mess, are you?"

"I'm wondering how you propose to extricate yourself from this?"

"Huh?"

"You won't be leaving this place, except in a dustbin."

Darcy and Joe stepped through the door. More of the SU team members peered through the window, crossbows and spear guns aimed at the three.

"Shit!"

"Keep one alive," Quentin said. In an instant, two sets of clothing crumpled to the floor.

* * * * *

Dressed in black, they'd taken up positions behind the concrete block wall that enclosed the property on the beach side. The incoming tide lapped just feet away, and the smell of rain was in the air. Light poured from windows. Music blared within. It seemed a party was in full flourish.

Hunkered down next to the gate, Quentin whispered, "Be sure to keep the rest of the unit back until I give the signal. They stink of gun oil. I can smell it from here."

"We're going in with you," Darcy said.

"No you're not."

"Look, I know you've got a bug up your ass about the sleeping arrangements," Joe said, "but Darcy and I are supposed to be your shadows."

"Darcy's made it abundantly clear, who's in and who's out," Quentin said between gritted teeth. "We aren't a team."

"Fine," Darcy said, laying a hand on Joe's arm. "You go right on ahead. We'll try not to get in your way."

"You're staying put."

She smiled, her teeth a white slash in the moonlight. "Of course. I always do what I'm told."

"Damn stubborn wench," he muttered.

"Pompous, arrogant asshole," she replied, still smiling.

"Darcy, keep clear of Nicky." If Nicky knew what the girl meant to him…

"Time's a-wasting," Joe whispered. He lowered the microphone on his headset to his mouth. "We're going in."

Quentin pushed open the gate and skirted the wall on the inside, keeping to the shadows and using the foliage of the palms and bougainvillea to hide behind as he crept along. Not that vampires couldn't see into the darkness.

French doors opened with a spill of light onto a slate tile patio. A lone figure stepped outside and lit a cigarette. The flare of the lighter illuminated the face of the vampire they'd come to kill.

The hair on the back of Quentin's neck rose. This was too easy.

"You may as well quit skulking in the bushes, Father. I see you received my message," Nicholas Powell said.

Quentin heard Darcy's gasp. He straightened and approached the monster he'd created.

* * * * *

Darcy glanced at Joe. His face had hardened to stone.

It couldn't be. Quentin couldn't be responsible for creating this evil vampire. But she didn't have time to consider the implications. They'd been made. She rose from her crouch and surveyed the courtyard. Her gaze lifted to the balcony above them.

Two vampires trained automatic weapons on her and Joe. The gun oil Quentin's keen sense of smell had detected hadn't come from the SU team. Then the thought came unbidden, had Quentin set them up for a slaughter?

"I'm flattered, Quentin. You've come all this way to see me. You and your friends must come inside." It wasn't an invitation. With an indolent wave of his hand, Nicky signaled to more vamps who spilled out the doorway. "After you. But first, drop your weapons."

Quentin raised the stake in his hand and then laid it at his feet. Joe and Darcy lowered their crossbows. It took every bit of her willpower to abandon her weapon.

Quentin stepped through the doorway. He didn't glance behind him to see whether they followed.

"Don't be shy," Nicky said. "Come inside and join the party."

Darcy stepped onto the tile patio. As she drew abreast Nicky, he held out his hand. "I'll take your headsets."

Inside the house, it became immediately apparent a trap had been set. There wasn't a human in sight, just five more vampires, unholy grins on their distorted faces.

"So what do you think of my humble abode?"

Darcy had just met the dark-haired vampire, but his voice, low and sardonic already grated on every last one of her nerves. She glanced about her, checking exits and for items that could be used as weapons if her weapon of last resort was taken from her. Slate tile covered the floor, and unless the beige leather sofas could be used to batter a vamp to the ground, only the glass and chrome tables offered any possibilities.

Quentin stood in the center of the living room and had yet to look her way. But his stiff posture and neutral expression reassured her that at least he was as much a victim as she was.

"So what do we have here? GI Joe and Jane?" Nicky said as he circled them. He halted in front of Darcy and looked her up and down. His dark eyes smoldered. Leanly built and muscular, Darcy didn't doubt Nicky would prove difficult to best in a one-on-one.

She glared at him, her hands fisting at her sides.

"Is she your woman?" Nicky turned to Quentin, one eyebrow raised.

Quentin remained silent.

"Hardly seems your type. She's rather plain. And not a curve to feast on," he said, his voice silky. "Rather like taking a boy. Do you like boys, Quentin?"

Quentin snorted. "Just for breakfast." He nodded to the vamps circling the perimeter of the room. "Seems your appetites are decidedly male, these days."

"I learn from my mistakes. Women are strictly for nourishment." He walked behind her and his fingers trailed down her throat. "They make lousy soldiers."

Darcy forced herself to remain still, although she knew her escalating heart rate betrayed her alarm. Her gaze sought Quentin's, but his stare remained on Nicky.

"Monica was a little unstable," Quentin replied.

"Fancied herself in love with me, can you imagine? How are our friends, Dylan and Emmy, by the way?"

Quentin shrugged. "I haven't heard from them."

"I must give them my regards when I see them next. I didn't have the chance before I left Seattle. I was rather rushed."

Darcy wondered how long the glib conversation would last. At this point, she couldn't have gotten a word past her lips. Nicky's fingers continued to trace her neck and jaw. She swallowed.

"So when will the rest of the team arrive?" Nicky asked so casually, it took a moment for the words to register.

She stiffened and feared her reaction had given something important away.

A little smile curved the corners of Quentin's lips. The smirk she'd come to love.

A short staccato burst of gunfire sounded from the front of the house. Quentin's gaze shifted to Darcy, and he lifted his chin. Darcy took it as a signal to act. She grasped Nicky's finger and bit.

"Bitch!" His fist punched her back, over the kidneys. Despite the Kevlar jacket she wore, Darcy nearly passed out. But she didn't let go of his finger.

In a blur of motion, Quentin leapt toward them and Darcy opened her mouth, releasing Nicky and rolling away. The sound of breaking glass and wood came from behind her, but Darcy continued to roll until she reached the back of one of the sofas.

When she made it to her feet, Quentin and Nicky were out of sight, although the sounds of their scuffle could be heard from the patio. She reached for the 9mm handgun strapped beneath her vest at the small of her back—and for the stake in her boot. A gun might not kill a vampire, but a headshot could incapacitate one for a moment—long enough to stake it.

Gunfire continued to explode, so near the sound was deafening. To her right, one of Nicky's minions inside the room had an AK-47 trained on a sofa Joe must have hidden behind.

When Darcy looked to her left, she found herself staring down the barrel of a Glock.

The vamp holding the weapon wore a gleeful expression. "Question is, should I shoot you first, and then suck your blood?"

Darcy held her hands up, her weapon pointing toward the ceiling. "Question is, do you have the safety off?"

The youth's gaze dropped to his gun, and Darcy fired a round through his forehead. Before he hit the floor, she staked him. "The safety's in the trigger, stupid."

No time to gloat, she headed for an unarmed vamp, fired off a shot and staked him. Another saw her coming and ran for the front door. Knowing the SU would catch him before he made it to the road, she turned to help Joe.

She saw his hand rise from the back of the sofa and fire several rounds toward the vamp who had taken cover behind the jutting edge of the fireplace. The vamp raised his machine gun and took aim. Before he got off a round, Darcy hit him in the temple. He dropped his weapon and cradled his head. "You fucking bitch," he screamed.

Darcy leapt for him, kicked the machine gun away and raised the stake. Only the wooden tip was blunted from the previous kills, and was stopped by bone at his sternum.

The vamp roared and quickly overpowered her, pushing her to the floor. Unable to do anything except stare in horrified fascination, Darcy watched his mouth with its jagged row of teeth descend.

Suddenly, the vamp screamed and crumbled into dust. Quentin leaned over her, his stake still poised. He lowered it and offered his other hand to help her to her feet.

She pushed the pile of dusty clothing from her body to the floor. "Thanks," she said. "Is that it?"

"That's everybody inside and the team's taking care of the strays on the grounds. But Darcy, Nicky got away."

Darcy felt ill. A niggling sense of doubt rose. Did Quentin deliberately allow him to escape? "At least he's lost his minions." She looked around the living room. It was pretty well trashed. Bullets had ripped through the furniture and the walls, in some places leaving gaping holes so large a fist could fit inside. Thank God she and Joe had escaped being hit.

Joe? Her heart went still, and a cold dread settled over her. She hadn't seen him since he'd battled it out with the vamp with the machine gun. She hadn't heard his voice.

She approached the sofa Joe had taken cover behind. Before she rounded the corner, she saw a crimson pool of liquid, which was spreading wider by the moment across the blue-gray tile. "No, no, no."

He was lying on his side, his 9mm still grasped in his hand, his face ashen. She knelt in his blood and felt for a pulse at the side of his neck. It was weak and slow. Her hands moved over him, looking for the wound. The blood appeared to seep from beneath his Kevlar jacket and she opened it, dreading what she would find.

The bullet had entered the top of his shoulder making a rather small, innocuous-looking hole. She reached inside the jacket, smoothing her hands around his back and found the exit wound. It was large and gaping. Joe wasn't going to make it, but she had to try. "Joe, you hold on. Don't you die on me. Quentin, help me get this jacket off him. I have to stop the bleeding."

Quentin's hand stopped hers as she began stripping away the vest. "Darcy, he's lost more than fifty percent of his blood. He's going to die."

She sought his gaze, her own pleading with him to help. "I have to try. Please, help me." She didn't realize she was crying until his fingers smoothed the tears on her cheeks.

"Sweetheart, no amount of modern medicine can save him. I might be able to turn him, though. It's not too late to try."

She shook her head, not understanding what he was saying.

"I can make him a vampire."

"No!" The word wrenched from her gut.

"His internal organs are shutting down, one after the other. He's going to die."

She leaned over Joe and cupped his face. "Joe, wake up. You have to tell me what you want. Please, wake up."

"Darcy, he's not going to answer you. He can't," Quentin said. "You have to choose."

The moments were ticking by and she could feel Joe's life slipping away. She raised her face to Quentin. "Do it. Save him, please."

Quentin knelt and gathered Joe's upper body off the ground to hold him in his arms. "I have to take more blood—to the point of his death. Go stand at the door. Make sure no one interrupts."

She didn't want to leave. She wasn't sure she trusted him enough to leave Joe's fate in his hands.

"Go!" Quentin lowered his mouth to Joe's neck.

Darcy rose and went to the doorway that led to the patio. She glanced back at Quentin and prayed she'd made the right choice for Joe.

Stepping outside she realized the storm brewing all day had broken. Rain fell in fat drops, soaking her uniform in moments. She welcomed the moisture and raised her face to let the drops mingle with her tears. *Will he forgive me?* As close as they had been—as partners and lovers—she knew he held a deep and abiding hatred for vampires. Yet she had just given Quentin permission to make him into something he believed abhorrent and unnatural. She'd made him into one of the monsters he'd sworn to fight.

Darcy heard the sounds of her team members as they combed the yard for weapons and vamps. Since stealth was no longer employed, she knew the vamps had been vanquished.

Max stepped inside the garden gate. "Darc, is the house secure?"

"Yeah."

"You okay?"

She nodded, and then realized he couldn't see the movement. "Sure."

"Joe and Quentin still inside?"

"Yeah." Darcy shook herself. She had to keep Max outside. He wouldn't understand what Quentin was doing. "Max, let the rest of the team know the inside's secure. We lost our headsets."

Max radioed the status. "Let's see if the rest of the team needs help."

"You go ahead. I'll be along in a minute. I have to let…Joe know where I am."

She returned to the doorway. Quentin still held Joe in his arms.

Joe's mouth was latched to Quentin's wrist, and he was drinking. He was alive. But had his soul survived?

Quentin's gaze was on her, wary and watchful. In the lamplight that bathed the two men, both glowed golden and beautiful. She couldn't be sorry for her choice. The two men she loved lived.

"I'll have to get him away from here, quickly," Quentin said.

Darcy sighed, weary enough to sleep where she stood. Another set of problems presented themselves. "We have an outbrief and after action reports. What do I tell them?"

"Nothing yet. Joe's alive, but we don't know if he's intact."

"Meaning, he's not a monster?"

"Make an excuse. He needs time to get on his feet. And he has to feed soon."

She looked at Joe, his eyes closed, suckling like a babe on Quentin's wrist.

"He needs blood from a source."

"Meaning not…recirculated?"

"Just enough to take the edge off his hunger. Then we can feed him steak or animal blood."

Darcy glanced away, sickened by the reality of what would be Joe's existence. "Take him to my place. I'll get there as soon as I can."

"Darcy, perhaps it would be best we found another host. The longer he waits, the stronger his thirst will be. He'll be out of control."

"I made the decision to make him what he is. His first meal won't come from a stranger."

CHAPTER SEVEN

Hours later, Darcy let herself in the front door, dreading the coming moments. She'd lied to the SU team and Captain Springer about Joe. In a few hours they'd know it and she'd lose her place on the team, and likely lose her job altogether. But that thought was the least of her worries. She had to face Joe and see whether her gamble had been for nothing.

The kitchen door slammed open, and she jumped. Joe filled the doorway, fury darkening his face, his chest heaving with suppressed rage.

Her hand crept to her throat, fear leaving a metallic taste in her mouth. She doubted Joe was going to thank her.

Quentin followed him out of the kitchen.

Her gaze shifted to him, but his expression gave away nothing of his thoughts, which made her even more nervous.

"You bitch!" Joe cursed. "You've made me into a thing. You didn't have the right."

Trepidation pumped her heartbeat faster and she opened her mouth to explain, but realized she really couldn't. He was right. She'd made the choice for him, knowing how he felt about vampires. She straightened her shoulders, ready to face his ire.

Quentin laid a hand on Joe's shoulder. "We talked about what happens next. You need to feed."

"Shut up!" He shrugged off Quentin's hand with a jerk. "This is between her and me."

"I'm not leaving you alone with her."

"Then you can watch," Joe snarled.

Quentin looked ready to strike him, but Darcy shook her head.

Joe stalked toward her and Darcy held her ground, refusing to back away. This was Joe. He wouldn't hurt her. He might be mad as hell, but he wouldn't hurt her.

Grim-faced, he reached for the front of her black T-shirt and ripped it away. "Get your clothes off."

Shaking, Darcy swallowed, her eyes widening as Joe crowded closer as if daring her to step back. "Can we at least go to the bedroom?" she asked, needing a moment to collect her courage.

"Strip now." He enunciated each word slowly, his nostrils flaring. "I smell your fear. Smart lady."

She lifted her trembling hands to the front of her sports bra, opened it and let it drop to the floor. His hand covered her breast immediately. He flicked the pad of his thumb on her nipple and it puckered, drawing to a tight point.

"My boots," she said quickly. "I need to sit down."

He shoved her back against the couch and she fell over the arm. He ripped at the laces and jerked her boots off, one at a time, then he pulled her to her feet again.

Her composure lost, Darcy sent Quentin a wild-eyed glance. *What are you going to do?*

His jaw tightened, but he remained still, his hands fisted at his sides.

"I said take off your clothes," Joe snarled.

Darcy grabbed for the snap at her waistband, popped it open, and slid down the zipper. He stood so close her head rubbed his belly when she knelt to push the pants down her legs. Her cheek glided along his straining erection.

Naked, she straightened, fighting to keep her hands at her sides rather than covering her breasts.

The corners of his mouth lifted. It wasn't a pleasant smile.

She shivered, alarm and a wicked thrill coursing down her spine.

Before she could protest, he ducked and shoved his shoulder into her belly. She folded over him and he straightened. Lifting her from the ground, he headed for her bedroom.

Darcy raised her head to find Quentin, hoping he would intervene. His jaw was set and his gaze a little wild. He followed them inside, turning on the lamp on the bedside table.

Her breath left her in a whoosh when Joe tossed her on the mattress. He stripped in seconds and fell across her. "No preliminaries, sweetheart. I'll fuck you before I eat."

His thighs forced hers apart, and he rammed inside her. Even as tears of outrage filled her eyes, she couldn't deny the ease of his entry. Her pussy was drenched with her arousal.

Joe allowed her no time to adjust nor room to breathe. He pinned her arms to the bed high above her head. He pumped into her, hot and fast, his chest flattened against hers. With his face inches above her, he forced her to see his anger and accept the pain he inflicted.

His cock pounded away at her womb reaching farther than she thought he could. His girth was thicker than she remembered and crammed tightly into her channel with each forward stroke.

While her mind protested his rough treatment, her body ripened. Her nipples swelled, the tips stabbing at Joe's chest. The delicate tissues lining her vagina released a wash of pre-cum that lubricated his cock and eased his passage.

"If I'd known you got off on violence, I'd have raped you long ago," he murmured.

"This isn't rape," she gritted out, finding it difficult to speak as he pummeled her. "I'm here of my own free will." Darcy decided to prove it. She raised her legs around his hips and gripped him, pulling him deeper into her.

With a growl, he pumped faster. His scowl tightened, and he closed his eyes and flung back his head. With a final thrust he came, his warm ejaculate spurting into her.

For a long moment they stared at each other. Then he released her hands and dropped his forehead onto her shoulder. Darcy enfolded him in her embrace and held him until his breath slowed.

"I'm sorry," he said, his voice strained.

She squeezed her eyes tight, relieved Joe was intact, and still her friend. Remorse meant he still had a conscience. "I know. It's okay," she said. "It's okay."

He pushed away and she unwrapped her legs and arms. Rolling to his back, he covered his eyes with his forearm.

Darcy lay sprawled on the bed, her legs splayed, tears leaking from her eyes, utterly defeated. Joe's soul had survived, but his unhappiness wasn't a matter of adjustment to his new state. He hated what he'd become. And it was her fault.

She heard the rustle of clothing and her eyes found Quentin. His face was taut, his gaze haunted. He removed his clothing and lay down beside her, opposite Joe. Darcy opened her arms to him.

They lay on their sides facing each other. Quentin wiped her tears away with his fingers then rubbed the moisture onto her nipples in slow circles.

Darcy leaned toward him and kissed his lips, her breath catching on a jagged sob when his mouth molded to hers.

He made love to her, sweetly, slowly—his hands soothing her frazzled nerves. He rubbed away the tension in her shoulders, circled each bump of her spine in slow, melting caresses until her sorrow eased. He built a slow fire that raised dimples on her nipples and drew the tips to hard points. His hand moved to her belly and he massaged away the tension she hadn't known was there, smoothing with his fingertips, gradually increasing the pressure using his knuckles to knead. She almost drifted to sleep beneath his tender ministration until his hands slid southward, dipping between her legs.

She eased her legs apart, allowing him entry, and he circled her opening without dipping inside, building a slow ache that had her arching gently into his hand, seeking more of his sensual solace.

He kissed her, his lips lapping hers in an undemanding kiss, and suddenly, she wanted more.

She wound her fingers in his soft hair and pulled his face closer to deepen the kiss, making kitten sounds in the back of her throat to tell him how well he pleased her.

He drew back from the kiss and her eyes opened. His face was taut, his nostrils flared, and she knew the cost of this sweet seduction to his control. "Love, Joe must feed, and you have to take him into your body again to ease his lust while he does it." He inserted a finger into her channel and swirled inside. "He's waited too long to drink without the bloodlust overcoming his senses—unless he substitutes sexual lust for bloodlust. Do you understand what I'm telling you?"

She nodded, not happy he prepared her for Joe's benefit. She bit back a moan when a second finger slipped inside her.

"You have her well primed," Joe muttered behind her. "She wants you."

"You made a ballocks of your previous opportunity, pup," Quentin countered angrily, even as his hands continued to gently seduce her body. "You'll do this under my guidance. A first feeding can take a man's mind. I won't let you harm her by forgetting yourself."

"But she wants you. The scent of her arousal is growing by the moment."

"Perhaps..." Darcy's voice was so soft and uncertain, she wasn't sure they'd heard.

Quentin's gaze met hers. "What is it, love?"

Darcy swallowed, not believing what she was about to ask. "Could you both make love to me?"

He grew completely still.

Behind her, Joe's soft, cynical laughter shook the mattress beneath her.

Her hands framed Quentin's face. "I want *you*, but he needs me now. Can't I hold you and take both of you inside me?" She knew her face flamed at the whispered suggestion.

Joe stopped laughing.

"You're very tight there," Quentin replied, his words spoken with deliberation. "He'll hurt you."

"Then help him prepare me…to take him."

"You try me, Darcy," Quentin said, his voice sounding hoarse. "I haven't any liking for sharing you with another man."

Her heart thrilled at his words. "Tonight ends it. I promise."

He drew in a deep breath. "You have a lubricant?"

Darcy couldn't believe he conceded so easily. "In the nightstand." As he turned to reach for the tube, a mix of dread and guilty anticipation stepped up her heartbeat.

"Such a nasty girl," Joe said, his hand reaching around her to cup her breast. His lips opened over the curve of her shoulder. He forced her to her back on the bed.

Quentin placed a hand in the middle of Joe's chest and shoved. "You won't treat Darcy harshly, not in word or deed or I'll dust you."

"Are you so sure you could take me?"

Darcy rose on her elbows. "Joe, put a sock in it. If you're going to suck my blood, you're damn well going to treat me with respect. You may be a big, bad vampire now, but you're acting like a brat. Cut it out."

Joe glowered, but his expression changed when his gaze drifted from her face and down her naked body. It grew feral. "Damn Darc! This isn't easy. I can feel changes creeping over me—some I'm fighting to control."

"That's why you won't feed unless I tell you," Quentin said. "Darcy needs to trust you won't hurt her, again. So for now, our attentions go to her."

Darcy felt liquid trickle from her cunt. It was downright embarrassing how arousing this discussion was becoming.

When two sets of male nostrils flared and sniffed, she thought she'd rather find a hole to hide in than face their knowing expressions.

Quentin's mouth curved into a smirk and Joe's eyebrow lifted in a *mano a mano* challenge.

Darcy's heart sounded a loud tattoo they couldn't fail to hear.

"How 'bout we start north and work our way south?" Joe asked, giving the lead to Quentin.

Quentin nodded and indicated Joe could start first. Quentin lay down on his side, resting on his elbow to watch.

As Joe leaned over her to kiss her lips, Darcy's eyes didn't leave Quentin's face. If he was still jealous of Joe's presence in her bed, nothing in his expression betrayed him. Darcy almost wished for a flush of anger or a frown.

So when Joe's tongue darted into her mouth, she clutched Joe's hair to deepen the kiss. Their tongues parried and stroked. Their mouths ate each other's lips in wet, sultry kisses.

When they drew apart, Darcy's mouth already felt swollen.

Joe left a trail of wet kisses along her jaw, down her neck, and lower to her breast. With his hand kneading the soft underside, and his mouth kissing the tops of her quivering flesh, Darcy reached for Quentin.

Quentin leaned down and licked her lips. Opening her mouth, Darcy touched her tongue to his without seeking a kiss. Their tongues mated softly, lapping at each other's tips. The kiss that followed sealed their mouths then slid, creating a soft suctioning that drew Darcy's belly tight once more.

When they parted, Darcy stared at Quentin for the longest moment. *I love you.*

Joe tongued her nipple, encouraging it to peak. Quentin nibbled on her earlobe.

Darcy tried to keep silent against their determined onslaught, but her gasps and soft moans caught her by surprise. They gave her no room to hide the depth of her growing excitement. Quentin's hand slid down to palm her neglected breast, and Darcy's hips moved restlessly on the mattress.

When both men's hot mouths closed over her nipples, Darcy's back arched off the mattress, pressing her chest high. The men worked in concert, sucking, chewing softly on her sensitive stems.

Then their hands smoothed over her belly and thighs, coming up the soft insides of her thighs, pressing them apart until her core was open and exposed.

Darcy's breaths became jagged and she shook—fine tremors that radiated down her belly and trembled through her thighs. Quentin made a shushing sound and kissed her belly, swirling his tongue into her belly button, then licking downward to the nest of damp hair.

Joe showed no mercy, he bit her—large open-mouthed bites, but never hurtful, that surprised and excited her. His hands lifted the leg nearest him onto his shoulder and he buried his face between her legs, nipping and kissing her thighs.

Quentin's fingers stroked around her labia, taking the fragrant glaze seeping from within her to tease the swollen kernel at the top of her nether mouth.

Joe's tongue darted inside her, fluttering, stroking, lapping her cream like a cat.

Darcy sighed noisily, watching the two heads, one with long silvery-blond hair, the other close-cropped black, circling over her flesh. "Ahhh, please," she pleaded. "Take me, now."

"Sweetheart, you're not nearly ready for us," Quentin murmured. He reached for two pillows. "Joe, help me get these under her hips."

Joe rose, and Darcy moaned at the loss of his mouth from her cunt. His hands cupped her buttocks and lifted her high enough for Quentin to slide the pillows beneath her. Then the two men knelt, staring at her splayed thighs.

"You have the prettiest asshole, Darc," Joe said, his voice deep and growling, his hand stroking his cock. "I'm gonna fuck it 'til you scream."

Feeling a twinge of fear, Darcy tried to close her legs, but both men tugged her legs wider and higher.

"I'm afraid we still have some work to do before she can take you." Quentin reached for the tube of K-Y. He squeezed it onto his fingertips and gave her a glance that sent prickly heat dancing across her belly.

"I'm going to stretch you with my fingers. Relax when I come inside you."

Joe apparently understood his role, his fingers dipped inside her cunt to finger-fuck her.

Darcy's hips rolled, trying to take his fist deeper.

Quentin rubbed the ointment around her asshole and Darcy quivered, her head digging into the mattress as she arched. Then he inserted one finger and swirled inside her ass.

She cried out and Joe withdrew his fingers. "No, you don't. Not yet."

The loss of the extra stimulation kept her from creeping over the edge of her climax. Instead, he stroked her thighs — teasing passes that glanced against her labia without ever giving her the deeper strokes she craved.

Quentin inserted a second long finger inside her and Darcy moaned, feeling herself tighten to resist his invasion.

"Relax, sweetheart," he crooned. "Let me in."

Darcy couldn't take it. The pressure burned. "This is too much," she whispered.

Joe's mouth latched onto her nipple and he suctioned, drawing the tip between his teeth.

With Joe's teeth gnashing on her nipple and Quentin fingering her ass, Darcy's sphincter gradually eased. Then she had to move. She needed *more*—and told them so—loudly. With her head thrashing on the mattress, her hand sought her other nipple and she tugged it, twisting gently.

Joe's hand pushed hers to the bed. "Not until *we* say so, Darc."

Darcy's ass burned, stretched beyond what she thought she could comfortably take, but it caused an exquisite pain. Her hands clutched the bedding.

Quentin pulled out partway then stroked back inside. Then he repeated the sweet torture, in and out, stretching and burning her tender tissue.

Darcy whimpered and circled her hips.

"You've been so good," Quentin said, his voice a deep rumble. He leaned over her, his fingers still shoved deep inside her and kissed her. "Darcy, can you take more?"

Darcy sucked his lower lip between her teeth, all the while her hips continued circling on his fingers. "Oh, please. Give me more. Come inside me."

"Joe, let's take her, now." Quentin pulled his fingers away and wiped them with tissues from her nightstand. Then he pulled the pillows from beneath her.

Joe tugged the sheets to the end of the bed and tossed them to the floor.

As she watched the men prepare the bed, Darcy hugged her belly, trying to still the tremors that grew stronger by the moment. Excitement so strong *she* could smell her own arousal created an ache that clamped her thighs together involuntarily. Her fingers crept to her clitoris and she rubbed herself.

"What did I tell you about helping yourself?" Joe knelt on the mattress and rolled her to her side to face Quentin. Then he snuggled next to her back, his cock flush against the crease between her buttocks.

"I'm only going to come a little way into your cunt, love," Quentin said. "Joe, you're to wait until she's ready. She's tensing up again. Here's the gel." He passed the tube to Joe.

Joe pushed her hair forward and swept his tongue over the vertebrae at the back of her neck. Quentin scooted closer to her, his cock brushing her belly.

Sandwiched between the two men, Darcy was starting to have second thoughts. The heat coming from their two bodies was drawing the air away from her lungs. She was panting, shivering, and neither had entered her yet.

Quentin extended his arm for her to rest her head upon and Darcy felt a moment's ease when she looked into his face. His watchful gaze searched hers.

She brushed her fingers over his cheek and caressed his shoulders.

His hand lifted to cover her breast and she sighed. She slid her thigh over his, opening her legs for him to fit between.

Quentin's hips pulled back, then his cock nudged her cunt, found her moist welcome, and he surged inside her.

Her thigh tightened around his hip, pulling him deeper into her, and he pulsed, shallow thrusts that slowly stoked her fire.

Joe's hands smoothed down her back to her buttocks and he squeezed, helping her press closer to Quentin. Then his fingers pressed inside her ass.

Her breaths shortened, catching on ragged sighs and moans. Her hips found Quentin's rhythm and she countered it, pressing her pussy forward to greet his strokes.

When Joe's cock slid between her cheeks. Her thrusts deepened, forward and back. He pulled his fingers out and pressed the thick, round head of his cock against her opening.

She whimpered, sure she'd never take him inside. The pressure became unbearable and she opened her mouth to beg him to stop. Then gasped when he shoved past the tight ring.

"Christ, you're tight, Darc." Joe's forehead rested on her shoulder and his hips stilled. A shudder shook his tall frame.

Darcy burrowed her face into the crook of Quentin's neck and moaned. "Give me more, Joe. Please, give me more." Her hips jerked when he surged into her, crowding her delicate tissues.

She didn't realize she was shaking, until Quentin's arms surrounded her. "Now, Joe. Prepare her neck."

As his cock stroked deeper into her ass, Joe's tongue slid along her neck.

Darcy gasped. Filled to bursting with masculine cock, she was on the brink of splintering into a thousand pieces. Her hands clutched Quentin's shoulders, her nails digging into his skin.

Joe pumped against her ass and Darcy had to move. "Quentin?" she asked her voice quavering.

His mouth settled over hers, his arm crooked beneath her thigh to lift it, allowing both men room to slide deeper into her. Quentin surged forward until he was fully seated.

Pinned between them, she couldn't move her hips. She quaked, whimpering and moaning, not recognizing the animalistic sounds erupting from deep within her throat. She accepted their deepening thrusts, their hips countering each other's moves.

Quentin's lips lifted from hers. "Now, Joe," he growled.

Joe's hands circled her chest to clasp her breasts, his fingers pinching her nipples. A rumble from behind her was all the warning she got before his teeth sank into her neck.

Darcy screamed, loud and long then closed her eyes tightly. Quentin kissed her again, his tongue sliding along hers and she bit him. He growled and thrust harder.

Joe's rumbling grew to a roar and his hips jerked out of synch, faster. Burning her ass, as his thick cock stretched her farther.

Faster, harder, deeper, their thrusts grew wild and Darcy writhed between them, sweat breaking over her body, cream gushing in her cunt.

Quentin's hips rolled and jerked, and his arm drew her thigh higher. Joe's hands moved lower to close over her hips, anchoring her to receive his hard, pistoning cock.

Beyond words, Darcy's body took their thrusts, forgetting to breathe. Then her orgasm rolled over her, clenching her belly, tightening her vagina and ass, pulsing, caressing their cocks. Both men growled and Darcy screamed as release washed over her. The men rocked, their cum spurting deep inside her body.

She didn't know she was crying until Quentin licked her tears from her face. As Joe closed the small wounds on her neck, he withdrew his cock, but Quentin stayed buried deep inside her. His arms pulled her closer and she turned her face to nestle in the crook of his neck.

Joe kissed her shoulder and drew away, leaving the sweat on her back to cool in the air. She heard the sounds of water running in the bathroom, but couldn't stir herself to move away from Quentin.

Quentin kissed her temple. "Come my dear, I'll help you with your bath." He offered his hand to pull her to her feet.

She was grateful for the support when her legs crumpled beneath her. With a shaky laugh, she let him lead her to the bathroom.

As Quentin passed Joe in the doorway, the two men exchanged nods. When the door closed behind the woman he loved and her vampire, Joe quietly left the bedroom.

CHAPTER EIGHT

Darcy woke to find the early morning light rimming the curtain and a heavy weight draped over her. She smiled when her scattered thoughts coalesced. She'd fallen asleep with Quentin's head upon her shoulder and his cock embedded between her legs.

"Good morning." He didn't open his eyes, but his mouth curved into a smile.

"Feeling pretty puffed up this morning?" she teased.

He arched an eyebrow. "You're very chipper, considering."

"Considering what? That I feel like a two dollar whore who has a hundred in her pocket?"

His eyes popped open. "That was rather coarse."

She wrinkled her nose. "I'm feeling rather...sticky this morning."

"I'm sorry, I'll move." He rose on his forearms, lifting his torso, which only pressed his cock deeper inside her.

She rubbed her heels on the back of his thighs and pressed down, keeping him firmly inside. "Not yet. Please?"

He lowered himself on his elbows, his face inches from hers. The smirk that was never far from his lips stretched lazily.

Blushing, Darcy covered her mouth immediately. "Maybe I should brush my teeth first."

Quentin shook his head. "A little tooth scum won't put me off. Not when I find myself buried inside someone so delightful."

"No, really. This isn't a minor case of halitosis."

"No. I'm not moving until you tell me what your first impulse was."

Beneath his watchful stare, she squirmed, but her gaze held his. "A morning kiss, then?"

"As in 'good morning', or as in 'morning after' kiss?" His eyes crinkled at the sides.

Darcy felt exposed—more so than the previous evening when her body had been examined and explored thoroughly by two men. Exposed and vulnerable. She pushed at his shoulders. "As in 'good morning, I need to get up'." She removed her feet from his thighs and waited for him to get the hint.

"I think I'll see for myself which it is." His head dipped and his mouth swooped down to take hers in a lazy, erotic kiss—his open mouth rubbing her lips, until she forgot her embarrassment and sighed.

When he ended the kiss, Darcy gave him a coy glance. "Well you didn't expire. So which was it?"

His mouth curved into a self-satisfied smile. "It was a 'Wake up, I'm horny' kiss."

She laughed and raised her legs to circle his waist. "You've got me there. Took you long enough. You are a slow riser." She gave his cock a squeeze with her inner muscles.

"I believe *we've* been insulted."

"*We* will think *you* lack stamina if you don't get down to business quickly." She tightened her thighs to hug his body close.

His cock pulsed inside her, edging deeper. "What business are you speaking of?"

Feeling deliciously wanton, Darcy quipped, "The business of giving me pleasure."

"What compensation will you give me for my services?" he asked in a haughty tone.

"Shall we barter? Service for service?"

His hips flexed, driving him deeper. "Hmm. Bears consideration."

"Like for like?" she said breathlessly.

"I think not. Wouldn't be a fair trade. We're not made the same."

"Because we're vampire and human?"

"No. Man and woman." His fingers skimmed her breast. "You're rounder here."

"Barely," she mumbled.

A growl sounded from deep inside his throat. "The tips of your *rounder* breasts are larger and longer…" He tugged on the stem of her nipple. "…and more sensitive than mine. Playing with my nipples won't make me nearly come. You have a distinct advantage."

Darcy mewled and curved her hips to encourage him to move.

"And then there are the more obvious differences." His hand crept between them and he fingered her clit and drove his hips upward to emphasize his point.

Not to be out-caressed, Darcy reached between their bodies, curving her hand around the cock embedded in her pussy and cupped his balls. "I envy you this…" Her fingers ringed the base of his penis. "…and this. I imagine just pulling off your clothes could excite you. And yet, when you come inside me you're still less vulnerable than I am. A woman must accept a man's intrusion."

"Love, we're made vulnerable in a different way." He pulled her hands away and pressed them against the pillow beside her head. His cock stroked inside her—deeply. "Your woman's body holds secrets a man can't understand. And you possess a treasure—a warm, moist place a man can burrow inside." He pulled back and stroked inside again. "Yet it's only when the woman is someone we trust that we choose to linger in her solace." Quentin stoked the slowly building fire with a series of gentle glides, pulling out and driving forward. Then he held himself still inside her, gazing down at her face, the heat and tenderness in his expression melting her from the inside out. "Your cunt is a place of solace, but my cock will always be an intruder and will always beg entrance."

She wrapped her legs around his hips and her arms around his broad shoulders. "You're wrong. Your cock fills the emptiness inside and I haven't the will to refuse your entrance. I want you inside me. I would hold you there forever if I could."

His face grew solemn. "This solace is transitory, love, as long as you remain human. Otherwise, I would keep you thus forever."

Again, he'd mentioned turning her. Each time, she was more tempted to accept. An eternity of loving him wouldn't be enough. She speared her fingers into his thick hair and pulled him down for another kiss.

The muscles in his arms bunched and he lifted his torso, giving his hips greater leverage. His strokes were longer—and to Darcy's mind—too damn slow. She planted her feet in the mattress and angled her hips upward to shorten the distance between them.

Their hips countered each other's strokes, pounding against each other; faster, sharper, creating a friction that built a spiraling coil of sensual tension. Darcy's legs quivered and her breath grew ragged. When her orgasm burst, she dug her fingers into his shoulders, held her hips as high as she could reach. His cock rested snug inside her channel, caressed from head to scrotum.

Spent, his weight crashed down on her and her legs collapsed. She rocked him, side to side, holding him as tight as she could, relishing the jetting release that bathed her.

Her lover yawned and kissed the crook of her neck.

If she didn't roust him now, she might be stuck beneath him for another long while. The thought was a pleasant one, but she really did need to get up. Drowsy and well-sated, Darcy traced the knobby vertebrae of his spine. "I should check in on Joe before he sleeps for the day."

Quentin's body stiffened above her. "You needn't worry about him anymore."

She pressed a kiss against his shoulder. "I'm not going to make love with him again, if that has you worried. Last night was goodbye. To tell you the truth, I don't really know why I wanted him, except I kept saying to myself it was right for me to love him."

"And not me. Because he's human?"

"Because we've known each other so long—as partners and friends. And I do love him—just not the way he wants."

"You know what I think?" he said, his voice held that droll note she was coming to treasure.

"Hmmm?" Her lips curved into a smile. He was going to say something outrageous.

He rose on his elbows to look down into her face. "I think you were using him to fight your attraction for me." His expression was as complacent as a cat's after licking cream.

"You're unbelievable!" She pretended outrage and made a half-hearted attempt to shove him away. "It has to be all about you, doesn't it?"

"Were you lovers before I arrived on the scene?"

"Of course not."

One self-satisfied brow rose. "Well then."

"That's it? That's your entire argument? You're an arrogant bastard." He was right, but she'd never admit that to him. He was already too sure of himself.

"I'm the one in the saddle, aren't I?"

"So now you're Roy Rogers?"

"Would you rather I was Trigger?"

"Hmmm." She pretended to take his suggestion seriously. "You do have a feature or two that remind me of a horse. Mainly your backside!"

"Not my cock? I think we're insulted again."

Gaiety fled, and she gazed solemnly at him. "Intellectually, I know you're an unsuitable choice for me, but I can't help myself. I want you still. Hell, I want you all the time."

"I'm similarly afflicted, my dear."

She drew a deep breath. "I really do need to make sure Joe is okay. I won't sleep easy until I do."

"Darcy, he isn't here."

"Did he leave to hunt for more blood?" Darcy asked, alarm rising as she imagined a hundred frightening scenarios.

He held himself perfectly still above her. "Darcy, he's gone."

"What?" she asked, not understanding.

"We talked about it last night, before you came home. He has a lot to adjust to and think about. His love for you was clouding the issue. He knew he'd lost, so he decided to leave."

"But the team—"

"He's taking a leave of absence."

Tears filled her eyes. "This is my fault. He's alone now."

"He's a man, love. Clinging to him would make him feel less so." He rolled to his side and pulled her closer into his arms.

"I don't like him leaving like this."

"Did you like having both of us love you, so well?" he asked, his voice tight.

Her answer was important to him. She couldn't make light of it or give anything but the honest truth. "It was frightening how much I felt—and painful. I couldn't concentrate on one sensation so much was happening. I wanted to cling to you to slow it down. Are you wondering if I will be satisfied with just one man now?"

He didn't answer, just stared at her steadily.

Her hand cupped his face. "You are quickly becoming everything to me. You enrage me, annoy me, fill me, and excite me. You're more than I ever knew I needed."

"How ungrammatical," he said drolly, but his eyes were warm and approving.

She understood. He couldn't reciprocate with loving words. He was a guy. Big, bad vampire was still just a man—and right brain-left brain challenged. Words of emotion might be impossible to draw from him, but his actions spoke volumes.

He'd kept her safe when Joe's storm had raged against her.

He'd prepared her body for another man to take.

He'd kept her warm and loved, and had been with her to soften her grief from Joe's departure.

Darcy let Quentin pull her close. Snuggled next to his body, she slept with her head resting over his heart.

* * * * *

Darcy took her seat in the conference room, uneasy with the silence from the rest of the team. Not a single glance met hers and her heart sank. She was going to be fired.

The Captain had called the meeting for late afternoon—before Quentin could possibly attend.

The conference room door swung inward and Captain Springer entered. He glanced at Darcy and his face grew solemn. "Sorry about your partner, Darc."

Darcy gave him a questioning glance. He didn't sound angry with her.

"Joe called me and told me what happened. That he'd asked Quentin to make him a vampire when he realized he wasn't going to make it."

Her shoulders lifted with her swift intake of breath.

"He did tell you, didn't he?" he asked, his expression full of sympathy.

Darcy nodded her head, blinking back tears. Joe had saved her ass. "Did-did he say if he was coming back?"

"He's got a lot to think about, but I told him his job was still waiting here for him. Hell, partnering with vamps might be the wave of the future."

Phil's arm slipped around her shoulder. "Tough break, Darc."

Murmurs of sympathy from around the table made Darcy feel about two feet tall.

Max's steady glare was the only exception. *Does he suspect the truth?*

She straightened her shoulders. "Boss, do we have any leads on where Nicky Powell is now?"

"Unfortunately, he's gone to ground. But he won't be able to stay there long. We found a stash of money in the house at South Beach Park. He can't go far without scoring more."

"Any clues how he'll put the money together again?" Phil asked.

Captain Springer's face lit with mirthless glee. "Word on the street is he approached a Jamaican drug runner to offer his special services to develop a new market and distribute the drugs."

Max cursed. "That's all we need. I suppose he's planning on making his own ring of pushers, too?"

"You got it," Captain Springer said.

"How do we know so much about his plans?" Darcy asked.

The Captain seemed entirely too pleased with himself. His cheeks were florid and satisfaction gleamed in his eyes. "We received the info straight from the horse's mouth. Seems the drug lord isn't pleased with his new partner."

"Who'd he go to?" Darcy asked.

"One of Rupe King's men."

Smiles lifted the tension in the room. Nicky Powell had made a fatal mistake.

* * * * *

Later that night…

"Why is it fortuitous that Nicky approached that particular drug dealer?" Quentin nuzzled Darcy's neck finding it impossible to keep his attention on what she was saying. What she was doing filled his senses. And her scent…

Her sweat-ripened musk lured him like a hound to a fox. He lapped moisture from her neck.

Darcy gripped his chin and brought his face level with hers. "Pay attention."

"Are *we* ready again?" He circled his hips under her to check for the depth of penetration.

Darcy rolled her eyes and pushed his hands from her breasts to the leather-upholstered sofa. "Business first."

"Of course." He smiled. "I love our conversations regarding commerce."

"Oh, you! I knew it was a mistake to let you divert me when we came inside the house."

"We *came* inside the car first to be precise. And what's this about letting you do anything? As I remember it, you left quite a few items of clothing on the lawn in your mad dash for the door."

He enjoyed Darcy's rosy-cheeked embarrassment immensely. Only she hadn't shown a hint of embarrassment when she'd shoved him down onto the sofa and climbed onto his lap. Nor had she blushed when she'd spread her legs wide around his hips and sank on his cock.

After she'd taken him, she'd been in an annoyingly chatty mood.

"If you'll just give me two minutes I'll explain everything."

"I'll give you nine inches."

"Huh! Is that all?"

"Give me a reason to exert myself further," he said, his voice dropping to a low rumble.

Her breasts were his barometers. He had only to watch the changes there to gauge her arousal. Her face was never as transparent. Even now, her chest was flushed pink. Time to escalate his seduction.

His hand rose to a tightly budding nipple. When he rolled it between his thumb and forefinger, her hips reacted. She couldn't help herself—he could tell by the ferocious frown she wore that she wanted to resist.

Simply watching her move on him, taking her pleasure of his body, pleased him. Her small breasts jiggled with each bounce. Her taut abdomen and sleekly muscled thighs clenched as she levered herself up and down. He could watch his cock disappear inside her pretty dark-furred mound for an eternity.

"Damn you," she moaned. "I'll never get my point across."

"Wouldn't you rather I did?" He flexed his hips to spear upward.

She gasped. "Just hold that thought." She circled on his cock again, driving him crazy with her tight twist and bounce. Her eyes squeezed shut and her small white teeth bit her bottom lip.

Quentin gripped her ass, his fingers splayed to "persuade" her to pick up the pace and height of her movements.

Darcy accepted his guidance with enthusiasm, moaning louder the harder and faster she bounced.

From the corner of his eye, he saw the front door push open. He stiffened, ready to toss Darcy to the side. Then he recognized the pair who appeared in the doorway.

Dylan O'Hara's expression reflected his wicked amusement at having found Quentin "occupied".

Emmy Harris winked and held her finger to her lips.

The two stood in the well of the foyer and waited for Quentin to finish.

Cursing beneath his breath, Quentin slid his hand beneath Darcy's hair and tipped her face to his.

Her lips closed over his, and then she murmured a protest when he tugged her gently back.

"We have visitors."

"Let's not answer the door," she groaned and ground her pussy over his cock.

"Ahem," his ex-best friend, Dylan, cleared his throat. "You left the front door open."

Darcy screeched and swung her head around.

Emmy raised her hand and fluttered her fingers. "Hi there. We're not interrupting anything, are we?"

CHAPTER NINE

Minutes later, Quentin's ears still rang from Darcy's loud scream. If he hadn't been so annoyed at the interruption only moments from orgasm, he might have laughed at how quickly the woman had sprung from the sofa *and his cock* and hidden in the bedroom.

Dylan, the bastard, had seated himself on the sectional, his arms outstretched and waited while Quentin picked up his clothes and dressed. He didn't bother to even try to hide his devilish smile.

Emmy's bright inquisitive stare embarrassed Quentin, because she made no bones about the fact her gaze was glued to his cock. She might even have mumbled something like, "I knew it was one of those vampire things—you're all hung like horses."

When the lower part of his anatomy was clothed, Quentin flopped down on the sofa. "Dylan, I thought we'd agreed that Emmy needed to be kept safe. Nicky's suffered a setback and is more dangerous than ever."

Dylan shrugged. "She wore me down."

"Yup! To a nubbin." Emmy grinned. "Now he can't satisfy me, I'll have to find my kicks elsewhere."

"Well come over here, sweetheart." Quentin opened his arms, feeling playful and fully enjoying his friend's jealous glare.

Emmy crossed the short distance and settled her shapely hips onto his lap. She leaned toward him and kissed his cheek.

"Uh huh!" Quentin pressed a finger beneath her chin and held her motionless while he gave her a wet, smacking kiss.

"Now see here!" Dylan said, his voice laced with irritation. "Get your lips off my wife."

Quentin broke the kiss. "Married? Now I really must kiss the bride." He bent her over his arm and pressed his lips to hers, again.

Emmy giggled and clutched his neck, and giggled louder when Dylan growled another warning.

When Quentin came up for air, he slung his arms around her and continued to hold her in his lap. "Have to hand it to you Dylan, your Emmy is all woman. I can see why you'd want to stake your claim. But Emmy, what do you see in this Paddy?"

Emmy's cheeks flushed with pleasure, and her eyes softened when she gazed at Dylan. "He's my big, bad wolf. He scares the hell out of me when he's making love."

Quentin understood her perfectly. Darcy scared the hell out him. His need for her grew stronger by the night. "So when did you two marry?"

"On our way here—in Vegas!"

Quentin released a bark of laughter. "Tell me you didn't..."

Dylan rolled his eyes. "Oh yes!"

Emmy's smile was beatific. "Elvis himself did the honors singing 'Hunk, Hunka Burnin' Love'!"

Quentin's mouth stretched with an unholy grin. "Must be love."

Shamefaced, Dylan shrugged. "What can I say? She had me by the shorthairs at 10,000 feet."

"Oooh!" Emmy bounced on his lap, her excitement impossible to contain. "Do you know what the 'Mile-High Club' is?"

Quentin quirked an eyebrow at his best friend.

"Navarro leant us his 10-seater to fly here. Emmy seduced the steward and he told her about the club."

"You make it sound like I had sex with the man," Emmy said, her lips pursed in an adorable pout.

"Damn close enough. He came in his pants!"

"I had to give him something in exchange."

"In exchange?" Quentin asked, knowing the answer. He was sure he'd enjoy Emmy's version better.

"For his blood, silly. Besides he was wearing an apron. No one but he and I knew. Except nosy over there. Of course, Dylan had to initiate me afterward — in the bathroom, the galley — "

"He gets the idea, love," Dylan said smoothly.

The bedroom door creaked open behind him and the scent of raspberry soap wafted over him. Darcy had showered. Quentin's cock twitched.

"I think you have the wrong woman in your lap," Emmy said slyly. She rose and walked toward Darcy. "I'm Emmaline Harris — "

"O'Hara!" Dylan reminded her.

"That rude man is my husband, Dylan *O'Hara*," she said, wrinkling her nose. "We're friends of Quentin's. Friends of the night, if you know what I mean."

Quentin turned to watch the exchange. Darcy had changed to a faded gray sweatshirt with the SU logo emblazoned across her chest and donned a pair of faded blue jeans and sneakers. Her hair was still wet from her shower. Two rosy spots of color warmed her cheeks.

The contrast between the two women was remarkable. Darcy was the taller of the two, but Emmy dwarfed her by virtue of her exuberance and statuesque frame. Emmy was dressed in a blood-red pantsuit that clung lovingly to her fleshy figure; her bright gold hair and ivory skin a vivid contrast to Darcy's severely understated appearance.

But Quentin knew how deceptive Darcy's beauty was. It was tactile rather than visual. Baby-soft skin stretched over taut, defined muscle. Soft hair, soft lips, soft kittenish cries when she grew excited...

Her curves were subtle. Her ass fit his palms, warm and round. Just the thought of her small, round breasts with their velvety-soft, rose-red nipples...

Quentin shifted on the seat and caught Dylan's amused stare.

"I never thought I'd see the day."

"Huh!" Quentin grunted. "I don't know what you're talking about."

"She's not what I would have expected," Dylan murmured.

Quentin's eyes narrowed in warning.

"Oh ho! How the mighty have fallen."

"Boys!" Emmy tossed her hair over her shoulder. "Darcy and I are going to scare up some steaks. Can we bring you anything?"

Dylan smiled lazily. "Whatever you're having, dear."

"See how he dotes?" she said, with a wink at Quentin. Emmy blew Dylan a kiss and followed Darcy through the swinging door.

Dylan's face grew serious. "So, tell me about Nicky."

"He's on the run. We found his new lair, but he gave us the slip."

"Us? I heard you were working with the local vampire hunters." He jerked his head in the direction of the kitchen. "I take it Darcy is one of them? Aren't you playing a dangerous game?"

"It's been interesting," Quentin murmured.

"I'll bet it has."

Darcy cut raw steak into bite-sized cubes, enjoying the sharp crack of her cleaver as it met the cutting board, while Emmy busied herself with washing potatoes and popping them in the microwave.

"My guy's Irish," Emmy said. "Strictly a meat and potatoes kind of guy," Emmy said.

"So you two are married?" *Hack!*

"Last night," Emmy replied happily, unaware Darcy was glaring holes at her back.

Hack!

"It's so hard to believe. Just a couple of weeks ago I was a bookkeeper and had sworn off men forever, and then there was Dylan. Don't you find vampire men impossible to resist?"

"Nope. The only thing I find hard to resist is slipping a stake through their hearts." *Hack!*

"Oh." Emmy's eyes rounded as she turned to watch Darcy. "Oh! You saw me sitting on Quentin's lap. That was nothing. Quentin's just a tease. A little jealousy goes a long way in the bedroom, if you know what I mean." She smiled. "Dylan will be reasserting his mastery when he drags me to a bed. There's never been anything between Quentin and I, so you don't have to worry."

"I wasn't worried." Darcy's words were clipped. "I don't give a rat's a—"

"Although he has seen me naked several times," her voice softened. "Actually, he's watched Dylan and I having sex several times."

Hack!

"Not that he did it on purpose, I'm sure. Dylan and I tend to get carried away and can never make it to a bed. You're not jealous, are you?"

Hack! "Of course not. What's it to me who he watches having sex?"

"Oh. I thought you two were…involved. You seemed to be enjoying yourself, earlier. Sorry about walking in on you and all. Are you mad about that?"

Darcy slid the meat off the cutting board onto a platter and handed it to Emmy. She turned her back to wash her hands at the sink.

"You know, you aren't at all what I expected Quentin to fall for."

Darcy's hand stilled as she dried them off. Emmy's comment mirrored her own thoughts. After seeing Quentin's hands curled around Emmy's abundant curves, she'd felt distinctly sexless.

"I never would have expected him to have such good taste. Dylan tells me he's strictly a munchable man. Any port in a storm. But you're not like that. You're in love with him, aren't you?"

Startled, Darcy let Emmy see her torment. "I'm not in love with him," she lied.

"Of course you are," Emmy said softly. "Who wouldn't be? He's an honorable, sexy guy. You know, he saved my life."

Darcy shook her head. "What we have is just sex."

"Keep telling yourself that," Emmy said with a slow smile. "I did. I thought there was no way Dylan would ever fall in love with me. I was too fat, too ordinary."

Anger melted beneath Emmy's thoughtful gaze. Darcy snorted. "Ordinary? You're beautiful. Any man would appreciate your curves. I feel like stick-girl standing next to you."

Emmy blinked. "Well thanks, but you're wrong. Men were not beating down my door. Only Dylan ever appreciated my big ass. And if I'm sexy now, it's because Dylan makes me feel that way."

Emmy set down the platter and stepped closer to Darcy. She reached to smooth Darcy's drying hair away from her face. "I can see why Quentin would fall for you. You have beautiful, expressive brown eyes." Her hand cupped her cheek. "And soft skin. And a willowy, yet strong body."

"No boobs," Darcy said with a crooked smile.

Emmy lifted an eyebrow in challenge and cupped Darcy's breast.

Darcy sucked air into her lungs, shocked by the intimacy of the caress.

"You have lovely, small, round breasts—with very, very responsive nipples. I'd do you."

Darcy blushed and pushed Emmy's hand away.

Emmy's expression grew serious. "You're not what I would have expected for Quentin. You're much better."

Desperate to change the subject, Darcy asked, "I take it you haven't been a vampire long?"

"No. Nicky Powell nearly killed me. Dylan had to turn me to save my life."

"Do you..." Darcy chewed on her lip. "...like being a vampire?"

Emmy's face beamed. "It's incredible. Every sensation is more intense. I can see in the dark. Scents are richer, fuller. My hearing is keener. And my lust!" Her laughter sounded like tinkling bells. "I'm insatiable! Poor Dylan thinks he has to follow me around everywhere I go, because I want it all the time."

Amen! "I'm not a vampire, but I want it all the time with Quentin," Darcy admitted.

"So, are you thinking about turning?"

Darcy nodded. "He's asked me."

"It's very dangerous. Think long and hard about it."

A blush heated her cheeks. "It's the long and hard part of him that nearly has me convinced!"

The two women giggled.

Emmy gave her a coy smile. "So is Quentin as good as he looks?"

"Better! But he always has to be in charge."

"Sounds like Dylan. They're both arrogant bastards, but I'll tell you a secret. Dylan loves it when I turn the tables on him. A little aggression—and a lot of up close and personal attention to his cock, and he's putty in my hands." Emmy picked up the platter. "Let's go feed these guys. They're going to need their strength."

* * * * *

Darcy stripped in front of the bathroom mirror. *So, I'm willowy.* She tweaked her nipples until they reddened and stretched to points Quentin couldn't help but notice.

She rummaged through the cabinet beneath her sink and found a tube of rose-scented cream and squeezed a generous amount onto her palm, then smoothed it over her hips, belly, and thighs. Next she found a tube of lip-gloss, cinnamon-flavored, and slicked her lips with the pink gel. She wanted him to pay special attention to her mouth. Then she searched for the perfume her mother had given her the previous Christmas. *Tuscany.* She pulled the cap off the bottle and inhaled the fragrance—floral, spicy, with a tinge of musk. A couple of squirts on her wrists and she was ready to go.

Pulling open the bathroom door, she found Quentin had already divested the bed of its covers and was sprawled in the center, two pillows behind his head. Both lamps on either side of the bed illuminated his body. He smiled and patted the mattress beside him. He was entirely too smug. This was going to be so much fun.

She sauntered toward the bed to join him.

Quentin's hot gaze traveled from her face to her breasts and his chest rose. When it slipped lower, Darcy increased the sway of her hips. His cock pulsed against his belly.

She climbed onto the bed from the end, crawling between his outstretched legs until her knee nudged his sac and her hands were planted on either side of his hips.

"Come over me," he commanded.

Darcy shook her head. Instead, she stared down at his cock for a long moment, and then looked at him from beneath the fan of her eyelashes. "It seems to me, someone's been neglected."

"Darcy?" His voice rose in warning.

She leaned down and opened her mouth. Her tongue darted out to lick a path from the base of his shaft to the tip. "I'm in charge this time, *Albermarle.*"

His eyes narrowed and a flush painted his cheeks red.

She scraped a fingernail up the inside of one thigh. "You can't move. You can't touch me. If you do, I'll punish you." She delivered a slap to his inner thigh near his balls.

His leg flinched and his jaw hardened. His gaze promised retribution. *God, she hoped so.*

She licked his lightly furred thighs, her mouth moving ever closer to his groin. She felt the tension building in his legs. When she reached his smooth sac, she mouthed his balls, smearing the cinnamon-gel over them.

His breath hissed. "It burns."

She slapped his thighs again. "I'll just have to lick it off, won't I?" She sucked first one, then the other ball into her mouth, laving his tender flesh with her tongue. Suctioning gently, she tugged and licked — swirling her tongue, mouthing him with her lips.

His breath grew ragged and his hips lifted, a shallow thrust that reminded her there was so much more to explore. Darcy felt an answering twinge of desire tighten her vagina. One last lap, and she lifted her head. "All better?"

His chest rose and fell rapidly, but he didn't speak.

Darcy grinned and hoped he was getting nervous. She walked her fingers up his cock and it pulsed. She tapped the engorged head. "Uh huh! Bad boy. Not yet."

Sliding her body over his groin, she decided to make a detour. When her face was level with his, she widened her legs and placed her knees on either side of his hips. Her open slit centered on his erection, and she rocked to caress it wetly with her labia.

His eyes were open and glaring directly into hers. Darcy leaned down and sucked his lower lip into her mouth. Then she slid her lips over his, smearing the last of the gel. His tongue darted out and licked her, and then he nudged her face with his nose to push her back. He proceeded to remove every last trace of the gel from her mouth.

"Mmmm," he groaned appreciatively.

Darcy held herself still over him, savoring the sensations. Her breasts speared his chest, her hips slid her open cunt over his cock, and she felt the rising tide of an orgasm.

She gasped and drew away.

His expression was triumphant as his hands clamped over her ass to hold her to him, pushing and pulling her hips faster, increasing the friction that was quickly building a fire in her loins. He'd turned the tables on her.

Darcy fought for control, but his body rocked beneath her spread legs and pushed his cock harder against her pussy. She shoved against his chest but only succeeded in increasing the pressure at the apex of her thighs. Her orgasm blossomed, taking her breath, tightening her thighs around him.

"Yes, baby. Come for me."

She shouted, jerking her hips faster, wanting to prolong the fractured ecstasy. Then it passed and her movements slowed. His hands continued to caress her buttocks. Then one slid to her chest and he fondled her breast as her heart slowed its rapid beating.

Darcy drew a deep breath and opened her eyes.

Quentin's calculating gaze held hers and he pinched her nipple—hard.

"Thanks," she said, her voice rasping. "I needed that to help me keep control."

A single eyebrow rose. He twisted her nipple, then scraped his fingernail over the sensitive peak. "Why would you want control?"

"I want you to beg," she whispered.

"*That* will never happen."

"Watch me." She pressed his hands to the pillow beside his head and scooted down his body, pausing to suckle his flat brown nipples until their tiny points hardened.

Her tongue swirled over the hair that covered his abdomen, and she smiled when his muscles tightened. He gasped when the point of her tongue dipped into his belly button and fluttered.

Lower, she slid down his sweat-moistened flesh, licking the soft skin of his belly. She nudged aside his cock with her nose and applied small, sharp bites on his muscled abdomen that caused his penis to jump and pulse.

Cupping his sac with one hand she smoothed her cheek over the length of his shaft. It smelled of her release and his own musk. But she wasn't ready to give him the ultimate kiss. She slid lower and tongued his balls, sweeping below the sac to the follow the line to his asshole.

"Sweet Jesus!" he muttered.

Shoving at his legs, she urged him to raise his knees and widen them. Now, he was at her mercy.

She tongued the tight ring and gloried in the sharp hiss of his gasp. She circled his asshole, lapped it with the flat of her tongue, then used the tip to tickle the center.

"Enough Darcy!" She loved the desperate tone in his voice.

"No. Not nearly enough. Have you ever been fucked here, Quentin?"

"No!"

"Then let me be the first."

Quentin started to sweat in earnest. Part of him wanted to wrest control from the vixen, the other part of him was dying to see where her curiosity would lead next. Would she really…

She did! One slender finger pressed inward where none had ever dared enter before. He squeezed his buttocks, resisting, but she was relentless. Finally, he felt the tight ring give and she was inside.

"So tight," she murmured. "I believe you." She swirled her finger and watched his face, no doubt to gauge his reaction.

He fought to school his features into a mask, but she touched something inside him that had his hips jerking off the bed. "Darcy!" he warned. He didn't dare move again, his arse burned already, his balls had tightened to stones, and his dick felt ready to burst. But he couldn't give her this victory.

"Poor baby. You look worried," she said, and rose on her knees, her face poised above his aching rod. "Will you beg me, now?"

Gritting his teeth, he refused to give her his answer, but his body spoke for him. His hips pumped, nudging his wayward little man against her lips.

Her mouth opened and she took the head of his cock into her warm, wet mouth. Her teeth nibbled on the crown—tiny, sharp bites that sent electric shocks throughout his body and he bit back a moan.

God, he needed her to take him into her throat. He pressed upward, trying to gain deeper access.

But she drew back. "Tell me what you want."

Quentin stared at her. Her eyes glittered with triumph. The witch knew how close he was to exploding, but denied him. He closed his eyes and willed his flesh to resist her lure, but he'd already lost. He'd die if she didn't take him now. "Please, Darcy. Suck my cock."

"Oh baby, you've made me so happy. But I don't think you're ready."

His eyes slammed open and he glared.

Her smile promised unimaginable torments and Quentin cursed. With her finger up his arse, he was shackled to her whim.

Her pink tongue lapped a lazy circle around the root of his cock, rising ever higher until she reached the head. He panted, hoping now she'd sink her mouth over him, but she pressed the tip of her wicked tongue into the small opening at the top, coaxing a drop of pre-cum.

She groaned and slid her mouth down his shaft, the sound vibrating on his swollen flesh.

His hips pumped upward, shallow, short thrusts that frustrated him. He craved her warm mouth, needed her deep, wet throat to swallow all of him.

Her free hand encircled him at the base and she scraped her teeth along the rigid pole of his sex.

Silently, he promised revenge. Promised to drive her mad with his tongue and cock. Until she begged for forgiveness for making him to plead. "Darcy, give me release. Take me, baby. Fuck me."

A second slender finger slid inside him and he couldn't hold back his shout. Pain and ecstasy warred. Then she moved her fingers, in and out, while she fluttered her tongue along his raging erection. His cries ripped from the back of his throat. Suddenly, she stopped all movement. He watched her, his body tensing to resist her next assault.

Her expression wasn't gloating as he'd expected. Her cheeks flamed, her chest rose and fell with each ragged breath. She was as seduced by her actions as he was. Her mouth closed over him and she sank on his cock, until his head bumped against the opening of her throat. Then she opened her jaws wider and he sank deeper into her.

He heard a lusty, hoarse shout and then he was driving his hips upward, slamming into her depths. When he came, his cries grew strangled, and finally, his balls exploded and cum spurted into her throat—long, hot streams of liquid fire. When he'd shot his load, he lay there, spent, allowing her to sooth him with her tongue and mouth, her low murmurs gentling his flesh.

He'd get his revenge later on the little witch. After he'd recovered from the greatest orgasm he'd ever experienced.

CHAPTER TEN

Darcy yawned and stretched easing the pleasant aches in her muscles, only to discover something impeded the movement of her arms. Her eyes shot open. Her wrists were wrapped in pink cotton — her panties, she realized, and they were tied to the headboard.

"Finally, you're awake," Quentin purred. He lay on his side, his head propped on one hand.

He looked like a man who wasn't in any hurry.

And why should he be? she silently grumbled. He'd come, roaring like a freight train, then promptly fell asleep. Darcy had lain at his side, frustrated and hurting for what seemed like hours afterward. She'd had her way with him, but her victory had backfired.

Now her body remembered where she'd left off. Every swollen, achy point throbbed with her heartbeat.

She groaned inwardly. He was going to make her pay. He'd torture her with the sweet, sliding promise of his cock, fingers, and mouth until she begged as loudly as he had.

She winced. Perhaps, she'd taken things a little far. Maybe, he'd accept an apology. "Quentin?"

"Yes, love." His voice was mild — with a hint of amusement.

Shit! Shit! Shit! What does he want to hear?

His body stretched beside hers, but not touching. The heat from his skin burned her. His mouth curved only slightly and his gaze never left her face.

His stillness made her nervous as hell.

"You know, everything you're thinking is written on your face, love. It's really quite remarkable."

Darcy wished she could school her features into a careless expression, but all her energies were spent holding her hips still. She clamped her thighs tightly and fought the quiver of arousal that threatened to shake her belly. *Where will he start? With my breasts or my pussy? Oh God, will he take my ass?*

She gave up trying to pretend fearlessness and glared at him. "Will you just get it over with? What do you want me to say? I'll say it." Her voice rose. "Do you want to spank me? I'll take it. Just get it over with, so you can fuck me."

Quentin's smile broadened. "What an imagination you have! Did I leave you in a bad way, sweetheart?"

"Yes!" Now she really would wail. "Touch me, please!" She rolled her hips toward him, pressing her thighs against his.

He settled his hand on her stomach and pushed her back.

"Are you going to leave me, again?" A sick panicked feeling made her stomach boil. "Are you going to make me wait? Because if you are, I'll scream so loud the whole neighborhood will think I'm dying. And I won't be so discriminating about who I beg to help me!"

His gaze narrowed, his eyes glittering dangerously. "I told you. You will not take another lover. Never again. I watched while your partner pounded away at you. I won't share you, again."

She thrilled at the possessive note in his voice. "Then fuck me. Make me yours. I'll be yours as long as you want me."

His hand hovered over one breast, then settled, warm and heavy. "And if I want forever?"

The nerve ending in her nipple fired, shooting a curling desire into her belly. She swallowed past the lump that lodged in her throat. "I'll give it to you."

"You'd give me your life for a fucking?" he asked, his voice casual, but his expression was alert.

She raised an eyebrow. "You are an extraordinary fuck," she purred.

"What makes me special? How can I know you aren't simply saying what I want to hear?"

Could he read her mind? "Baby," she moaned, "I love the way you smell—of the sea and warm musk."

He raised a single eyebrow. He wasn't impressed.

"You only have to look at me and I melt. Your mouth torments me." She writhed and arched her back to raise her breasts. "My tits are so tight and hard, they're begging for your kisses."

"Huh!" he grunted, but molded her breast with his palm.

She raised her knees and let them fall open.

His gaze zeroed in on her moist slit.

"I need your mouth and your huge cock. Take me."

His jaw rippled as he clamped his teeth tightly. "Tell me about my cock." Was his voice hoarse?

"You fill me to bursting. When you're crammed up inside me so tight I can't breathe, I don't ever want to let you go."

Heat was in his gaze and he flared his nostrils. "There's the little matter of what you did to me tonight."

"I'm sorry. I took it too far. I know I did. But you were so wonderfully responsive. I felt powerful and so goddamned turned on. Then you fell asleep…"

"Did I leave you wanting?"

"Yes!"

"Good." He reached over her and released the knots that bound her wrists.

"That's it?"

"I find I can't prolong your punishment. I'm hard as oak and I haven't had the pleasure of your warm *solace* this evening."

Darcy opened her arms joyously.

Quentin lowered himself over her, stretching his body, pressing her deep into the mattress from her shoulders to her toes.

"I'm going to fuck you until you shout the roof off the house." He pushed her hands onto the pillow and nudged her knees apart.

Eager to begin, Darcy wriggled beneath him, wanting her legs free to clasp his hips, but he didn't allow it.

His cock nudged between her thighs, poking against her soaking slit.

Darcy's hips widened just far enough so he slipped between her thighs and pressed against her slick folds.

Quentin's jaw clenched and he drove his hips forward, pushing past her labia, into her channel, all the way inside her until he butted her womb. He released a groan.

Darcy echoed it.

But he didn't move again. "Well, here we are."

Darcy waited for the storm to erupt, but he remained still. Her eyes narrowed. She knew he'd conceded too quickly.

She tugged her hands from beneath his and traced the center of his spine, lightly, teasingly.

"Darcy," he growled, "You're not going to wrest control from me."

Oh yeah? I know your hot buttons, baby. She dug her nails into his back and scraped them down to the top of his buttocks.

"Witch." His mouth descended and he circled his lips over hers. She tempted him with her tongue, reaching out to lick his closed lips, stabbing at the seam.

He resisted her invitation.

But she'd just started. Her hands glided lower and she cupped his firm ass, giving him a squeeze.

His cock pulsed, but he didn't move inside her. He dragged his lips from hers. "Have you no patience? Is it not enough that

I'm inside you, filling you? It is for me. You're cunt is hot and moist, and your lust is fragrant."

Darcy glared at him. The bastard was going to make her wait. This was almost more diabolical than her last "lesson." He was there! All the way up her. How could he resist their heat? Her hips longed to squirm and flex, but his weight trapped her movements.

But he'd forgotten about one set of muscles over which he had no control. She tightened her pussy and released, tightened and released.

And her hands were free. She reached until her fingers found the crease of his ass and trailed downward, then pressed his tightly furled anus. Grinning, she said, "Can you resist? Hmmm?" She circled one finger and felt his thighs tremble atop hers.

Leaning upward she bit his lower lip and dragged his mouth down to hers, sucking his lip inside her mouth, while her hands continued their torture below.

Sweat broke out on his face and chest, his arms began to shake, and his dick moved an inch deeper.

With a hoarse cry, he rammed a knee between her legs, shoving her thighs wide and pulled out of her entirely.

Darcy moaned a protest and pressed her finger into his ass.

Holding himself above her on his arms, a deep rumble built in the back of his throat.

Darcy chuckled and poked her finger in and out. The man did love a finger-fuck. "What's it gonna be, Bat-boy?"

Quentin broke into a full-fledged growl, and Darcy knew she'd won.

He grabbed her and rolled her roughly onto her stomach. Then he pulled her hips up and drove his cock straight into her, cramming himself inside her.

Darcy yelped and rose on her hands — the better to meet his powerful thrusts.

Each forward drive jerked her whole body until she grasped the headboard to brace herself.

It was almost too much—too deep, too hard, too fast. His hands gripped her cheeks and jerked her higher. He rammed forward as far as he could go, grinding himself inside her, lifting and lowering her hips to increase the friction where her pussy met the crisp, wiry hairs at his groin.

Darcy hung onto the bars, her hips jolting, until her orgasm hit—an explosion of sensation that tightened her vagina and seared the breath in her lungs. Quentin was right there with her, his steel rod pistoning against her buttocks faster, his hands squeezing her ass in a bruising grip, and then he released a roar that should have rattled the windows.

As he slowed, Darcy gasped, her breath hitching on a burst of laughter. "I'm going to have to check the shingles on the roof in the morning."

Quentin collapsed against her back, taking them both to the mattress. "Madam, will you ever let me have the last word?"

* * * * *

Quentin stirred three teaspoons of sugar into his tea and ignored the amused smiles from his two companions.

Seated around the kitchen table, the three vampires took turns yawning sleepily.

Emmy stretched her arms above her head and giggled. "Well, I'm going to say it. No Dylan, I know you think it's impolite to comment, but I swear Quentin shouted loud enough to wake the dead last night." She ignored Quentin's scathing glance. "What on earth did she do to you? I think I could use some pointers."

Quentin remained tight-lipped. His dignity demanded he keep mum. Darcy's "pointers" were the culprits, after all.

Dylan cleared his throat. "Speaking of your tormentor, where's Darcy gone off to?"

"She left a note. Said she'd stop by the house after dark and give us the scoop." He didn't add that he'd been too caught up in sex-play the evening before to let Darcy tell him the latest developments in the case. It was too bruising to his ego how the woman managed to distract him.

"Quentin…"

Emmy's voice held a tentative note that snagged Quentin's attention from his cup.

"Darcy told me last night that she's thinking of becoming one of us."

"I've asked her to consider it," Quentin admitted.

"It's not a good idea," she said quietly.

"I know the procedure is dangerous, but I have done it before. If she wants it enough, I'll do it for her."

"You mean if she wants you enough," Dylan murmured.

"Well that, too."

"I think you should wait," Emmy whispered, her face reflecting sympathy.

Quentin stared. Something was wrong. "Was your experience so terrible?"

"You know I didn't have a choice, but no, it was less frightening than the alternative. But that's not why I'm asking you to wait."

A sick feeling of dread descended on him. "Well then, out with it, Emmy."

"You can't turn Darcy. She's pregnant."

* * * * *

It was early evening and the sun still winked on the edge of the horizon. At the gate guard's direction Captain Springer, Max, and Darcy exited their unmarked squad car.

"I have to take your weapons," he said, his expression unapologetic. "Mr. King's orders."

At the Captain's nod, Darcy reached beneath her jacket for the Beretta holstered at the small of her back and handed it to the guard. Max pulled a gun from his ankle holster, but the Captain merely shrugged. "I knew he'd shake us down."

They were instructed to leave their car inside the gate and walk to the front door. The house was split-level and long. The grounds were lush with vegetation. A flagstone path led to the front door where another guard held the door open for them to pass. "Go straight back to Mr. King's office."

The interior of the house was more impressive than the exterior, if the long corridor they traversed was any indication of the rest of the house. Dark wood floors, white stucco walls and high ceilings were enhanced by a large heavy oak armoire and high-backed leather chairs. At the end of the corridor was an open door.

"Drugs sure pay good," Max said beneath his breath, halting in front of a large display case filled with baseball memorabilia. "Damn, he's got a signed Sosa game ball."

Darcy gave him a gentle shove to keep him moving toward Rupe King's office. As they neared the door, a large man with the shoulders of a linebacker held it for them, indicating they should pass. After they filed in, he stepped out and closed the door behind him. Darcy had no doubts he would remain just outside the door in case Mr. King needed him, and the bulge she'd detected beneath his vanilla-colored suit jacket had certainly been a gun.

"Come in, come in," a low, melodic voice, with a hint of Jamaican accent beckoned them inside.

Darcy turned to see a tall, thin man wearing a long-sleeved linen shirt rising from behind his desk. His hair was close-cropped, his face a dark ebony, his mouth wide, and his dark brown eyes were wary.

"Mr. King?" the Captain asked.

"Indeed." His gaze swept over the three resting on Darcy. "You and your people may take a seat here." He indicated a brightly upholstered couch and two armchairs before a large picture window that looked out into the tall pines in the back yard.

Her two associates took the armchairs, which left Darcy sitting on the sofa with Rupe King.

There was a long silence, and then Captain Springer cleared his throat. "Mr. King, you contacted our department regarding a man who approached you with a business proposition."

Rupe King's lip curled in a sneer. "A vampire! A goddamn vampire wants a share in my operation. I'd as soon fuck with the devil himself."

"This particular vampire is of interest to us. He's responsible for numerous deaths of young people here and in Seattle, where his string of murders originated."

"His name be Nicolas Powell," Rupe all but spat the name. "And I too have particular interest in this vampire."

The Captain's expression became intent. "I understand you recently lost your brother."

"Yes. One of Nicky's minions devoured him before his companions' eyes." Rupe King's eyes held a bitter rage. "I will see my brother avenged, whatever the cost."

"We've had one confrontation with him a couple of nights ago. We took out his followers, but Nicky gave us the slip. He's wary of us now. We need a way to set a trap for him."

The Jamaican's eyes glittered with interest. "I must admit that while I have a well-trained staff, I do not feel they are adequate for this challenge."

Captain Springer's chin lifted toward Darcy and Max. "My unit's been hunting killers like these for four years. We have the experience."

Rupe King gave Darcy an assessing glance.

Darcy kept her expression impassive.

"Will I be left alone, if I help you get him?" the wily drug lord asked.

"For the duration of the op, yes."

Rupe King relaxed against the sofa. "I will sacrifice a shipment. It arrives tonight. Two of my trusted men will be aboard the boat to act as the deliverymen—they must be mine or he will smell a double-cross."

Captain Springer nodded. "Just tell me the dock. Also, I have a vampire of my own who will help with the sting. No harm must come to him."

"Three actually," Darcy murmured. "Two more came in from Seattle last night to help. Friends of Quentin's."

Captain Springer shot her a startled glance, then quickly recovered. "The three who work for me will not be harmed."

Rupe King did not look pleased. Obviously to him, the only good vampire was a dead one.

Only a week ago, Darcy would have agreed.

"So be it," he said with a nod.

While Rupe and the Captain finalized the details, Darcy's tension grew. Things were heating up fast. Tonight they'd trap a killer and Quentin's mission would be over. And she still had a choice to make. Leave the life she'd built for herself, or join with Quentin as his companion of the night.

On one hand, she had a career. And she'd worked damn hard to be accepted by the guys, even earning a good measure of their respect for her fighting skills and dead aim. Although of late she'd taken hits due to her liaison with the vamp, she took great pride in what she had accomplished.

On the other hand, outside of her work she had no life—and no one to share what she had built.

Quentin offered her an eternity of companionship and love—oh, and mind-blowing sex. Although he drove her nuts with his insistence that he be the master of their relationship, she relished the challenge of shaking him up. Last night's victory still had her grinning. If only inwardly.

"You will not see me, again." Rupe King's voice drew her attention back. "My operation has been compromised by this business. Gentlemen, and lady, I wish you good luck this evening." He rose signaling the end of their interview.

As she passed Captain Springer, he captured her elbow and ushered her out of the room. When they were out of earshot of King and his associates, he leaned toward her. "Do you think you'll be able to keep your mind on the operation, or do I need to replace you on this mission?"

Darcy's cheeks flamed. "I'm in, sir. I won't let you down."

"When we get to the car, you'll have to tell me how we acquired two new team members," he said, his voice huffy.

Darcy gulped, he really was pissed. Quentin was a distraction she could ill afford in her line of work. After tonight, whichever way she chose, she wouldn't endanger others by her inattention.

The three retrieved their weapons at the gatehouse and headed away from the drug lord's estate.

Darcy sat in the back seat aware of Max's accusing glare in the rearview mirror. He continued to disapprove of her actions and it hurt her more than she was willing to admit. Max needed to get over it.

Darcy ignored him, and instead, filled the Captain in on what she knew about Emmy and Dylan, which was embarrassingly little considering the two knew a whole lot about her—like what she sounded like when she came and the exact shade of pink her nipples were.

"We'll head straight to Darcy's, Max. The team will be gathering. Is the van loaded up?"

"Yes, Captain," Max replied.

"Well, let's go nail this devil!"

CHAPTER ELEVEN

Quentin sat quietly while the team entered Darcy's home. He noted that Emmy took care of the introductions and proceeded to charm the pants off the hard-nosed bunch.

Dressed in her version of night camouflage — a wrap-around black T-shirt that exposed her deep cleavage and black jeans that hugged her fleshy derriere — Emmy drew every male eye in the room. No one seemed immune to her artless charm.

No one, that is, except Max Weir. The muscle-bound man watched her with a cynical eye. While he appeared resigned that the three vamps were part of this operation, Quentin doubted Max would ever let go of his deep-seated prejudice.

As had become the team's habit, they brought food to share among the group while they reviewed what they had learned. Emmy's plate was piled high with tidbits from every dish that was lined up on the table. The woman had an appetite.

Quentin's had disappeared. He felt like he was watching the group from a great distance. Since Emmy had made her announcement, he'd been reeling. Darcy was pregnant! And the child could only be Joe's. That fact ate at his gut. A child was the one thing Quentin could never give Darcy.

"Could you be wrong?" he'd asked Emmy after her bald statement.

She'd shaken her head. "I can sense the difference. Smell the blood gathering in her womb."

"Couldn't she be menstruating?"

"This feels different."

"Well that's definitive. It 'feels' different," he'd said, knowing he sounded snide and small. "Isn't it too soon for you to say? It's only been a few days, since..."

"Darcy's body is already changing, Quentin."

Why hadn't he noticed? Of course, the scent of her skin and hair, and yes, her arousal, tended to overwhelm his senses whenever she was near.

A child certainly changed everything. No vamp—at least none with a conscience—would turn a pregnant woman. The results were too horrific.

Thank God, Em had noticed.

"Quentin, you aren't eating," Emmy said, taking a seat beside him. "You really should try these meatballs. Phil's wife, Bets, made them. They're barely cooked—in our honor. Wasn't that sweet?" She used a toothpick to spear one of the sauce-covered balls and popped it into her mouth. She held up another and offered it to him.

Rather than let her see how morose his thoughts had turned, he opened his mouth and accepted the offering. If Emmy sensed he was disturbed, she'd never leave him to stew in his own thoughts.

The door opened suddenly and Captain Springer strode inside, followed closely by Darcy. Quentin wondered why the Captain had detained her. The Captain's broad face held a look of determination that hardened his square jaw.

Quentin's gaze followed Darcy into the room, then fell to her flat tummy. *Damn!* Something hitched in his chest. Something he didn't want to put into words.

His desire to make her his mate for eternity was slipping through his fingers. She'd been ideal—with a passion strong enough to match his. For the first time in his undead life he'd been ready to commit to one woman.

The right thing to do would be to give her up. Now.

But despite her pregnancy, he couldn't bear the thought of letting her go.

Darcy offered him a tight smile and waited for Emmy to scoot down the couch. Then she slid onto the couch beside him — so close his thigh heated with the contact.

"Listen up," Captain Springer called for their attention. "It's going down tonight. Rupe King's boat is coming in with a shipment of coke. When Nicky meets it at the dock, he'll get a little more than he bargained for."

Having been filled in on Rupe King's role in the bust by Max, Quentin listened as the Captain issued instructions to the team.

"I'd like to extend a welcome to Dylan and Emmy O'Hara." The Captain nodded to the couple, then glared at Darcy. "I'd appreciate your input as this goes down, but this is my operation. My team is trained and I wouldn't like either of you to be hurt in the crossfire."

Dylan nodded his understanding. "We'll be standing by to assist."

Unexpectedly, Darcy's hand settled on his thigh and Quentin covered it with his own, giving her a squeeze. No one seemed to notice as all eyes were on the Captain.

"We'll go in with Kevlar, crossbows, and assault rifles. The Vero Beach PD have already cleared the dock of civilians." The Captain paused and his gaze swept each of his team. "It goes without saying that we're going to take out every one of Nicky's gang. Give no quarter!"

The team came to their feet and filed out the door. Quentin caught Darcy's hand when she rose to follow.

Her glance was questioning.

"Perhaps, you should sit this one out, love," he suggested quietly.

A frown furrowed her forehead. "Not now, Quentin. You can't wrap me in cotton wool. I'm part of this team and this is our biggest operation to date. This is my job."

Quentin knew she'd refuse. He should just tell her. Or better yet, tie her to her iron bed and let her rage at him.

She tugged her hand from his, and Quentin sighed and stood up to follow. He hadn't the right to come between her and her ambitions. But tonight, he'd stick close to her shapely ass and make sure she didn't run into trouble.

This would be her last dangerous assignment for a while. He'd tell her why later.

* * * * *

The radio crackled in Darcy's ear. "Nicky and his crew just pulled into the marina," the Captain said from the command post—the team's van in the parking area. "Remember, we'll wait to strike until he brings his men in to move the cargo."

Thank God! She'd been afraid she would disgrace herself. The wait had been interminable. The storm that threatened to break over their heads had whipped up waves in the inlet, setting all the boats tied to the dock bobbing in the water. Her stomach pitched right along with them.

"I'm gonna barf if this doesn't go down soon," Phil moaned.

Soft chuckles sounded from seven mikes. Darcy commiserated with Phil. Glad she hadn't eaten any dinner, she kept silent beside Quentin, nausea roiling in her belly and clammy perspiration breaking on her forehead. This was one stakeout she'd be happy to see the end of.

"Too many of Bets' meatballs, Phil?" Emmy broke in, her voice full of sympathy.

"God, don't mention it," he groaned.

Above the sound of the gathering wind, footsteps echoed hollowly on the wooden planks of the dock. Quentin crouched so close behind her she felt his body grow rigid. It felt right to have him watching her back even though she still missed Joe. They'd taken up a position on the cabin cruiser tied next to Rupe King's. Hunkered down behind the gunwale of the boat, they listened tensely for the order to move in for the kill.

Quentin had stuck to her like glue all evening. It was annoying, but sweet, how protective he was of her. And totally unnecessary. When things turned ugly—and they would—she'd be moving fast. She didn't want to trip over him.

The rumble of voices sounded in the next boat, but they were too low to make out their words. There was a sudden burst of laughter and a door opened, spilling light from the cabin onto the dock.

Darcy rose up to peek over the rail, but Quentin's heavy hand pushed her down. She turned to glare at him. "What do you think you're doing?" she whispered angrily.

"Shhh." He lifted his chin in the direction of the other boat.

Darcy saw one of Nicky's boys on the bow with a radio next to his ear. "Tell them it's clear," the teen said.

Ignoring Darcy's glower, Quentin whispered into his headset, "Get ready. Nicky's given the all clear. The others will be closing on the boat."

"Roger that," Max replied quietly. "No one moves until I give the signal."

With the team in position on neighboring boats and inside cars in the marina, the gang would be encircled in moments.

Darcy held her breath. Once the noose tightened, Nicky would react like a trapped animal. She'd seen the mayhem he was capable of when he held all the cards, now she'd get a glimpse of a monster in full rage.

The heavy tread of half a dozen of Nicky's "soldiers" echoed dully in the night. Darcy hugged her crossbow to her chest and concentrated on the sound of her breaths to make her racing heart slow its pace and give her thoughts focus.

Slower, calmer, centered. She drew on her inner reserve of peace, visualizing the team's victory.

She was ready.

"Get cocked," the Captain said.

Darcy rose on her knees, lifted her bow, and sighted down the shaft of her arrow, and then rose a fraction higher to point it over the railing. In the dim light provided by the lamps strung from boat slip to boat slip, Darcy couldn't sight on Nicky.

"I don't see Nicky," she whispered.

"Must still be in the cabin," Max replied. "Take out the men on the dock you can see when I give the order."

With the deck of the boat pitching beneath her knees, Darcy struggled for balance. "I'll take the first in line."

"I've got the second target," Max replied.

Once the team had selected their marks, the airwave was silent. The only sounds coming from boats nudging their slips and booted feet on wood.

Suddenly, one of Nicky's men lifted his nose into the wind.

"Now!" Max shouted.

Darcy pulled back on her trigger, letting her arrow fly. Her first target staggered, and then disintegrated. When she reached for her next arrow, Quentin leapt over the gunwale and landed on the narrow walkway between the two boats.

The rapid tattoo of gunfire erupted and her team members shouted in their mikes as they took cover.

Cursing beneath her breath, Darcy quickly pulled back her bowstring, latched it in the spring clip, and slid the arrow along the track. Armed, she slid over the gunwale, intent on following Quentin.

From all along the dock came the sounds of the ensuing battle. Curses, and the sharp staccato of machine fire ripped through the night.

"How many?" Max's voice demanded.

"I counted nine," the Captain said, his voice sounding raspy as he ran along the dock to join the fight.

"That means six to go." Max grunted, and then roared. The sounds of fists meeting flesh filled Darcy's headset.

"Emmy, get back to the van!"

"Dylan, I have a stake in this too. You're not leaving me behind."

"God dammit to hell!"

As she crept aboard the drug lord's cruiser, Darcy ignored the voices in her ear and the flashes of gunfire that burst brilliantly around her. Getting Nicky was her sole focus. Oh, and saving Quentin's butt. They were partners now. He shouldn't have proceeded without her.

She climbed up the gangway and slipped over the side, making her way toward the steps leading down into the cabin. The lights had been doused, but she sensed movement inside. Careful not to make any noise, she inched her way toward the shadowed compartment.

"Well, if it isn't GI Jane." The voice came from behind her and she stiffened, her heart lurching in her chest. "I'd recognize your sweet scent anywhere."

The team went instantly, eerily, silent. With her heart picking up its pace, she slowly turned to face Nicky Powell, her bow raised level with her chest. All she could think was where the hell was Quentin?

Quentin watched from the shadow of the cockpit, his hand tightening around the puny stake he held. Nicky had a gun pointed at Darcy. Quentin didn't dare make a move or he might distract her.

Nicky took a step toward her.

"Don't come any closer," she warned.

He sniffed the air. "I smell Quentin. He's been all over you, hasn't he?" His smile sent a shiver down Quentin's back.

"You're surrounded," Darcy said, her voice steady. "You may as well lay down your weapon. You aren't stepping off this boat."

Quentin's chest filled with pride at her courage.

"But I have you, therefore I have the advantage."

A soft click and the blur of her arrow flying toward Nicky's chest happened so quickly, Quentin didn't have time to react.

The arrow sank only to its tip.

Nicky's laughter, soft and ominous rang in the air. "Do you think you're the only ones who own flak jackets?" He plucked the arrow from his shirt. "Let's stop wasting time. Come here." He waved her closer with his gun.

Quentin watched Darcy's face and knew the exact moment she'd decided not to cooperate. She drew a deep breath and her hands clenched at her sides. He started to rise from his hiding place when she took a step toward Nicky. Suddenly, she feinted to the side.

The roar of Nicky's gun spurred Quentin from his hiding place. From the corner of his eye he saw Darcy pitch forward and over the side of the boat, her body splashing softly in the water below. He roared and launched himself at Nicky, desperate to get to Darcy.

He raised his stake and Nicky fired again, striking Quentin in the abdomen. He dropped the stake, but the bullet didn't slow his advance. His charge carried him into Nicky and down onto the bow of the cruiser. His progeny roared, his face transforming and pulling Quentin into his bloodlust.

Quentin's body and face expanded and he flung back his head with a roar of fury. He rolled with Nicky, fighting to keep his "son" beneath him. He spotted a coil of rope and reached out his hand to close around it.

Nicky pounded at Quentin's sides with his fists, but Quentin was undeterred. He grasped the rope in both hands and wound it once around his opponent's throat.

Nicky's eyes bulged as the noose tightened. His mouth gaped and his body bucked in powerful surges, trying to unseat Quentin, but Quentin pulled tighter until the nylon cut into the other vamp's throat.

With adrenaline surging through his veins, Quentin snapped the rope, severing Nicky's head from his shoulders.

When the din of his bloodlust quieted in his head, he heard the shouts of the team and Dylan as they ran toward him. He lurched toward the side of the boat and jumped into the water. As he entered it, he heard splashes all around him and bright lights shown into the murky depths.

He swam deep to the bottom of the inlet, but he didn't see her. His heart breaking, he reached into the silt and waving fronds of seagrass, searching for the place her body had settled. How long had it been? *Please God, I have to find her.*

His lungs burning from the lack of air, he refused to return to the surface. Every moment was precious. His hands sank below the swirling green seaweed as he swam along the bottom.

Then he saw a pale oval glimmering among the fronds. He reached and snagged Darcy's braid, pulling her into his arms. He swam for the surface, his lungs nearly bursting, praying he wasn't too late.

When he surfaced, many hands reached for his burden. Although reluctant to let her go, he lifted her body gently into their waiting arms, then heaved himself onto the planks beside them.

Max made quick work of removing her Kevlar jacket and her T-shirt. Then he placed two fingers to the side of her throat. "Her heart isn't beating."

A raw, burning sensation tightened Quentin's throat. With every fiber of his being, he fought the need to push everyone aside and gather her close to him and howl. Darcy couldn't be gone. Eternity without her was unthinkable.

His breath sounding harsh in his ears, he watched Max press his clasped hands against her chest. Captain Springer knelt beside her head and lowered his mouth to hers, breathing into her lungs. Dylan pressed her T-shirt against the furrowed wound high on her shoulder that seeped slowly with her blood.

An arm settled around his shoulders and Quentin looked up into Emmy's misty face. Then he realized he was crying. She kissed his cheek and hugged him tightly to her breasts. His arms slipped around her while his eyes burned, watching the men work over Darcy's still form.

"Breathe dammit," he whispered, willing her to live. If only, he'd moved more quickly, he could have taken the bullet for her.

The men continued to work and Quentin's dread grew. He was responsible for this. He had made Nicky. God damn his soul.

Max stopped the compressions and checked her pulse again.

Quentin saw a flutter of an eyelid. "Wait," he said, his breath catching. *Please don't let me have imagined it.*

Darcy's body convulsed and water burbled from her mouth. Max rolled her to her side and she choked, vomiting water. Her eyes remained closed and the group waited to see whether she'd recover.

Slowly, her hand fisted and she coughed. Her eyes opened and she stared straight at Quentin.

Quentin didn't care that everyone saw the tears that streaked down his cheeks. He crawled toward her and reached out his hand to cup her cheek. "Don't you ever give me another scare like that," he said, not recognizing the sound of his voice, it was so clogged with emotion.

Darcy's hand settled over his. "What? You think I planned to suck down the entire Atlantic?" She coughed again, the sound rattling harsh inside her chest.

"Let's get this one to a hospital," the Captain said.

Darcy's eyes sought Quentin's. "Nicky?"

"He's dead," he said flatly.

"As are the rest of his minions," Max said.

Darcy settled back against the wooden planks, her eyes closing. "So tired."

Quentin gathered her into his arms and lurched to his feet. "Sleep, baby. I've got you now."

She sighed and pressed a kiss to his throat.

Quentin held her to close to his heart as he followed the Captain toward the waiting van. He'd never let her go.

CHAPTER TWELVE

Darcy followed the sound of soft laughter into her kitchen on wobbly legs, rubbing her sore, itchy shoulder. As she pushed the door open, three sets of vampires' eyes swung guiltily toward her.

Suspicion aroused, her gaze darted around the kitchen but didn't land on anything that would inspire the uncomfortable silence—except an open package of calves' liver. Quentin shoved something on the counter behind his back and leaned indolently against the counter.

Darcy's eyes narrowed and she reached around him. She pulled out a cold container of her favorite ice cream, Cookies N' Cream. She lifted an eyebrow, but Quentin simply pulled a laden spoon from behind his back and slipped it between his lips.

Emmy snickered. "So you're up at last? Should you be out of bed?"

Darcy frowned at her attempt to change the subject. Something was up. "What's going on here?"

"We were just discussing the merits of organ meat," Dylan said, then quickly pressed his lips together.

Emmy jammed him in the belly with her elbow and smiled brightly. "And Quentin's odd cravings."

"Emmy!" Quentin's narrowed gaze looked just plain mean.

"I think we'd better leave these two alone, darling." Dylan grabbed Emmy's elbow and herded her out of the kitchen.

"Sweetheart, how are you feeling?" Quentin asked—too quickly.

Tired of everyone changing the subject and talking in riddles. Darcy crossed her arms over her chest. "Everyone has been treating me with kid gloves."

"You were injured, love. Everyone's been worried about you. Even Captain Springer and the team make it a point to stop in every day."

"And talking in whispers when they think I'm sleeping."

"Right. I suppose you've been wondering about that." Quentin straightened away from the counter.

Darcy's breath hitched. This was the first time she'd stood next to him since being shot, and she'd forgotten how tall he was. Even unconsciously, he was able to distract her. "Mmmm-hmm."

"Well, we felt it was for the best."

Ignoring the sensual awareness that made her skin tingle, she drummed her fingers on her arm.

"We didn't want to impede your recovery."

Impatient now for him to get to the point, she blurted, "Out with it."

"Alright," he said, blowing out his breath. "But first, let's go sit down. You're looking a little flushed."

She let him lead her into the empty living room and settle her on the sofa, fussing unnecessarily with the pillows until he was satisfied of her comfort. He'd been this way all week—ever since she'd been released from the hospital. Solicitous. Kind. Distant.

"Have you changed your mind?" she asked quietly, not seeing any need to draw this conversation out. The suspense was already killing her.

He squatted on his haunches in front of her. "Changed my mind?"

"About turning me."

His gaze slipped from hers and Darcy felt her heart squeeze tightly.

"I suppose you're eager to leave now," she said, although the words seemed to stick in her throat—behind the lump that threatened to choke her.

"Leave?"

"With the investigation over, I thought you'd be itching to get back to Seattle."

"It rather depends," he said quietly.

She knew her heart was in her eyes, but she couldn't help the hope she knew was reflected in her expression. Her emotions were too raw to conceal. "What does it depend on?"

"On you."

She swallowed. "You don't want to turn me, do you?"

"Not now."

"Because it's dangerous?"

"Because it wouldn't be right."

Shaking her head to clear her confusion, she said, "I don't understand."

"Love, you're going to have a baby." His expression was stark, his jaw tight.

"What?" Of all the reasons, that would have been last on her list. Pregnant? How—"Oh." *Joe. Oh God.* "Everyone knows?"

"Yes, love."

"But the hospital—"

"Captain Springer told them I was your fiancé. I asked them to let me tell you."

"My *mother*?"

He nodded.

"But I've spoken to her on the phone every day." *My own mother kept a secret like that?*

"She thinks the child is mine. She'd have been on the first plane here if she hadn't caught the flu."

She inhaled a ragged breath. "Joe?"

"He hasn't called in. And I thought you'd want to be the one to tell him." Quentin reached to pull away the pillow she clutched between nerveless fingers, and then closed his large hands around hers, warming them. "You don't have to make any decisions now. You have a lot to think about. And there are some things I want to tell you."

Her eyes pooled with tears, but she nodded. *Are you going to tell me it's over? That you can't love a woman with a child? Because I won't give it up.*

"I never told you how it was I came to be…what I am." He squeezed her hands, and his gaze held hers. "I was a spoiled, reckless young man. I left England in search of adventure because I suffered from boredom. I'd never experienced a grand passion for anything." He lifted his shoulders and shrugged sheepishly. "Except sex, that is."

A little smile curved her mouth. This she could well imagine. He was describing the Quentin she'd first met.

"I never loved anything or anyone. I was a younger son, so my family was only too glad when I headed to the Caribbean." He smiled crookedly. "My behavior was causing a bit of a scandal, you see.

"Anyway, in the Caymans I met a dark, honey-skinned woman. Her appetite matched mine and she taught me things — wicked, sexy things that bound me to her. I craved what she meted out. Even believed I was falling in love with her."

Darcy knew where this was headed. "She was a vampire."

"Yes. We spent weeks in her cottage next to the beach, and I never once questioned her aversion to the sunlight or odd cravings for raw flesh. Her brand of sexual sorcery enslaved me for a time. I pleased her, and she gave me the one 'reward' that was in her power to give."

"Eternal life," Darcy whispered.

"Yes. Only once I'd changed, I recognized her dark seduction and she ceased to hold power over me. And I was damned to walk the Earth at night—forever seeking relief from my never-ending boredom."

Tears finally slipped down her face. "And now?"

"I tried to bind you to me in the exact same way that witch did —but with my own brand of dark seduction."

"Because you were bored and you could?" She had to know what was really in his heart, however much it hurt.

"Because I love you, and I don't ever want to let you go."

Darcy closed her eyes and breathed a sigh of relief. When she opened them, his worried expression prompted her to ask, "What do you fear?"

"That one day you'll wake up and discover I've bound you with desire."

"Would that be so bad?"

"It is, if there isn't true love in your heart, as well," he replied, his voice thick with emotion.

Darcy pulled her hands from under his and reached to cradle his face between her palms, her heart bursting. "I love you, Quentin. For however long I live, I will always love you."

Quentin's eyes squeezed shut. "And I will love you for all my life."

Darcy's heart raced and her hands smoothed over his broad shoulders. "Love me, Quentin."

"I do," he breathed.

"No, *love* me."

His eyes popped open. "I see. Your shoulder?"

"Aches like the devil, but I have a deeper ache somewhere else."

"I think I have just the cure," he purred.

"*Hurry.*"

Quentin stood, swept her into his arms, and walked briskly to their bedroom. There he laid her on her pink-flowered sheets and swiftly, gently, removed her clothing, and then tore his own from his body.

Darcy grinned. "A little anxious, are we?"

"*We* have suffered an entire week of purgatory, madam."

"Poor baby. Is that why you slept on your side of the bed?"

He stalked toward the bed, his expression intent, his gaze locked on her open, welcoming cunt. "I was afraid I'd hurt you if I so much as touched your soft skin. I've been going mad."

"Come to me," she said, opening her arms.

He stretched his body over hers, braced on his arms, careful not to jostle her shoulder. "I don't know if I can be gentle," he whispered.

"Fuck me, Quentin," Darcy moaned.

"Oh love, invite me into your solace." He nudged her portal with the smooth, broad head of his cock.

Darcy's body glazed the tip with her creamy invitation.

He entered her with a single, endless glide, and then held himself still.

Darcy closed her arms and legs around him and held him tight. "No one will ever fill my body or my heart like you do." She circled her hips on his cock, screwing them both to distraction.

"*Christ*, you're not making this any easier for me." He moved then, flexing his hips to drive into her, surging, pushing her up the bed with each hard stroke.

All her love poured from her body, bathing his cock with welcome.

Quentin groaned and leaned down to take her lips in a searing kiss, eating her mouth. "I won't ever let you go. You're *mine*." His hips moved faster, his thrusts grew sharper. His face tightened, but didn't transform.

Even in the throes of passion, he protected her.

"Please, please. Harder. Oh come deeper!" Darcy clawed his back, pumping her hips against his, seeking the sweet release his body promised.

Quentin reared back on his haunches, hooked his arms beneath her knees and drove deep, pounding relentlessly into her, lifting her hips from the bed with his powerful thrusts.

"Yes!" she cried out, and writhed beneath him, her channel convulsing around his shaft.

Quentin shouted and his hot, liquid release poured into her.

As the last spasms of her orgasm milked him, Darcy reached for him again. "Hold me."

He covered her, once again holding his weight above her on his elbows. He rested his forehead on hers, while he gasped for breath.

Darcy soothed him with her hands, caressing his moist, sweaty back. "Will it always be like this for us?"

"Always. I promise."

"Even when I grow older?"

He lifted his head and searched her gaze. "I'll love you when you're old and wrinkled and frail. And I'll always think you're the most beautiful woman I've ever held."

Darcy sighed and settled her hands in the small of his back. "I have a child to rear. School and PTA meetings. I'll need to be with him during the day until he's old enough not to need me."

"Do you think my love is so shallow I won't wait?"

"I'll grow older, my body will change." She wrinkled her nose, trying to inject a little levity into the most important conversation they would ever have. "My boobs will droop. People will wonder what a handsome thing like you is doing with a soccer mom."

Quentin's hand caressed her breast tenderly. "These little gems will remain perky into your dotage, madam."

Her heart twisted. She had to tell him. "I may choose never to turn. What if I want to grow old and be a grandmother?"

Quentin's eyes misted. "I'll hold you every night and love you gently until the day you die, and then I'll watch over our child and *her* children. I won't ever stop loving you."

Tears streaked down the side of her face and she sobbed, clutching at his shoulders. When the storm passed, she sniffed and gave a little laugh. "Look at us, blubbering like babies."

He smiled tenderly and smoothed the tears from her cheeks with his fingertips.

"You know, I have the oddest craving for Cookies N' Cream."

Quentin closed his eyes, a look of intense euphoria on his face. "Yes, with liver chasers."

Darcy's face stretched into a grin. "Was that what you were hiding in the kitchen? Sympathy cravings?"

His frown didn't dim her mirth. "It's not funny. I'm afraid what other indignities the next nine months will hold."

Darcy laughed. "I can see you in the emergency room. We'll need two cots."

His expression held horror. "Do you think so? Bugger me!"

She grew serious again. "What about Joe?" she asked. "Can you share our child with him?"

"I'm resigned that he'll be a part of our lives, if he wants it. But I will not share a wife."

Afraid she might start crying again, she said, "Are you asking me to marry you?"

"No. I'm telling you what will be."

"I like it when you get all mastery."

His eyebrow rose, and the smirk she loved tipped the corners of his mouth. "Oh, I can give you mastery, love. Shall I show you?" He leaned over her.

Her palm against his shoulder, she held him back. "One more question first."

He waited, his expression alert.

"Will our son be born in Vero or in Seattle?"

The smirk deepened. "Seeing as we both work for the SU, I think that question is already answered."

"You and Captain Springer have been doing a lot of talking while I was out."

"We're like this," he said, crossing his fingers. "Besides, did I ever tell you how much I detest the cold?"

"Some members of the team won't be very happy about a vampire joining the team permanently."

"Three vampires, love. And Max will just have to get over it."

"Three?"

"Emmy's determined to be a doting aunt. And Dylan and I have a mind to institute a governing council of vampires to help keep the peace."

"So I'm marrying a politician?"

"You're marrying a Master. Think you can handle it?"

Her hand crept around his cock. "I already am."

Enjoy this excerpt from
ALL KNIGHT LONG
MY IMMORTAL KNIGHT III
© *Copyright Delilah Devlin 2004*

His research had told him the professor was considered an expert in vampire lore. She'd written papers, magazine articles, and books, and even been consulted by more than one movie producer.

All his research told him she might hold the answer, but it hadn't said anything about how young or *drinkable* she was. Her hair was neither blonde nor brown, but the warm color of whiskey. Her eyes, hidden behind a pair of wire-framed glasses, glinted cognac. Her lips were a pale rosé.

The hunter within him woke.

Realizing he'd been staring, he cleared his throat. "You're Professor Lily Carlson? The author of 'Vampires: Myth and Reality'?"

Her gaze swept over him. An action so swift, he thought he might have imagined it. "And you are?" she asked, leaning over the table to extend her hand.

Joe froze. That indefinable scent was all over her. He had the urge to rub on her like a kitten in catnip. He eyed her small hand, afraid to touch it and feel the blood humming below the surface of her creamy, white skin. He was *that* close to jumping her. "I thought the survey was anonymous."

"Oh, it is," she replied quickly, withdrawing her hand. "You're responding to the ad, then?" At his nod, she looked vaguely disappointed. "Well, I suppose I should review your answers. Please have a seat," she said, waving him toward the bench seat opposite hers. "Thank you for taking the time to help me with my research."

Bemused, Joe slid onto the seat. He knew he should get straight to the point, but he stalled. For just a few minutes, he wanted to be with a woman while she looked at him as if he was just like any other man. Well, perhaps like he was a man with a serious mental disorder. But at least, she wasn't recoiling in horror or inspecting him like the Bearded Lady at a freak show.

Not that she was a great beauty, nor even as strong and fierce as his ex-partner Darcy. Dressed in a boring-beige suit, her whiskey-colored hair piled in a loose knot on top of her head, and her glasses sliding down her shiny nose, she looked like the schoolmarm she was. But while all the beige and brown should have made her look muddy, she glowed golden in the lamplight. And her scent — richly textured with something wild and animalistic — was extraordinary.

The woman opened his survey and glanced at his answers, then flipped the page. Her lips pursed for a moment, drawing his gaze to her full lower lip. "There are a few more questions I need answered. Do you mind if I learn a little more about you?" she asked, glancing up at him from beneath her gold-tipped lashes.

The surge of heat that centered in his groin was way out of proportion to her innocent question. Afraid he'd stutter over a tongue that suddenly felt too large for his mouth, he merely nodded.

"You understand the questions I'm about to ask you are part of a sociological study I'm conducting about our vampire subculture?"

Again, he nodded.

"All information you provide," she recited as if from rote, "will be completely confidential. I hope you will answer me honestly," she gave him a doubtful stare, "or to the best of your ability."

She looked expectantly at him, so he nodded again.

Her gaze returned to his survey and she cleared her throat. "You...are a vampire?"

"Yes." This was the first time he'd admitted that fact out loud, and he knew how ridiculous it sounded.

"So, are you a Psy or a Sang?"

"There's more than one kind?" Joe asked.

"A Psychic vampire feeds on a human's energy; a Sanguinarian is a blood-drinker."

"I guess I'm a Sang."

"You drink blood once a day?" she asked, her head still bent over the paper.

He shrugged, hoping she'd glance up at him again so he could see whether her eyes really were a warm, golden-brown. "More or less."

She scribbled something in the margin of his survey. "Well, which is it?"

"Sometimes more."

"Do you drink human blood?"

Joe wished she'd end this line of questioning, or he'd be drooling shortly. Her scent had every appetite revving into high gear. "Yes."

She glanced up from the survey. "How long have you had the urge to drink blood?"

"Since I woke up, tonight."

She blinked. "No, I meant...since ever."

"Last winter."

"Did you by chance suffer some sort of emotional trauma?"

Joe stiffened. *If you consider I died, and the woman I loved had her boyfriend turn me, then hell yes!* "Yes."

"Was the trauma centered around a love relationship?"

He drew a deep breath. The professor was determined to hit every sensitive nerve he owned. "Yes."

"A woman?"

He glowered at her and didn't respond.

She did another of those little sweeps of her eyelashes that left him feeling confused. "Woman," she said softly and annotated his answer. "Was it a sexual relationship?"

Every muscle in his body contracted. The memory of the last time he'd seen Darcy, the last time he'd been inside her, had his flesh straining inside his jeans.

"Was it?" she insisted.

Joe nodded, feeling his face harden, knowing he looked as dour as the Grim Reaper right about now.

"You say, you drink blood during sex."

He felt like howling. "Sometimes."

She looked up, her head canting to the side. "Why?"

"To give myself and my host greater pleasure. The orgasms are worth dying for," he said, hoping to give her a taste of his discomfort.

"Oh." Her face suffused in pink, and she cleared her throat. "Do you use lancets to bleed your host?"

He didn't understand her question and stared.

"Do you use something sharp to pierce your host's skin?"

"My teeth. I bite them." He lifted his lips and let her see the teeth he couldn't convince to recede into his gums—he was just too damn hungry.

"Oh." Her expression remained professionally frozen, but Joe had the feeling she wanted to roll her eyes. She reached into her handbag and pulled out a silver cross, and then held it in front of him. "Do you get a burning sensation when you see this object?"

"No."

"Does this produce any sensation at all?" She touched his hand with it.

Air hissed between his teeth at the first touch of her hand. He was on fire. His hand curled beneath hers, curving into a fist.

Her eyebrows lifted and she quickly scribbled something else on his survey. "Do you believe in Satan?"

"Yeah, if he's the evil that lurks in a man's heart."

"Do you worship Satan?"

"Uh, no."

She reached into her purse again and pulled out a tiny bottle of water and a sharpened stick.

Joe stared at the items she stacked neatly in a row in front of him and his blood began to boil. Silver crosses, holy water, and a stake. The woman had studied *Buffy 101*! She was a fraud. She didn't know the first thing about vampires—hell, she didn't believe they existed.

"I don't suppose, Professor, that in all your research you've ever actually met a vampire?"

About the author:

Delilah Devlin dated a Samoan, a Venezuelan, a Turk, a Cuban, and was engaged to a Greek before marrying her Irishman. She's lived in Saudi Arabia, Germany, and Ireland, but calls Texas home for now. Ever a risk taker, she lived in the Saudi Peninsula during the Gulf War, thwarted an attempted abduction by white slave traders, and survived her children's juvenile delinquency.

Creating alter egos for herself in the pages of her books enables her to live new adventures. Since discovering the sinful pleasure of erotica, she writes to satisfy her need for variety--it keeps her from running away with the Indian working in the cubicle beside her!

In addition to writing erotica, she enjoys creating romantic comedies and suspense novels.

Delilah welcomes mail from readers. You can write to her c/o Ellora's Cave Publishing at 1337 Commerce Drive, Suite 13, Stow OH 44224.

Why an electronic book?

We live in the Information Age—an exciting time in the history of human civilization in which technology rules supreme and continues to progress in leaps and bounds every minute of every hour of every day. For a multitude of reasons, more and more avid literary fans are opting to purchase e-books instead of paperbacks. The question to those not yet initiated to the world of electronic reading is simply: *why?*

1. *Price.* An electronic title at Ellora's Cave Publishing runs anywhere from 40-75% less than the cover price of the <u>exact same title</u> in paperback format. Why? Cold mathematics. It is less expensive to publish an e-book than it is to publish a paperback, so the savings are passed along to the consumer.

2. *Space.* Running out of room to house your paperback books? That is one worry you will never have with electronic novels. For a low one-time cost, you can purchase a handheld computer designed specifically for e-reading purposes. Many e-readers are larger than the average handheld, giving you plenty of screen room. Better yet, hundreds of titles can be stored within your new library—a single microchip. (Please note that Ellora's Cave does not endorse any specific brands. You can check our website at www.ellorascave.com for customer recommendations we make available to new consumers.)

3. *Mobility.* Because your new library now consists of only a microchip, your entire cache of books can be taken with you wherever you go.

4. *Personal preferences are accounted for.* Are the words you are currently reading too small? Too large? Too…**ANNOYING**? Paperback books cannot be modified according to personal preferences, but e-books can.

5. *Innovation.* The way you read a book is not the only advancement the Information Age has gifted the literary community with. There is also the factor of what you can read. Ellora's Cave Publishing will be introducing a new line of interactive titles that are available in e-book format only.

6. *Instant gratification.* Is it the middle of the night and all the bookstores are closed? Are you tired of waiting days—sometimes weeks—for online and offline bookstores to ship the novels you bought? Ellora's Cave Publishing sells instantaneous downloads 24 hours a day, 7 days a week, 365 days a year. Our e-book delivery system is 100% automated, meaning your order is filled as soon as you pay for it.

Those are a few of the top reasons why electronic novels are displacing paperbacks for many an avid reader. As always, Ellora's Cave Publishing welcomes your questions and comments. We invite you to email us at service@ellorascave.com or write to us directly at: 1337 Commerce Drive, Suite 13, Stow OH 44224.

Discover for yourself why readers can't get enough of the multiple award-winning publisher Ellora's Cave. Whether you prefer e-books or paperbacks, be sure to visit EC on the web at www.ellorascave.com for an erotic reading experience that will leave you breathless.

WWW.ELLORASCAVE.COM

Printed in the United States
31447LVS00001B/1

9 781843 608950